THE FAIR & FOUL

PROJECT GENE ASSIST
BOOK ONE

ALLIE POTTS

Axil Hammer Publishing
2020

To Jason

For cheering me on no matter how far the distance, steep the hill or bad the weather. We crossed this finish line together.

ONE

Vials of various colors and volume filled the medical refrigerator. They shone like jewels on display. Juliane shifted in her chair on the other side of the lab to better follow her colleagues' movements, however, the straps keeping her in place made it difficult to watch everything.

Alan glanced over his shoulder at the man seated in the chair closest to him. A wrinkle crossed his brow for a moment, but turned back to the refrigerator and selected a ruby red vial from the rack. He then fit the tube into a pneumatic apparatus resembling a tattoo artist's needle with a snap.

Freed from its holster, the pneumatic tool emitted a hum. The tip of the device flickered with a bright glow. Alan held it in the light and shook it with an exaggerated flourish.

"Can you try not to look like you are enjoying the idea of sticking us with a needle?" asked Juliane.

"It's not every day you get to be the one to usher in the next evolution of mankind. This is a big moment," responded Alan with a laugh as he leaned in, ready to pierce the occupant of the other chair's skin with the needle. "Now count back from sixty. This may pinch a little."

Alan swapped the needle tip with a fresh one and approached her while his assistant, Betty, disposed of the old one. Juliane watched the needle enter her arm and felt the liquid push against her veins. It created a sensation that somehow was both ice and burn. Then it was replaced by a feeling Juliane couldn't quite describe.

"It will be easier on you if you don't resist," Alan whispered in her ear as he began packing up their supplies.

"What do you mean?" she asked. Her heart raced. Beads of sweat dampened her forehead. Her stomach flopped like she'd descended too quickly in an elevator. Her vision blurred.

"Your immune system is attempting to repel the serum. It is after all, effectively a virus. You know full well it's the best way to deliver the software to your DNA."

"Is that why I'm still strapped to this chair?" She pulled at her restraint.

Alan nodded and tapped her arm. "Right. As I was saying, it's best not to fight. Over the next few hours, you will feel feverish and may experience some other unpleasantness. You need to let whatever happens, happen. No matter what."

Juliane narrowed her eyes in an attempt to see him more clearly. "No matter what? That sounds rather ominous."

"Well, yes. It was meant to be. You see, a person's will has a remarkable influence on their physical well-being. Perhaps, one day we'll better understand the how and why . . . Right now, you need to will your body into accepting the spread of the virus."

"There's a chance my body won't?"

"Correct."

Juliane frowned. "What happens if my body rejects it?"

Alan's words began to sound muffled to her ears as if the air around them had transformed into sludge. "If your body tries to fight it, then, unfortunately, it will fail. This is not the sort of virus it is used to dealing with. Your body will consume itself, trying to halt the inevitable. If that happens . . . "

"We can die from this?" Juliane blinked until her vision was clear. "You should have mentioned that before!" *What have I done?* "You said upstairs the trials were successful!"

"And they were, but the subjects were all animals and animals trust their instincts so much better than we do. They don't have to be told to adapt and survive. They just do. There is bound to be a higher rate of success."

"You said this was safe," she shouted. She pulled at her straps again.

"Did I?" Alan shrugged. "Or did you simply hear what you wanted to hear? We wouldn't be in this room if I didn't have the utmost confidence that, in your case, the risk of rejection is low. However, the downside of being first to do anything is it always involves the chance for failure. I thought you of all people accepted that." The corners of his lips quirked up. "Ah, I know what it is. You're feeling feverish already and not thinking clearly. Would it make you feel better if I told you I injected myself yesterday?"

A bead of sweat rolled down the side of her head as she thought about his question. Alan had given her ample experience to hone her willpower—she might have told him off at least a half-dozen times otherwise, and certainly, he was a genius. If he could make it, so could she. "You did this to yourself, already?" Her mouth felt like a desert.

Alan grinned. "Don't worry, you'll feel like a brand-new person before you know it."

Juliane's gaze darted to the occupant of the other chair, Louis. He was slumped over, a sheen of moisture covering his face. "You told him too, didn't you?" she demanded. Not waiting for an answer, she tore at her restraints. This time they gave way. Freed, she attempted to race to his side, only to be stricken with such intense vertigo that she dropped to the floor.

Alan sounded far away. "Betty, we need some cots in here. I believe Dr. Faris has her assistant on speed dial. Would you mind giving him a call?" The lab alternated between arctic freeze and volcanic heat. Juliane couldn't have given Louis any further assistance if she tried. An image of Louis crumpled in his chair swirled around her vision. Juliane took a deep calming breath, closed her eyes, and willed herself to remain alive.

TWO

six months earlier

Juliane gingerly touched Dr. Henderson's inscription on the worn children's book. Its binding had long since faded to illegibility, and the cover was likely to fall off altogether if she jostled it too much. Even with all her care, a yellowed newspaper clipping managed to escape from the pages.

She knelt to retrieve Dr. Henderson's obituary. He left the school system shortly after she did, hoping to achieve publication, but he had succumbed to a rare blood disease only a few years later.

Juliane understood his original motivation for leaving. Why should he limit himself to teaching a small population of students when he could improve the lives of so many?

She smoothed out a crease as she reinserted the clipping into the book's pages. The world lost an amazing teacher. It was too tragic to be tolerated. Dr. Henderson had recognized her potential before anyone else. His legacy would be her legacy.

Juliane sighed as she closed the book and placed it back between a volume on theoretical computer science, which was her graduate focus, and one of several texts with a psychological focus, which had been her postgraduate work. She glanced at her watch. A message flashed, reminding her that her presentation was scheduled to begin in fifteen minutes

If she arrived too early, she risked appearing unnecessary. But if she waited too long, Alan could start without her, sending the same message to the audience.

Her gaze slid to the right of the bookcase. Off to the side, hidden from casual view, was a small framed photo of a pair of Bullmastiffs laying in the sun. It was the only photograph on display in the entire room. She closed her eyes, blocking the image.

Silencing one sense only served to enhance another. Her heartbeat began to race in anticipation. Juliane inhaled deeply, filling her lungs to their capacity. She savored the air's pressure as she counted to ten before releasing the breath. Repeating the cycle, she felt her heart calm. *Get it together. It's not like this is your first time,* she thought.

She did not need to see the minutes change on her watch to know that it was time to make her move. The only other personalization in the room was a small bronze paperweight shaped like a chameleon, which sat atop a filing cabinet near the door.

Her mother's friend, Daphne, had given it to her after it became clear that Juliane's mother was never coming back. It was the only thing Juliane kept after her brief guardian's heart attack. Juliane reached over and rubbed its forehead as if the physical activity would simultaneously crush the butterflies in her stomach.

Summoning as much swagger as she could muster, she pulled down the door's handle. Anyone watching her as she made her way down the hall would think she was the embodiment of cool confidence.

Her destination was in sight as a young woman with brown hair pulled back into a ponytail sprinted across the courtyard, cutting her off. The woman's toe caught on an uneven paving stone, sending her tumbling to the ground. Her face turned crimson as she attempted to collect a stack of papers that had littered the ground during the fall.

"Are you okay?" asked Juliane. She could feel seconds pass waiting for the woman to answer.

"No. I mean yes. I mean, other than being mortified that you just saw that, I'm okay." As the woman attempted to stand, Juliane noticed the woman's pant leg was torn at the knee. The woman took a step toward her scattered paperwork and winced.

Juliane bent to help collect a few of the scattered pages. "Are you sure?" she asked.

"It's just a scrape. It looks worse than it feels. Dr. Than is going to kill me for getting her paperwork out of order."

"I'm sure she'll understand."

"Have you ever met her?"

Juliane smiled. "I'm sure she is no worse than some of the people I've worked with over the years. I also think she'd probably be even less understanding if you bled all over her office. How about this? I need to go into a meeting, but I'll have someone swing her precious paperwork by her office before the end of the day. In the meantime, you go clean yourself up."

The woman glanced at her torn clothing and the stack of papers. "You wouldn't mind?"

Juliane held out her hand. "Aren't we all here to make life better for others?"

THREE

The heavy slam of the auditorium's double doors punctuated her entrance as a similar sound echoed on the other side of the room. Even with the delay in the courtyard, she must have arrived at the auditorium at the same time as Alan.

Juliane had been right to be concerned about the timing of her entrance. Alan never wasted an opportunity, not even a minute. He'd launched into basic introductions without preamble as he made his way to the stage.

The audience, of course, was captivated the second Alan entered the room. He could have been reading the ingredients from the back of a cereal box. They would still be eating out of his palm.

Juliane began handing out carefully-bound supplement materials without needing to be cued. Presentations changed, but some tasks were routine as muscle memory.

The words "My lovely assistant" caught Juliane's ears. It was all she could do to keep her face expressionless. *Now's not the time.* She fought the urge to grind her teeth in annoyance.

It will all be worth it, she thought to herself for the hundredth time during these project review board presentations. She and Alan both worked for the ACI. It was a multibillion-dollar entity, part private-enterprise, part university-partnered think tank, whose breadth of technology product offering was only surpassed by the size of its research and development.

Alan was its superstar. Juliane had been aware of his reputation even as a postgraduate student at Berkley. He had received his doctorate in biotechnology before he was fifteen, and had published the same year. His inbox was always stuffed with peer submissions awaiting his review.

"In 2013, a team of researchers was able to find methods to not only store a megabyte's worth of data into a speck of human DNA, but they were also able to retrieve that stored data. This, of course, has allowed us to move away from semiconductor technology over the years for memory storage; however, we still have not been able to find a means of accessing that data without some computer interface to interpret the results. That is until now." The audience stood in rapt attention as Alan continued. Juliane didn't blame them. She too had once been awestruck in Alan's presence, especially when he discussed his work.

When he called, inviting her to join his team, the phone call had sounded like a validation of every sacrifice she had ever made. She'd followed his career. She knew he commanded the best audiences whenever he presented. From what she could see, all the premier journal editors jumped at the chance to take his call, and if the various co-eds that always appeared to fill the background of his interviews were any indication, he possessed more than a few groupies.

Partnering with him, then, seemed like the only logical choice, especially if she was ever going to join the upper echelons of science. She took what she could carry on the first plane to the East Coast within hours of hanging up.

It had been nineteen degrees the day she arrived in Meriden, Connecticut, but the weather soon proved to be the least of her surprises. After only a few weeks of working together, her hopes became her dismay.

Alan could have easily gotten what he wanted out of a teammate by enlisting the help of a coat rack. She was relegated to a mere prop in his presentation, her contributions overly simplified time and time again, rather than relied upon as an expert in her own right.

"And I am sure you will be happy to report to the junior Mr. Evans that initial trials with synthetic tissue have well exceeded our wildest expectations."

Juliane's attention snapped back to the present as Alan's words registered. She was certain that only a nanosecond of surprise had flashed across her face, but equally certain that Alan had noticed it. While the ACI had ties to the university, it was controlled by the Evans family.

The Evans family had been generous in their endowments over the years, not only in their company investments but to the global community as well. The elder Mr. Evans was respected and admired even by the competition.

His son, Louis, however, was rumored to be a completely different matter. From what she knew about him, he'd grown up near the coast of Italy, enjoying hobbies such as windsurfing and extreme sports. She knew he had attended the Swansea University in Wales and that he had led the boating team to victory year after year only because she had witnessed more than a few individuals try to cite similar experiences as a way to earn favor with the board. The efforts had always backfired.

To her knowledge, Louis had nothing to do with the company. At least he hadn't for as long as she had been employed. But Alan's offhand remark implied that Louis's role was now much larger. Juliane cringed at the thought. Putting a jock like Louis in charge of the ACI could have only one outcome. *Epic disaster.* She needed to make a name for herself, do so quickly.

Alan did not appear to share her concerns. *Why should he? It's not like he has to worry about his reputation. He could quit tomorrow and get ten job offers without sending out a single resume.* He was now strutting around the room making broad gestures. He was proud as a peacock displaying his plumage. She mumbled under her breath, "Showtime."

Alan paused for effect. Juliane could see the attendees practically salivating in anticipation. They should. It was a discovery that would indeed drastically impact society. The things they would be able to do once the technology was further proven would cement the ACI's place in history.

Juliane absently patted the back of her hair, which was knotted viciously in a dark and glossy bun at the nape of her neck, as if to reassure herself that each strand was still in its proper place. A weaker-minded individual might be satisfied watching history be made from the wings; however, her mind was the least weak part about her. She was more than just Alan's lovely assistant, and it was time the rest of the world knew it. She had to find a way to inject herself into the conversation.

As the lights dimmed, Alan turned to verify that the projection on the wall matched his talking point. He caught her eye and paused. *This is my chance.* Juliane's heart raced. *Time to show them exactly what I can do.* She fought to control the excitement from showing on her face.

The presentation, which at this point had been filled with standard two-dimensional charts, graphs, and data points. Not trusting that a digital designer would properly understand her vision, Juliane had spent the last several weeks programming the next section herself.

Alan's lips turned up, but the smile he directed her way was anything but sincere. She knew in that split second that Alan understood this was the type of work that reputations were made on, but had no intention of sharing those honors with anyone.

"Ladies and gentlemen," he said before she could get a word in. "Today we can say that we have mastered the ability to access data through the mind alone!"

The audience leaned forward in their seats as the presentation on the screen spun into a breathtaking computer-rendered simulation. The only sound, aside from Alan talking, was a pen being dropped.

She suppressed the urge to interject or cry. Neither would earn her any points with the board.

"And it is all thanks to a simple firefly." An insect crawled across the screen and launched itself into an artificial twilight. "The science behind how these simple creatures illuminate the night, its bio-luminescence, is nothing new."

More insects joined the first on the screen. "But what we've been able to do with that enzyme certainly is." Their bodies flashed randomly at first but then settled into a coordinated symphony of light.

"Through a process of genetic imprinting, we believe we can now signal human epidermal cells to release a similar enzyme." The sky surrounding the insects condensed and warped until it was the outline of a human hand.

"You want to make people glow in the dark? Like bugs?" asked a man seated in one of the center rows.

There was a collective intake of breath in the room. No one interrupted Alan during a presentation. No one. Juliane would be surprised to see the man in the auditorium ever again.

Alan's lips tightened, but he continued without addressing the audience member directly. "Note that this technique would also allow for a degree of cellular control unmatched in the animal world. A person's skin would illuminate only just enough to be recognized by a receiving node. Then, through a series of high-frequency flickers—so rapid that they are nearly imperceptible to the human eye—a person's cells would then be able to transmit data packets similar to data transmitted by LEDs."

Alan paused to drink from a water bottle, although Juliane suspected the pause was more for the audience's benefit than to address his thirst.

"So where are the receiving nodes?" the man asked.

The corners of Alan's lips twitched as he turned his attention to his questioner. "The better question is where wouldn't they be? Traditional routers would still work, but they could just as easily be found in the person next to you. After all, a sunflower can track the position of the sun even though it has no eyes. It can do this thanks to yet another specialized cellular protein. The same sequence that can force the production of one enzyme can be used for another."

As irritated as she was with Alan, Juliane couldn't help nodding like a proud parent. While Alan's work centered on getting the data to interact with a person's internal cells, her algorithms were the key ingredient in making the system dynamic and adaptable. Together, what they had accomplished was almost magical.

"Imagine a world where no one has to worry about another ugly wireless tower going into their backyard, a world with ageless infrastructure. Imagine a world with Internet-enabled telepathy. I call it, Project Gene Assist."

As the lights came back up, Juliane readied herself to answer whatever questions would come her way. Her algorithm was designed to automatically calibrate performance regardless of skin tone, age, or gender. It was perfect. She could still salvage this opportunity. All Alan had to do was hesitate long enough to give her the opportunity.

As the minutes passed, her shoulders ached from refusing to slump in defeat. Alan was able to answer every question with ease and confidence, never once looking her way for assistance. She had to acknowledge he had come to this meeting well prepared.

Not for the first time, she wondered how things might have been different had she not taken his call that fateful day. The projects she would have worked on might have been less impressive, but she would have had an easier time distinguishing herself from less capable team leaders.

Juliane frowned and shook her head. She hadn't gotten this far in life by taking the easy route. She just needed to change her tactics. That smile had proven Alan knew exactly what he was doing. Perhaps it was time to take a different approach and confronting the issue directly.

As the last of the board members filed out of the room, Juliane dropped her statuesque calm facade. "We need to talk."

"What about? Do you think something went wrong? I rather thought our presentation went perfectly."

"Oh, now it's our presentation?"

"Your name was on it, was it not?"

"Oh yes, in small print on the opening slide. Very memorable."

"As was mine. I'm afraid I don't understand what the issue is."

"The issue is, as far as the board is concerned, that's the extent of my involvement."

"What is?"

"My name. On a single slide. In small print."

"They knew you were involved more than that. After all, why else would you be on the stage with me?"

"That's a great question. Why was I on the stage? You certainly don't act like you need me here. If my name wasn't on that one slide, no one would have known I had any input on the project whatsoever."

"You could have chimed in at any time during the question-and-answer round."

"No, I couldn't. You answered every question."

"And were any of my answers wrong?"

"No, but it was my area of expertise." She knew she had started to sound like a whiny child, but trying to regain her self-control was like trying to plug a broken dam.

"I see, and had they followed up with a question about how the data is stored in the proteins, or how the brain can access the information, could you have followed up on that?"

"We both know I wouldn't be prepared for that."

"So, you agree that we both knew enough about your *contribution*"—she didn't need to see his fingers make the air quote gesture to hear it in his tone—" to provide expert answers, but only one of us knew enough to provide complete answers on any topic." Alan paused. "If we had done things your way, this entire process would have continued twice as long, and for what? Your ego?" As he paused his eyes bore into her own. "What is that thing you like to say? Our purpose here is to find ways to make life better for others. There is no place for ego in the pursuit of the greater good, only efficiency. We make our presentation, get our funding, and go on to the next project as quickly as possible."

Juliane said nothing as she absorbed her words twisted against her. He was as prepared for her accusations as he had been for the presentation. She was forced to concede that he had won this round. She would leave, lick her wounds, and come back to fight another day.

"I am going to interpret your silence as agreement." He shut down the wall projection and put together the balance of his belongings. Without waiting for a reply, he turned and disappeared. Juliane closed her eyes and clenched her fists, swallowing a scream of frustration before it could consume her. Her time would come. She just had to be patient.

FOUR

Shadows stretched across the greenway as she exited the building that housed Dr. Than's office. It hadn't taken much effort to organize the woman's paperwork before handing the stack over to an idle runner in the lobby. Her office and lab space was in the Gould Building near the center of the ACI campus. When it was constructed, Louis Evans Sr. had just begun expanding his company's holdings. He had always been quick to invest in technology. As a result, the building was one of many structures built in the 'experimental' style loathed by the town's historical community.

It was a cylindrical structure with a glass dome top that provided spectacular views of campus. While the glass was clear, the dome acted as a solar collector, powering the entire building. At its base, the architects had installed a series of camera and pixel displays, which would then project whatever the view was on the other side, rendering the base invisible to the casual observer. The effect made it appear as if the top of the building was a floating hemisphere. Supposedly, Louis Evans Sr. had thought the town needed modernization to counter other structures such as Castle Craig, a tower made to look like a medieval castle set within nearby Hubbard Park.

To Juliane, the building was a testament to the ACI's willingness to invest in the unproven, but not all experiments are successful. The panels were enough to achieve the effect the designers were looking for, but what the architects hadn't anticipated was the extent of injuries their design would inflict upon those who never looked up as they wandered about the campus.

The entrance to the building was easy to miss. It was only identified by a subtle alteration to the otherwise repeating layout of brickwork that cut through the commons. As she approached, she noticed a man lounging against a walled planter near the base of the building. He looked to be about her age, in his early thirties, dressed more sharply than one might have expected at this time of day.

Juliane would have expected a person dressed like that to stand at attention, careful to avoid contact with anything that could mar its appearance. But based on his relaxed posture, he couldn't care in the least if his clothes were damaged by their proximity to dirt or brickwork.

His skin was gorgeously tanned and unblemished, his hair stylishly tussled. His face was partially covered by a full yet manicured mustache. Juliane decided it suited him.

He spoke as she grew nearer. His voice was velvet smooth with a singsong quality about it. It was not an accent she was familiar with. She was so caught up listening to the sound of the words and not their content that she did not immediately realize he was addressing her.

"I'm terribly sorry, Ms., but would you happen to know where in the blazes the entrance to the Gould Building is? I must have circled this spot nearly a dozen times and all I've gotten for my trouble is a bruise to my leg." Unlike the dozens of times she had heard similar complaints from new visitors, the man seemed more amused than annoyed.

Juliane remembered all too well her first visit to the building and offered him a sympathetic smile. "Sure, you've almost found it. Follow me." Juliane led the way, and within moments, several panels ceased displaying projections from the other side of the building, allowing a door to become visible. "The trick is to look for changes to the pattern of the brickwork. Around here the pattern is everything."

"Why in the world would a building be made with a door so hard to find?" he asked.

"I am sure the designers thought a door would destroy the effect," Juliane answered while sparing a glance upward and toward the dome. "Architecture aside, it also helps provide a higher degree of security. Several projects are being reviewed inside that the competition would give anything to know about."

They entered the building together. The marble of the floor tile shone in near mirror quality with images of the high-end fixtures reflecting on its surface. The interior of the Gould Building was more typical of a *Fortune 500* tower rather than most research and design facilities. Juliane had expected the man to stop to fully take in their surroundings, but his stride never broke. He nearly walked into Juliane's heel.

They continued through the building's lobby, finally reaching the elevators. "The directory is on the wall over there. Do you think you will be able to find your way from here?"

The man laughed. "Not if the interior of this place matches the exterior. I've been sitting out there waiting for someone to either enter or exit for probably the last thirty minutes. I was already late for a presentation before I arrived. I've likely missed it entirely by now, but I suppose there is a chance that I could go directly to the source for a download—assuming my contact is here." He looked around the empty hallway. "There doesn't appear to be a lot of traffic in this building."

"No, I suppose not. We tend to get lost in our projects and forget about the basic human necessities. Some of us even prefer to sleep here."

"We? I thought this building was nearly solely occupied by research and development. Are you one of the academic liaisons then?"

Academic liaisons were part-time employees, full-time students, and basically a step above servants. Within any other organization, they would have been called interns. However, the ACI had chosen the unique title as a way of acknowledging that in addition to being tasked with all sorts of menial work in support of assigned research teams, these individuals were also expected to serve as a bridge between the ACI and their various universities.

They had helped the ACI make millions, yet they were expected to put up with any number of indignities for little more than the hope that their indentured servitude might one day grant them the recognition that they had never been able to achieve on their own, and for what? Recognition that they might one day be invited to join the ACI full time and given the opportunity to repeat the cycle. Juliane wrinkled her nose at the thought.

It was common for new recruits to spend a year or two in such work, but a person still doing that work at her age? Juliane shuddered. *If an AL is my age and hasn't been recognized by now, they never will be.* It was a matter of personal pride that Juliane had never spent a second as an AL.

"I have had the pleasure of maintaining my own office here for the past few years."

He stopped in mid-stride, and Juliane batted her eyelashes, returning his false sincerity with her own. His gaze swooped over her body from head to toe, while his head cocked to the side and his thumb stroked his chin as if appreciating fine art. "What did you do then, graduate high school when you were twelve?"

She found herself wanting to shake her hair free from its bun in slow motion like women in the movies did whenever they were attempting to be seductive. *Where did that come from?* she wondered. Juliane was relatively certain that had she gone through with the move; she would have looked ridiculous. Juliane knew she was attractive, and had even gone on a couple of dates, but had found that most men were a complication she hadn't missed. Instead, she heard herself giggling. "Sixteen." *What has gotten into me?*

"Well, you don't look a day over twenty."

Juliane decided the banter had gone on entirely too long. As much as she enjoyed the moment, she shouldn't allow this smooth-talking stranger to turn her into a person she didn't recognize. She reminded herself that women before her had fought too hard to penetrate her otherwise male-dominated field. She had fought too hard. She would not allow herself to play the role of the vapid female, even if that's exactly the sort of person her mother would have raised her to be—if her mother had bothered to stick around. She rolled her shoulders as if shrugging off a coat while tightening the control on her expression.

"You mentioned that you were here to see someone? I'm not completely surprised that they didn't come down to see you when you missed your appointment; as I mentioned, we tend to lose track of time. Do you know what floor they are on?"

The stranger seemed oblivious to the effect he had had on her and her internal struggle. "Well, if I am being honest with you, even if I had managed to attend the presentation on time, it would have been a surprise visit. I'm here to see Dr. Faris."

Juliane froze, her finger on the elevator call button. She fought the rush of fire that sought to consume her cheeks. "If you were intending to surprise, you certainly did. I'm Dr. Faris, but I don't believe I have a meeting with you on my calendar."

She risked a glance in his direction, only to be disappointed to see that he did not share in her embarrassment over their prior exchange. If anything, he looked as if he enjoyed himself more knowing who she was. His eyes twinkled in amusement, and the corner of his lips turned up in a sly grin. "Okay. So that's not the only thing I need to be honest about. I've known who you were since before we met. I just wanted a chance to break the ice before we got to the formal introductions."

"Oh? And why is that?" The fire in her cheeks was immediately extinguished, replaced by a sick feeling in the pit of her stomach.

"Well, I have reason to believe that you might have made excuses not to meet me otherwise."

Juliane wondered if she might be dealing with some sort of stalker, an attractive, smooth-talking stalker but a stalker nonetheless. She knew it was only a matter of time before her success earned her one.

"And who might you be then?"

"I'm Louis Evans. I believe you might have heard of me?"

FIVE

Juliane and Louis rode up the elevator together in silence. Mentally, she replayed her words over and over again, analyzing them to see if she had said anything she might be ashamed of, now knowing who her companion was. By the time the doors opened on her level, she was still far from making a ruling.

"My lab is down this way." Juliane gestured toward a door with J. Faris displayed on the nameplate. Not waiting to see if Louis followed along, she picked up her pace. As she pulled open the door, she was greeted by Chad, her academic liaison and research assistant.

While he was an asset most of the time, Chad was hardly what Juliane would describe as dependable, due in large part to his involvement with another AL, Nadia. His girlfriend seemed to demand more of his time and more importantly, his attention than Juliane ever could.

Frustrated one afternoon after yet another missed assignment, Juliane lodged an official complaint, but that hadn't made an impact. She'd learned Chad's family had sway within the ACI—much more than it seemed she did. Juliane had concluded that until she found a way to be taken more seriously, his flighty personality would have to be just another inconvenience she'd learned to live with, much as a rock exists with moss.

"How'd the presentation go, boss?" Chad came to her side with a clipboard and a cup of coffee. His burnished red hair, pale skin, and freckled face combined with his earnest expression made him look like a child playing doctor in his white lab coat.

"As well as could be expected. Brace yourself, we're about to have some company." Juliane took the cup from his outstretched hand, grimacing as she realized the liquid was long out of the pot.

The door opened behind her as Louis entered, sending Chad back to his desk in a scurry. Juliane rolled her eyes. Why Chad had even bothered to apply to the AL program remained a mystery. She would have thought that a person with his level of social anxiety would have looked for a position that required less interaction with other people.

"Chad, I'd like to introduce you to Louis Evans, here to . . ." Juliane trailed off as she realized that Louis had never mentioned the reason for his visit. Louis spoke up before the pause became uncomfortable.

"Please accept my apologies, Dr. Faris. I realize I didn't give you any advance notice, but as I've recently become more active in the company, I decided I'd like to take a more hands-on approach, especially with some of the more promising work." He held up a hand. "But before you start to worry, I want to be clear. I'm just trying to get my finger on the pulse, not decide whether or not to pull the plug. And I've found all the pomp of a planned visit tends to get in the way."

Juliane's forehead knit as he spoke. His vague answer left her wondering what his role in the company truly was. Whatever it was, Alan and their audience earlier had been more familiar with it than she was. However, it didn't explain why Louis was meeting with her and not with Alan. Juliane frowned. She hated unknowns.

"I'd heard about your father. I am sure he'll be back behind his desk in no time."

Juliane nearly jumped when Chad spoke, it was so out of character. Her frown intensified. She had no time for office gossip and used advanced filters to mute sensationalized stories, but in doing so, she must have missed some momentous news. *Whatever it is, it must be really terrible for Chad to speak up. It has to be a scandal.*

Juliane contemplated changing her filter settings. If she relaxed them, she might be better prepared in the future, but then she would also be bombarded by all the garbage news that wasn't worth her notice. The frown deepened into a scowl. *No.* She would leave her settings as-is. What was the chance that she would ever be blindsided again to this extent?

Chad must have seen her frown and misinterpreted its cause because he quickly bowed his head and returned to his work.

Louis shrugged. "In any case, I am here now as acting CEO."

Juliane felt as if the floor dropped out from under her feet. She had prepared herself for Louis to say that he was in some training program, or come up with some bogus title designed to keep him from causing too much trouble, like Assistant Coordinator of Cool Research. She did not expect her career to now be in his inexperienced hands, even if his comment that her work was 'promising' was a point in his favor. Whatever had happened to his father must have been truly awful for the board to favor this decision.

I've run out of time. "So how do you intend to do that?" Juliane asked. She bit her tongue before her doubts about his abilities could spill out. "I mean what do you know about my work?" She once again fought against the rush of blood threatening to color her face. Questioning the big boss's competence wasn't the best strategy for distinguishing herself within the new hierarchy.

"Well, I know that our financial statements show a recently signed purchase of three, large, top-of-the-line three-dimensional scanners to a J. Faris with only the barest description of their intended use. Additionally, I saw requisition paperwork for several holographic projectors. Based on your association with Dr. Dronigh, I might have thought the scanners were being used to grow synthetic body parts, but that can't be it for three reasons." Louis held up his hand, counting off each point on a finger. "His reports are much more complete, there is no tie-in at all with the projectors, and finally because I know of at least three other groups who are decades ahead on that front."

Louis toyed with his mustache. "I would hate to think I paid for a poor copy of someone else's work. So, I am wondering, Dr., just what *did* the requisitions buy?"

Juliane's hands froze by her side. As much as he claimed to only be attempting to get a feel for current projects, he sure sounded like an ax man verifying his target before swinging the blade. *I have nothing to be ashamed about.* She straightened. *I followed standard operating procedures. The request went through the entire approval process. It's not my fault no one realized it wasn't for one of Alan's projects.*

Before she could say anything at all, Chad spoke up again. "Oh no, it's not like that at all. Dr. Faris is brilliant in her own right. She doesn't need to copy anyone else's work."

Juliane beamed in pleasure at her assistant. He might be as unreliable as the rain, but at least he was loyal. She told herself that she would try to be more forgiving the next time Nadia's demands caused him to come in late or leave early. *At least, I'll try. After all, I can't allow that sort of behavior to go on indefinitely; otherwise, nothing would get done.*

Louis's lips turned up. "Brilliant, eh? Well then, feel free to elaborate."

Her eyes narrowed at his grin. He'd known who she was downstairs and yet willfully led her to believe he was just another lost visitor. *Why?* So, he could make her look like a fool? Did that mean he thought she was a joke? Admittedly, she might have implied he wasn't qualified for his job either, but that had been an accident.

His behavior on the other hand, from the moment they'd met, had been deliberate and intentionally deceitful. She grit her teeth before her temper got the better of her senses. "How much do you understand about deep learning and artificial neural network processing?"

Louis's smile broadened. "I'll do my best to keep up."

"Hmm . . ." *How do I explain my work in terms this man will understand?* "Maybe it would be best to start with a demonstration instead?" she suggested. *Could this day get any worse?*

"By all means. Demonstrate away."

"Follow me." Juliane led Louis to the center of the room where a large tower made up of a trio of metallic arches took up most of the floor space. "You enter it here," said Juliane, gesturing at the blackout fabric hanging from the interior of each arch. "But put these on first," she said, handing him a small wireless earpiece and a clip-on microphone.

"Guess it's a good thing I'm in charge here, otherwise, I might ask if I need to sign a release," asked Louis with a twinkle in his eye as he immediately placed the fob in his ear. He affixed the microphone as he entered the tower. Juliane shook her head. He jested, but there were several other projects on the campus that dealt with strange radiations or otherwise unstable force. Only a person lacking a healthy sense of mortality would make a joke like in the campus labs.

Juliane clipped a small microphone onto her collar. "It's perfectly safe. I wouldn't dream of suggesting you do anything that could harm you. You have better lawyers than I do." Sound did not carry well from inside the tower by design, but she heard a hearty chuckle in response even before she attached her own earpiece.

She nodded at Chad to begin the power-up sequence, while she turned on a series of display screens. A series of lights illuminated the center of each column, pulsing up the length of each pillar.

Her screens lit up in an exact match to what was displayed on the inside of each archway wall for Louis. Without having to be told, Chad brought her digital notebook before returning to his post by the desk. He leaned into another small microphone. "Test Beta 152. Subject Louis Evans, male, Caucasian, systems scan complete. Initiating simulation."

Juliane took a brief sip of her coffee. It had somehow defied the laws of physics by becoming colder. "Chad, would you please get me a fresh cup? This is awful."

"No problem." Chad pulled out his phone. "Uh, er . . . it's Nadia." He waved the device. "I need to take a quick break. I'll bring it immediately afterward."

Juliane looked at her display and was met with the sight of the Italian coastline. It was a gorgeous day, fit for the movies, and pulled directly from a scan of Louis's mind. She sighed remembering her promise to be more patient. "I suppose can manage this from here. Just make sure it's still hot this time." Juliane waved, but Chad never looked away from his phone's screen as he hurried off.

Louis's voice spoke up in her ear, bringing her attention back to her demonstration. "This is incredible! It's like I'm there. Wait. I know that beach. I used to come here every summer. My father's cell phone reception couldn't reach this far, so we'd come here to escape for a little bit. It's so off the beaten path, it shouldn't be on anyone else's radar. My dad would be annoyed to see that it made it onto a computer's stock footage."

"It's not stock footage. My system has tapped into your neural processors. The landscape in front of you is what my algorithm has determined you most want to see. Based on a series of readings, it continuously takes on what neurons fire as well as changes in your body's chemistry." It was hard to keep the pride from entering into her voice.

"So, you are basically reading my mind."

"Well, yes, to an extent, if you want to simplify it like that."

"Should I be worried?"

"That is up to you. There are several layers of consciousness, and the system can only display so much before the images would get lost in mental noise. We just see what is in that topmost layer of your thoughts."

Juliane watched as the brilliant blue sky within the seascape display faded to an equally gorgeous sunset. A ring of rocks appeared on the beach surrounding a small fire. A tin filled with ice-cold beers materialized aside the fire.

Juliane had grand visions for her 'side project.' Seeing thoughts on a display was seeing your imagination take life, but there was so much more her algorithm would be capable of doing once she had proven the concept. As a stand-alone system, she saw applications beyond augmented reality. It could be used as a means of easier diagnosis and treatment of those with mental illness or those who otherwise lacked a voice. As a networked system, it had even more potential.

"You are getting the hang of it. But I need to warn you, the system does not differentiate between intended thoughts versus unintended tangents."

Silence. *First rule of effective communication, Juliane, know your audience.*

"Sorry, I'll try to explain it more simply. Right now you are thinking about a gorgeous day at the beach, but maybe while you are looking at that beer cooler, you allow a stray thought to bubble up about an incident in which you, I don't know, cut your hand on a broken piece of glass or step on a broken bottle. Suddenly, you might find yourself surrounded by distinctly less pleasant images and unable to regain control."

Louis made no comment to indicate he understood.

Juliane sighed. "In other words, you could go on a very bad trip."

While Juliane watched the screen, a woman draped in semi-sheer cloth leaving little to the imagination began approaching the fire ring, her black hair dancing in the virtual sea breeze.

"Careful, Louis. I was just telling you about how important it is to control your thoughts while in there." The features of the woman's face, which had been somewhat blurred, sharpened until Juliane realized that she was viewing a scantily-clad version of herself.

She hung her head. It wasn't even out of beta testing and already her work was being perverted for the adult entertainment industry.

Juliane clenched her fists. This entire demonstration had been a mistake. While she hadn't expected him to completely master his thoughts while in the simulation, she hadn't anticipated his tangent thoughts would take the same route as a sixteen-year-old male.

Juliane grimaced as the virtual woman wearing her face on the screen slowly lowered onto her knees, one hand reaching around to clasp her hair in a loose ponytail, while the other stroked the length of her body seductively.

Louis's thoughts would have to be fairly strong too, for the display to show that level of detail. Juliane's shoulders slumped. If she wasn't already apprehensive about the future of the ACI with Louis in charge, the last few minutes would have been enough for anyone to consider updating their resume.

Grateful that her assistant was not present to witness this latest mortification, Juliane began the shutdown sequence. "I believe that's enough."

When Louis did not respond, she continued. "I have to say I am sorely disappointed, and now, my entire official test records are sullied." She waited with arms crossed. Louis did not immediately emerge. "I am sorry, but there is no cold shower. You'll just have to come out as you are."

The curtain lifted and out stepped Louis. Tears of laughter streaked his face. The microphone was no longer attached to his shirt and not even the faintest hint of shame colored his skin. In fact, he looked even more confident and at ease coming out of the emulator than he had going in. He took one look at her stormy expression and laughed harder until his entire body shook.

He'd never lost control of his thoughts, Juliane realized. *Not even for a second.* Righteous indignation was replaced with an indecisive paralysis. She wanted to slap him. She wanted to shake his hand.

Other than herself, no one previously had been able to gain that degree of skill and control in her interface on the first try. Admittedly, the number of subjects who had logged time in the emulator was limited to Chad and the occasional passing AL they managed to flag down in the hall, but those early results couldn't be described as anything other than failures.

Her entire world had just been turned on its head. The taste of disappointment fled her mouth, leaving her lips dry by its sudden absence. She bit them to return their moisture.

Only time would tell if there was more to Louis than the crude exterior he showed the world, but if a person could display mental strength like a bodybuilder displayed muscles, the man standing before her might just be Mr. Universe. *Perhaps the ACI has a chance after all.*

SIX

"That's a fun toy."

Juliane shook herself back into awareness. Now seated at Chad's desk, he appeared to scan some of their notes from previous recordings. His cheeks were no longer wet from spent tears, although he still maintained a glow.

"I beg your pardon. My Total Immersion Reality Emulator is not a toy," replied Juliane, like the mother of the school's overachieving valedictorian being told that she had a 'good' student.

"Well, that's a pity. Add in a little haptic feedback and you'd be able to print money from red-light districts to the gaming industry."

"Haptic feedback? Oh, no. I will not cheapen my work by putting my software in little video booths with air jets."

Louis looked up. Juliane thought to herself that he must have been born with an amused expression on his face; there was just nothing that could spoil his mood.

"I do so hate to remind you that it's not just 'your' technology or 'your' software." He rested his head on a propped-up arm. "But just for the sake of argument, what would you do with it?" He gestured at the machine. "I will give you that you have probably developed one of the most realistic virtual reality programs I have ever seen, and the fact that you don't have to use of one of those ill-fitting sensor caps is a nice touch, but beyond that, there isn't all that much difference from what has been out there for the last fifty, sixty years." He raised his eyebrows as if challenging her to contradict his last statement.

Juliane straightened her back and shoulders, pushing out her chest. She noted that Louis's head tilted ever so slightly, a gesture she begun to interpret as one of appreciation. "Perhaps, had you arrived earlier and seen the presentation about the other project I've been working on, you might have realized the bigger implications too."

Louis's eyes twinkled. Juliane couldn't decide if she wanted to slap the grin off his face or if she wanted him to do something else with those lips. "Yes, that was rude of me, wasn't it? Please feel free to school me."

Juliane felt her body begin to tingle in a flush fueled by pride in her vision. "Had you been there, you would have heard that Alan and I have found a way to turn the human body into, essentially, an Internet server."

Louis's expression showed no indication he grasped the synergies between that news and the demonstration he had just experienced. But his performance in the emulator proved that his mind was vastly more capable than he let on. *Or maybe he just plays a lot of video games.*

"Just as the Internet is made up of a series of electrical connections, so is the human brain—both are simply processing data. Thanks to my mind-mapping algorithm, information, like the images you saw in the emulator, can not only be read onto a screen but could be potentially transmitted directly to a person's brain by mimicking pulses sent by optic and nerve endings. At least, in theory."

"Like augmented reality contact lenses?" Louis asked.

Juliane's shoulders loosened. Louis wasn't unimpressed due to not understanding the technology. He was just making sure that there wasn't something already on the market.

"Those lenses are limited to what information can be processed by sight. One-dimensional. You can improve the experience with an earpiece, but even then, the experience is limited. However, thanks to my algorithm, we will now be able to transmit things like taste, smell, and even touch—all with a thought. My virtual reality would look and, more importantly, feel real to anyone accessing it at any time. It wouldn't just be a virtual reality; it would, in fact, be a synthetic reality—and the data transmissions—well beyond what we call the Internet today."

Juliane felt more than a surge of satisfaction as she watched the amusement finally leave Louis's face. "So, what if two people logged in to your system at the same time? Might they think they are . . . I don't know . . . sitting by a fire drinking wine together, even though they are physically thousands of miles apart?"

He certainly has a one-track mind. "Yes, to them it would feel as real as if they were in the room together." *Fine. If this is what it takes to keep my project alive.* Juliane stepped closer. "They both would feel the heat of the fire, the taste of wine on their lips." She caressed her throat. "The carpet they were sitting on would feel just as soft or scratchy as they believed it should feel like." *Wait, that came off too naturally. Am I flirting?*

"I can think of a number of ways that could make life interesting."

Juliane felt ridiculous. *Now, who was being unprofessional? Of course, I'm not flirting.* Louis was technically her boss, even if he didn't want to act like it. She had every right to go to human resources and report him, if she wanted to, for his emulator joke. *Not that it would do me any good.*

"It's only a theory for now," said Juliane, hating that she had to include the disclaimer. "It will require people to agree to modify their DNA, which I don't see happening anytime soon. This is why my emulator is so important. It allows people to visualize the benefit—assuming the majority of people have more maturity than a teenager." Juliane looked pointedly at

Louis, who still lacked the decency to blush; if anything, his grin came back with a greater vengeance.

"But even so, your system is a long way from being perfect," Louis stated.

"What do you mean?" Juliane's forehead wrinkled. Her program was exquisite.

"Well, as you said, all it takes is for one errant thought and the system can take a user down a path that they didn't want to go down. Therefore, in a shared experience, who would really control the simulated reality?"

Juliane paused, surprised. It was a complication she hadn't considered. "I suppose whoever had the strongest will would take over the entire simulation."

"And what if a shared reality was, I don't know, hacked or hijacked? Espionage isn't limited to the movies. What then?"

Juliane's fingers tapped absently across her equipment as she thought through his question. She realized she had no ready answer. "I suppose there is some potential for abuse. I'll design in a system limiter."

"How much would that cost?" asked Louis, pantomiming the motion of pulling out and opening his wallet.

"It doesn't have to cost *you* anything. It's just a matter of programming time."

Louis raised his eyebrows briefly as he snorted. "And who do you think pays for your programming time, exactly?" He clapped his hands. "How about this—I will be presenting new advances in our technology in Vegas in two months. You need to convince the masses. Yes? That's all the publicity you could hope for."

He extended his hand. "I'd like you to be there with me, with this . . . What did you call it? The Total Immersion Reality Emulator?" Louis twisted his expression as if he had tasted something unpleasant. "I'll need to ask the marketing team to help with that one. TIRE doesn't exactly scream high tech. In the meantime, you'll need to figure out a way to get those limiters in place. Do you think you can do that?"

Two months. It took a minute for Louis's words to register. *That's not enough time to properly reconfigure and test the system. At least, not at that scale. It's . . . it's . . . it's my one and only chance to prove myself.* Juliane plastered a smile on her face and shook his hand. "I'll be ready."

Chad returned as Louis turned to leave. Seeing Louis approach, he jumped to the side. Coffee sloshed over the rim of the cup and onto his hand.

"Did you burn yourself?" Juliane asked, glancing around the room for something to blot the liquid.

Chad shook his head. "It's okay. It wasn't all that hot anymore. Is the demonstration already over?"

Juliane sighed as she took the cup from his hand. She wondered if she could put an on-demand coffee maker on the list of requirements for Louis. "Let's just say I showed him enough."

Louis turned at the room's exit with a grin. "I do believe Vegas will be a memorable experience—for both of us. Looking forward to seeing what you can do. Two months."

SEVEN

Chad was late again. Juliane's earlier promise to be more patient with him had long since expired. The symposium was only a month away and she still hadn't figured out how to demonstrate her technology to a large audience, short of forcing them each to file into the chamber one by one.

Even if that was an option, she wasn't convinced that the average person coming in off the street would be able to grasp its greater potential. The more she had thought of it, the more worried she had become that Louis's use of the chamber would be considered the norm.

She needed to adapt her algorithm to better serve the mental capacity of the average person coming in off the street. To do that, she needed another brain in the room for it to reference in testing. Chad's continued absences were causing delays she couldn't afford.

Juliane was just about to write him off for the day when her assistant burst through her office door. "I'm so, so sorry, Dr. Faris! I know I am late, but Nadia needed to finish telling me what I need to expect this weekend."

Juliane rolled her eyes skyward. "I hesitate to ask, but what is happening this weekend?"

"Nadia believes it is time we took our relationship to the next level. I'm meeting her parents, and I have to make a good impression—"

"Oh, and this announcement delayed you by . . ." Juliane glanced at the clock even though she was already very much aware of what time it was. "Fifty minutes."

"Really? Eh . . . I feel terrible, but you don't understand, she's daddy's angel," Chad stuttered as he was prone to do when he became particularly agitated. Juliane gave him a pointed look; she had previously given him tips on how to center himself, as she couldn't stand listening to his pained attempts to force out words.

Chad took a few calming breaths and continued. "If this conversation doesn't go right, well then, I might as well consider our relationship over. She's written out a list of everything I need to do to prepare for tonight. I hate to ask, but can I leave early today?"

Juliane took a calming breath herself. It was too close to the symposium to find and train a new assistant. If he would only apply himself toward his career with half the energy his relationship consumed, he might just have a chance to get through the academic liaison program. Juliane fought the urge to shake her head in disgust; wasting your talent was worse than having no talent at all.

A familiar voice spoke up from the doorway before Juliane had a chance to reply. "Oh, Jules, you know if you ever wanted to come by my office, I would be more than willing to provide you with some one-on-one mentorship on how to inspire those under you."

Juliane schooled her expression. She would not give Alan the satisfaction of seeing how much his words agitated her. "Alan, please, we've been through this nearly half a dozen times. Please don't call me Jules."

"Yes, we have, and yet, I still don't understand why you insist on getting angry about it? You are a gem, and it makes sense that your name reflects how dazzling you are."

Juliane fought the urge to gag. If the condescension rolling off Alan's tongue was any thicker, it would be visible to the naked eye.

"You know, Jules," continued Alan, dragging out each sound of the word, "if you ever tire of the whole ice princess thing, you might try to learn how to accept a compliment. You aren't that hard on the eyes after all. Who knows? You might even learn how to land yourself a prince. I'd be happy to give you some one-on-one mentoring for that as well."

Alan was good looking, but Juliane was attracted to more than surface appearance. "I assume that you had other reasons for coming down from Mount High to see me?"

"Now, Jules, why do you hurt me when you know I have only ever wanted to look out for you? What other reason might I need?"

When Juliane didn't speak, he continued, "Ah, but you are right. This isn't strictly a friendly call. I know that you landed yourself a direct assignment from Mr. Evans. I also know you'll be with him at the New Tomorrow Tech Symposium."

"I expect most everyone in our building knows that by now."

"Yes, well, I imagine you're probably getting pretty nervous and starting to think you aren't ready, but I just want you to know that the ACI wouldn't have signed off on you going—no matter who backed your invitation—if they thought for a moment that your work was going to reflect negatively on them."

"How unexpected of you, Alan. I appreciate your concern, but no, I'm not nervous at all." Juliane lifted her chin and rolled her shoulders back in an attempt to ooze confidence. *Alan can't possibly know how far I am behind schedule, can he? If Chad said anything to the other ALs . . .*

"Excellent. I am glad to see that you aren't wasting any energy on an emotion like that. It isn't as if you will have that large a crowd anyway." Alan turned to leave, placing his hand on the doorframe. Juliane remained silent. She would not ask for clarification. She would not.

"Our hall fits 200," Chad said.

If Juliane hadn't been working so hard to show only a calm and cool demeanor, she would have slapped her forehead at Chad's remark. This was not the time for him to attempt to defend her honor. She knew how Alan operated and was therefore unsurprised when Alan responded.

Without acknowledging Chad's presence, Alan directed his answer to her. "Well, that's a pity, as the majority of attendees will be in *my* presentation hall, but at least, on the bright side, you won't have to worry about violating any fire codes."

Juliane nearly bit her tongue in two as Alan departed. "Do you never think ahead? How could you set him up like that?" Juliane watched a rather impressive color change sweep through Chad's features. His skin became alabaster before blazing with a red that could put his hair to shame. She slumped down at her desk, rubbing a hand over her eyes as if it might somehow wipe away the sudden exhaustion she felt.

"I'm sorry, Chad. I know you couldn't help yourself. He's very good at reading situations and manipulating people to get the outcome he wants. I've seen him do it over and over again, and you are a particularly easy read. Just—word of advice—don't ever play poker with him." She began to massage her temples.

Chad also returned to his desk and picked up a ball made to look like an eight ball from a billiards table. Juliane watched as Chad looked at it, returned it to its spot on the desk, only to pick it up again and repeat the process a few seconds later.

"Why do you keep doing that?" she asked.

"Oh, this is a Magic 8 Ball."

"Are you asking it to grant you back the last hour?"

"It's not that kind of magic. Did you know my family agrees with you?" Chad's words were barely audible. He continued to look toward the toy.

Somewhat intrigued, she caught herself asking, "As well they should, but about what?"

"That I don't think ahead. But unfortunately, I do, and that's kind of my problem. For example, you might ask me if I want to watch a movie. If I say yes, I'll have to answer a slew of follow-up questions."

He turned the ball over and over. "What movie do you want to see? What theater? Are you going to want popcorn or a drink?" His eyes pleaded for her to understand. "There are any number of choices. But what if, as a result, we go to this one particular theater that has new kids on the staff who don't know how to properly pop the corn. What if they are always leaving too many kernels? What if the restrooms have doors that stick? What if after drinking too much soda, you leave the movie with a handful of popcorn to go to the restroom. You don't want to take food with you into the bathroom, so you try to eat it in one bite, but a kernel mixed in with the handful of popcorn sticks in your throat, blocking your airway, and the door back out is jammed."

He grabbed his throat and made a gagging sound. "Then, no one notices that you choked to death alone in the restroom until it is far too late, and it is my fault because I decided that we should go out to the movies rather than staying in."

Juliane sat in stunned silence. It was probably the longest conversation she had ever had with her assistant outside the topic of their work. "How do you manage to leave the house at all, thinking like that?"

Chad shrugged, returning his focus to the oversized Magic 8 Ball. "There are even more terrible scenarios for those who remain home alone all day. My parents gave me this," Chad waved the plastic ball in Juliane's direction, "as a joke."

She had seen the sphere before on his desk but had assumed it was just some random knick-knack. Now, she could see that the missing piece of the ball was filled in with a dark, flat surface.

"It was my grandfather's."

"What? That plastic thing is an antique?"

Chad shrugged. "Well, they don't make them anymore, so I guess it is a bit of a collectible."

Juliane rolled her eyes. She never could understand people who would pay an arm and a leg for an old toy when the new toys were so much better.

Chad, lost in his thoughts, continued, "I remember it sat on the top shelf at my grandfather's house. I was told I wasn't allowed to touch it until I was tall enough to reach it. He said it was magic."

"And, of course, you believed him."

"He told me it could tell the future."

Juliane snorted.

"Laugh if you want, but I was a kid. For that reason, I couldn't wait. One day, I stacked a footstool on top of the desk and climbed to the top, but it was still just out of reach. I stretched out as far as I could go, but I lost my balance and accidentally kicked the footstool out from under me. I grabbed hold of the shelf in an attempt to right myself and wound up bringing the whole shelf down with me."

"Obviously, you survived." Juliane knew she should be more sympathetic, but she needed Chad's attention to be back on their work.

"I did. But I wound up breaking my grandmother's favorite vase. That was the first lesson on unintended consequences."

It became clear to Juliane that Chad was not going to return his focus on the present until she allowed him to finish this little trip down memory lane. "So, tell me, how does it work?" she asked.

That question caught his attention. Chad eagerly showed her its underside. "It's filled with water, and there is a twenty-sided die inside with things like yes, no, or maybe printed on the sides. You think of a question, turn the ball over, and then, poof! It tells you the answer." Chad put the globe back down on his desk. "I haven't needed it much, though, since meeting Nadia."

Juliane bet he hadn't. As far as she could tell, Nadia made all the decisions for both of them. "Fine. I'll bite. What have you been asking it?"

"Whether or not I will impress Nadia's father later."

Juliane closed her eyes, intending to count to ten, but all she could see was Alan's gloating face in her mind. As a result, she asked, more shortly than she might have a mere minute ago, "And what does it say?"

"Outlook cloudy, try back later."

"I see." Juliane looked straight at their Total Immersive Reality Emulator. Her eyes darted to the side, and her head cocked ever so slightly as she grasped a stray thought. "So, your toy is just a random answer generator."

"I guess so."

"But people still believe it?"

"Well, I don't know if anyone believes it can predict the future, but it's nice to pretend."

"But what if it wasn't? Random, I mean."

"What? Like as in destiny?"

"No. Not destiny. Weighted probability," Juliane chided. She stared at her emulator. "Okay. I'll make a deal with you. I'll let you leave early today to study up on Daddy Dearest, but tomorrow, if I have a way to show you your potential future, do you think you might just be able to return to our work at hand?"

"Absolutely. You won't regret this."

Chad disappeared through the doorway before the sounds reached Juliane's ears.

"I'd better not," Juliane muttered to the empty room.

After an all-night marathon of software tweaks, the Total Immersive Reality Emulator was ready for another round of testing. Chad fidgeted by the side of the fabric entranceway, his earpiece and microphone already fixed in position.

"Whenever you are ready."

Juliane watched as he stepped through the archway, the LEDs on each pillar beginning their familiar scan. She clipped on her microphone while her displays came to life, showing an image of the exterior of one of the local restaurants from the vantage point of a car pulling into a parking space. Nadia was in the passenger seat, and she remained there even after the car came to a complete stop as if waiting for Chad—who had been in the driver's seat in this simulation—to open the door for her. He must have also made this realization as the display showed him acting like a classic gentleman.

Nadia entered the restaurant first, and a man rose from the bar area to greet her. Nadia was an attractive woman, and this man possessed a more than passing resemblance, obviously her father.

Her face lit up as they embraced, and she gestured over in Chad's direction. Juliane's earpiece throbbed with the din of the restaurant bar area. "Dad, I'd like to introduce you to Chad." Her father nodded his head briefly in acknowledgment, but the smile that had been on his face when greeting Nadia was severely diminished. The hostess came up to let them know that their table was now ready.

Juliane watched as the dinner scene played out. As she had expected, Chad allowed himself to forget that he was essentially in a program and began to react more naturally. They spent perhaps five minutes talking about his life as an AL and his most recent work; the rest of the conversation focused on Nadia, but Juliane could tell that Nadia's father hadn't warmed to Chad during this time.

Juliane's fingers flew over her display, toggling a keyed sequence. The simulation jumped ahead. Chad and Nadia were in an apartment, most likely Nadia's from its interior. Nadia explained to Chad why they just weren't going to work out.

Chad made repeated attempts to change her mind, but nothing worked. A glowing light shone under the apartment door. Chad went toward it, and the simulation started over, once again in the car.

The entire process repeated, beginning at the restaurant. Each time, Chad tweaked his response per Juliane's instruction, until dinner ended with Nadia's father shaking his hand and Nadia showing her appreciation back at the apartment. Juliane shut down the simulation.

"So, do you feel more ready now?" she asked Chad as he exited the arches.

"It was nice to have a reset button, but you can't know for certain that he was going to react that way. I mean, I've never even met him. I've only seen his photograph."

"That might be true if I based the simulation on only your brain patterns. But while you were obsessing over the unknown, I was adjusting the program to look up supplemental digital information. Now, the system doesn't just create a simulation based on your brain patterns; it also creates a response profile based on digital history—in this case, Nadia's and her father's social media interactions, browsing history, and spending behaviors. Using that data as a reference point, the system was able to incorporate their probable reactions into its prediction of your future, even though it has never taken their readings."

"Er . . . not that I am not completely impressed, but doesn't that violate their privacy somehow?"

"It might have been more black-and-white fifty years ago or so, but it's more of a gray area today. The data is out there, just waiting to be utilized, as long as you know the right channels to go through—and I do. Now, I believe you made me a promise yesterday."

"Well, you technically can't say you showed me the future."

"I never promised that. I said I would show you your probable future. You have to admit what I've done is far better than your silly Magic 8 Ball. Shall we get back to work?"

"Forget about the presentation. You could make billions with this playing the stock market."

"Please. We've only barely begun to scratch the surface of its potential."

"Well . . . you're the boss. What do you need from me? Should I go and get you some more coffee?"

"You should get a few cups for yourself as well. Neither of us will be sleeping again anytime soon."

EIGHT

Juliane smiled. Her system's predictive model wasn't perfect. A butterfly had flapped its wings in the Amazon, triggering a breeze that changed the weather pattern, resulting in Nadia wearing a light jacket. There would always be some element of chaos, but it was pretty impressive nonetheless.

Chad reported that the evening as a whole had played out so close to the simulation that it almost felt scripted. He'd also surprised her by making good on his promise as the last few weeks leading up to the symposium passed without further interruption.

Even though Chad was correct in stating the new predictive capabilities could gain the attention of analysts on Wall Street, but they both knew it would be impossible to capture the market's attention if the only exposure to the technology was from one-on-one demonstrations.

They had to make it bigger, much bigger, and make it a shared experience. With that in mind and Louis's signature on the bottom line, Juliane and Chad built up several other scanner pillars. These pillars, once assembled, would transform the entire presentation room into an emulation chamber.

Satisfied that all her equipment had been packaged and shipped to her standards, she made her way to the airport. After the grueling pace, Juliane was grateful that the ACI had taken care of making all of the arrangements.

The gate assignment on her ticket stub had brought her to a portion of JFK she had never known existed. It was a private hangar on the far side of the airfield, and she had reached it only by boarding a small trolley car.

When she entered the hangar, she was met with the sight of a single aircraft, whose image was mirrored in the high-gloss hangar floor. The aircraft itself could be considered a work of art by some circles. It featured a blended wing and body rather than the more traditional tubular fuselage and separate wing design.

Several aircraft builders had talked about migrating over to a similar design for the past several decades. Supposedly, the intent was to make aircraft quieter and more fuel-efficient, but as far as Juliane knew, none to date had been willing to risk their stock valuations on a design with unproven commercial results. And yet, here was a working concept with the ACI logo visible from every angle.

Juliane smirked as she found herself wondering if the Evans men were the type to overcompensate for shortcomings through the acquisition of large, fast, and expensive toys, and she attempted to muffle a chuckle before someone overheard and forced her to explain herself.

A glance around soon proved that she hadn't needed to worry. Louis was nowhere in sight. Juliane realized she was relieved yet disappointed. As she entered the craft, she paused in the entranceway. Louis might not be there, but she wasn't flying alone. Seated in one of the many swiveling, leather-clad chairs, was a man pouring himself a drink who she'd never seen before.

Juliane's eyelashes were longer than the man's hair, which was so blond it was nearly white. He wore a tailored suit similar in style to one of Louis's, which had to cost more than what she paid for rent in a month. As she crossed the threshold, he stood at attention, like a gentleman of old, but had to be close to the same age as Louis.

He stepped toward her while placing the drink to the side in one graceful motion, and he clasped her hand in his own. She was taken aback at how very strong his grip was.

"Ah, you must be Dr. Faris. I'm Durham Ladensham, professional entourage, and part-time legal counsel, at your service." He must have seen Juliane's wince at the strength of his handshake as he immediately softened his hold. "My apologies. I've recently taken up fencing and occasionally forget that my grip is a bit tighter than it used to be."

Juliane attempted to smile back in understanding but wasn't quite sure how to process his statement. She'd never encountered anyone who had taken up fencing as a sport. The people she interacted with tended not to take up any sport unless required to by their doctor; even then, it was typically either jogging or golf.

He continued, misinterpreting the cause of her hesitation. "I'm a longtime friend of Louis's. He asked me to serve as your unofficial tour guide while he wraps up a few other details ahead of the symposium. Don't worry. He'll be joining us in Vegas."

Juliane raised a single eyebrow. Louis thought she needed a traveling companion, did he? What did he think she was going to do? Wander off and miss her chance to stand in the spotlight?

"He's not told me much about what you are getting ready to present," Durham continued, oblivious to her reaction. "I am hoping that you might be a little more loose-lipped." He smiled, daring her with his eyes.

Juliane met his gaze and shrugged. If Louis wanted to play coy with his friend, she could play along, but first, she had to dispense with any suggestion that she was some dainty maiden in need of an escort.

Without breaking eye contact, she moved to the aircraft railing and swept up the drink he had been in the process of pouring. She raised the glass to her lips, halving its contents. She tasted smoke as the rich scotch warmed her belly.

It was the type of drink one might suggest would put hair on your chest. Certainly not one a stranger would have poured for a lady. She savored the flavor before asking, "So, fencing?"

Juliane felt victorious as his eyes left hers, tracking the motion of the glass. His smile deepened in appreciation along with the tone of his voice. *Message received.*

"Well, it's hard to keep up with the old lacrosse circuit when you travel as much as I do. I felt like the ultimate FOGO. I figured that this way, all I have to do is find a club nearby." He shrugged.

"Sorry, I have no idea what you are talking about."

"Oh, well, some of us aren't as lucky as you are, and have to find other ways to maintain our girlish figures." Durham snorted at his joke.

"It's not been that hard. I just don't go out to eat much." Juliane forgot to eat altogether some days. It depended on how engrossed she was with her work and whether or not Chad was around to remind her that Nadia was waiting on him for their next meal. "No, what I meant was I have no idea what FOGO is."

"Oh, I see. Louis and I played on the same team for a while. FOGO: Face Off, Get Off. I felt like I would only show for a game and then wouldn't see the team again until the following season. Louis has this huge banner of the WLA, er . . ., Welsh Lacrosse Association, on one of the walls at his place. I tend to forget that not everyone grew up with the terminology."

The crew must have completed their final safety checks because the aircraft door was closed, and an attendant interrupted the conversation, motioning them to take their seats. Juliane sank into the plush cushion. "I may never be able to fly coach ever again," she sighed, sinking even further with the jet's rapid acceleration.

"Well, if your presentation goes even a fraction as well as Louis anticipates, I suspect you may never have to. Welcome to the good life." He had poured himself another drink right before their ascent and raised his glass from his seat. She returned the gesture, emptying the balance of her glass.

Their ascent was over before Juliane could put her glass down. As soon as cruising altitude was reached, Durham swiveled in his chair toward her. "What is the big hush-hush project anyway?"

"Does Louis normally keep you in the dark?"

"Normally? No, which is why I am now so intrigued. I'm not just a pretty face here. I like to know what is going on so that I can advise him on what he needs to do to come out on top."

Juliane shrugged. "Well, I suppose he has his reasons. I would hate to ruin whatever he has planned." Juliane watched the smile slip from Durham's face for a moment. He bowed his head, and when he raised it again, he did so with a fox's grin.

"Well, we are heading to Vegas with some time to kill. How about I play you for the information?"

"What kind of game do you have in mind?"

"How about the game of kings?"

"What? Chess?"

"The fact that you even caught that reference tells me that it's a great choice. You're a genius, right? Well, then, you've got nothing to fear. What do you say?"

"Chess." It was a question as much as a statement. Lacrosse in Wales, fencing around the globe, and chess as his go-to game of choice. The man sitting before her had quite a different upbringing than she had.

Durham didn't waste time waiting for her to answer. He pulled out a chess set from a small compartment located near his seat. Then he pushed a small button and a table rose from the floor.

"Convenient you have the board ready."

"Isn't it, though?" Durham grinned like a child. The pieces were set up in a matter of minutes. "Ladies first."

Juliane marveled at the board as Durham placed the final piece. It was a beautiful set; each piece appeared hand-carved out of marble and polished to a high shine. She hesitated to mar their surfaces with her fingerprints. She moved her first pawn as if it might shatter on impact.

A few moves later, several of her pieces had been captured. As she suspected, Durham was quite skilled with the game. She watched as he swooped in to take out another, this time a knight. With each move, he had grown bolder and bolder while her available moves dwindled.

"Really, my fine doctor, you ought to pay more attention to the game at hand—a couple more moves like that and your king will be completely exposed." He paused.

She had been hunched forward, studying the board, but looked up when he had begun speaking.

His smile widened to a near leer. "Or are you hoping for an excuse to bare all your secrets?" She glanced down to realize that her neckline had drooped low, providing him with a display of cleavage. She successfully fought back a blush. *Stay confident, Juliane,* she told herself as she acknowledged his comment with a quick tilt of her head and a single raised eyebrow.

She watched as he raised his eyebrows in surprise. She saw his Adam's apple bob in a quick gulp before he regained his composure.

Juliane turned her face back toward the game at hand, although she continued to look up at Durham through her eyelashes. "Oh, I think I might still have a chance. Don't you?" Her voice deepened to a near purr as she reached out to caress one of her chess pieces. "You know, we never did agree what I get if I win."

"In full disclosure, I feel that I do need to tell you that I've beaten some of the best in the world, including Louis. But in the event that happens, you can name your reward."

"Anything I want?"

"Anything at all."

"Day spas, shopping sprees, fine dining?"

"Sure. I'll hand over my card, but you might find yourself needing a big strong assistant to take you to all those places."

"And you'd be willing to do all that if I win?" Juliane drew the piece she held ever so slightly along her face so that its tip rested just beside her lips.

"All that and more. If you win, I'll be your personal slave as long as we are in Vegas," Durham responded eagerly.

Juliane shifted her head so that it rested on her other palm as she placed the piece back on the board, rubbing her thumb along its head. Durham took a quick glance around as if verifying that they were alone in the cabin. "Well then, I believe you should hand over your wallet, as do I believe you have found yourself in a back-rank checkmate."

Durham's eyes darted back to the board. His king was firmly trapped behind his ranks with no available moves, and it was at the mercy of her queen. Juliane smiled, batted her eyelashes, and said, "Oh, and while you are at it, would you please fetch me another drink?"

The look of shock upon Durham's face was too much to resist, and Juliane threw back her head in a burst of unrestrained laughter.

"What just happened?" Durham asked as he moved to refill her beverage.

"You don't play women often, do you?" she asked as she shrugged a shoulder with a look of mock innocence.

"You play dirty. I'll remember that the next time we play," he replied.

"Who says there is going to be a next time?"

"There is always a next time. Just ask Louis."

"Oh, dear. It sounds like I may have bitten off more than I can chew."

Durham launched into tales of he and Louis's various exploits. By the time they landed, Juliane felt much more knowledgeable about her new boss.

However, she now understood why Louis hadn't told him the details about her project. Durham was a voice in need of an ear. Even so, he was entertaining enough, and before long she found herself looking forward to sharing his company in Vegas.

NINE

She had gone into the first boutique more out of curiosity than need. A sideways glance at an exposed tag showed a price well beyond her average means. As she moved through the rows of clothing, Juliane had selected garments without hesitation, interested to see how far Durham would let her take her victory.

Rather than stopping her, he had given an indulgent grin along with his credit card. However, she didn't swipe it once, much to the chagrin of the sales clerk, who was denied a significant commission. While she might be willing to employ some of her mother's tricks, others left a sourer taste in her mouth.

"You know you really could have gained an entirely new wardrobe," Durham announced as they made their way toward her hotel.

"Thanks, but it wouldn't have been right."

"Why not? You beat me fair and square."

"That was just a game. I'm not going to spend your money on my clothes. Especially not here. Did you see those prices?"

"Chess is so much more than just a game. It's about strategy, and our strategy for the presentation should involve getting you outfitted in something that will take the room's breath away. Please, let's make one more stop. You earned it."

Not waiting to hear her protest, Durham steered Juliane into another boutique. Juliane's eyes widened at the outfits on display. Before she could turn around and leave the shop, Durham flagged the attention of the store's clerk. This clerk was not as willing to abandon a commission, and within short order, she pulled a white suit from the back of the shop.

It was made of some newly-developed material that put standard cashmere to shame. It was the color of Antarctic snow and accented by subtle lines of silver piping. The sales clerk dragged Juliane to one of the fitting rooms. Juliane couldn't help herself. The fabric was so soft, she had to try it on. The outfit fit as if it had been designed for her and her alone. It complimented her every curve.

"Gorgeous. Simply gorgeous," exhaled Durham as she exited the room.

"I still can't accept this," Juliane sighed.

"That's too bad, because I paid for it while you were in the fitting room, and I am sorry to say this shop doesn't have a return policy. However, to complete the look, you really need to do something with your hair. Good thing I've already made you an appointment at the hotel's spa."

"You really shouldn't have," protested Juliane. She ran the numbers in her head. *If I put aside a few dollars each paycheck, I might just be able to write him a check in . . . five years.*

"Yes, I should, and you shouldn't pretend you don't want to go. This could be your regular life soon enough." Durham's expression softened. "The world won't know what hit them."

Durham left her at the spa entrance to go check in with Louis. She had been plucked and trimmed with near surgical precision. Her skin, normally pale, had taken on a rosy hue after their ministrations and shimmered due to a post-treatment moisturizer containing a subtle body glitter. Without a single split end to mar her hair's shine, her dark hair cascaded down her back as if it was a blackened waterfall. Looking into the mirror, she had never felt so stunning. *I'm never going to be able to pay him back if I'm only ever seen as Alan's lovely assistant.*

Before he left, Durham had arranged private transportation for her between the spa and the auditorium. Seeing how the bright white shone, she was relieved not to have to risk her new clothes on the monorail shuttle.

She entered the recently renovated convention center like a queen, basking in the admiring glances turned in her direction as she made her way down the hallway, all the while pretending it was just another day.

Though the common areas were crowded, she recognized Alan's voice. He was seated under bright lights and giving an interview to a reporter. She acknowledged him with a subtle nod of her head as she passed.

The reporter repeated his question. Alan's response had none of its usual polish. Her lips turned up ever so slightly as she continued toward her room.

Finally, she arrived in her auditorium. All the pillars were positioned exactly where she had specified. It was an arrangement four times larger than the original configuration at the ACI campus. Everything was going to plan.

The pillars nearly encircled the room but were placed in such a way that they blended into the room's perimeter. She could see Chad's red hair behind the array of equipment as she strode up to the podium.

As she approached, she had to stifle a laugh. The tan suit he had chosen to wear, combined with the black cords in his hands, made him look like a meerkat. The image was further strengthened when he froze in place at the sound of her approach.

"If that's how you clean up, I have to find an excuse to get you out of that ivory tower you call a lab more often." Juliane spun around to see Louis leaning casually against the auditorium entrance. As if sensing a predator, Chad immediately dropped back down out of sight, continuing his work.

"Durham's probably relieved to be off escort duty," Juliane replied.

"The last I saw him, he was happy enough with the assignment, and I can see why."

Juliane stifled a laugh. Within moments, his long strides had brought him nearly an arm's length from her.

Louis changed the subject. "Durham also tells me you beat him at chess. I should have warned you against that. Now he is going to be gunning for a rematch every time he sees you." Louis rolled his eyes. "He can be a little like a dog playing fetch that way."

He chuckled at his joke before becoming more serious. "I should have warned you about that. Now that you've demonstrated that you have some skill, if you ever do lose to him, you are going to hear about it until the end of time. Trust me, I know from personal experience."

Laughter entered back into Louis's voice. "I swear he is going to make sure that people thousands of years from now know that he once won a game."

A venue representative ran up beside Louis with a clipboard in hand. "Mr. Evans, sir, I believe we have everything set up as requested. Video and sound checks were great. Guests should begin filing in within the next twenty minutes. Do you want to be in here when that starts or be announced?"

"Yes, I think it might be better to make an entrance. I'll stand over there and will come on stage after the introductions."

Juliane looked at Louis and the man, her brows knit in confusion. "What do you mean? I thought I was giving the presentation?"

The man looked nervously from side to side, avoiding eye contact with her. Juliane waited for Louis to respond, while a terrible but oh-too-familiar feeling began to grow in the pit of her stomach.

"I know that this is your project and, therefore, your baby," Louis answered. "Nobody in this world would be able to tell the world about its inner workings better than you, but that's just it, you know too much about its inner workings. You said it yourself. We have to convince the masses that their need for this technology outweighs the risk. We want to sell people on its potential. We want them to dream."

Louis paused as if waiting for Juliane to come around to his way of thinking. She kept her silence.

"If we tell them exactly what it can do, they are going to focus on what it can't." He finished as if it were the most obvious logic in the world.

"But what about the script I submitted?" Juliane asked.

"Yes, thank you for those talking points. They were extremely helpful. Have I mentioned that you look positively amazing? The media is going to have a field day trying to figure out who the gorgeous woman is beside me."

He gestured toward the crowd. "Trust me, by keeping an air of mystery about you beyond the initial introduction, you are going to have journalists practically selling out their own mothers to get your name and your entire backstory out into the news sphere first. Why pay for marketing when they'll do it for you?"

"And why should I trust you?" Juliane exclaimed. "You were planning this for some time, but didn't bother to tell me."

"You should trust me because my family has been doing this sort of thing successfully since before you were born." Gone was his friendly demeanor and in its place was all business. She was reminded that the subject of her anger, was also her boss.

Juliane's shoulders slumped. She had no argument that would change his mind. She was going to have to suffer through being a prop once again. Alan would no doubt make a point to stop by and gloat the minute they were back in the labs.

Juliane glanced over to the coordinator by Louis's side. The man studied his clipboard as if it contained the secret formula for eradicating cancer in all its forms.

She noticed he also had a few programs of the day's events clutched under his arm. She snatched one quickly, adding a glare that dared him to object her rude behavior. She scanned the page until she found her event. Printed on the page in black and white was Louis's name beside her topic.

Louis's tone softened. "I am sorry you misunderstood my expectations for today. The management group or someone from our public relations department always takes the lead on the topics that we feel have the greatest chance of success. Considering how many people fear public speaking, most people we work with thank us for doing this. I just assumed you knew about the standard arrangement."

Juliane's lips had tightened into a fine line. "I guess I missed that fine print. If that is the case, then would it be fair for me to assume that someone has at least briefed you on the latest benefits of the new algorithm? "

Juliane's barb landed as she knew it would. As the deadline had approached, her progress reports had only covered the barest details. She hadn't felt the need to include everything at the expense of her program. Back when she thought she was going to be presenting, she didn't think the lack of complete documentation would matter.

Louis had the decency to allow the fairest hint of blush to pass over his face. "The last report on your progress was a couple of weeks ago. I was planning on just presenting based on that lovely demonstration you provided when we met, just on a larger scale. What should I know?"

"You wanted something that dazzled. Think of this as virtual reality meets one of those ancestry websites meets documentary."

Juliane could tell that he failed to see the connection. "Ah, well, I guess the show has to go on. I'm better winging it on the fly anyway."

The nervous little man coughed. "Well, if everything has been worked out, it's probably time for you both to take your places."

Sparing Louis one more glare, Juliane whirled around and marched toward the stage, each step sharply punctuated by the click of her heel. At least her time with Alan had given her plenty of experience standing around in someone else's spotlight.

As she passed, Chad gave her a quick sympathetic nod. She hoped for his sake that he had merely seen the program at some point while she was away at the spa rather than knowing about it in advance and not informing her.

The lights began to dim as visitors filed into the room. Each was given a pair of slim glasses as they entered. Louis had disappeared into the shadows. Juliane saw Alan pass by the auditorium doors on the way to his room and plastered a killer smile on her face. She tried to at least take some measure of satisfaction in the knowledge that every person who entered was one less person attending his presentation.

Eventually, the room reached its capacity. The nervous little man with the clipboard made a few welcoming remarks as other staff in the back closed the heavy doors. She flicked her wrist ever so slightly, signaling Chad to begin the show.

Remaining lights abruptly switched off, sending the room into absolute darkness. Juliane listened as a few of the guests shifted nervously. The pillars' lights began to pulsate. The ceilings were replaced with the impression of a starry night. This, in time, was replaced with the dawn of a sunrise as the display panels came on-line.

The walls became a panoramic view of a seashore. On the horizon was a tall wooden ship. A smaller rowboat was slowly coming closer. Then the rowboat hit the shore.

Men and women dressed in garb hundreds of years out of date crawled over the railing, some with joy radiating from their faces, others with trepidation. Juliane heard at least one person in the crowd gasp. The figures were so real, you thought you could reach out and touch flesh. Her skin prickled in response to where it was hit by virtual ocean spray.

The scene changed once again. The ocean transformed into a land worn to dirt and scarred from heavy wagon wheels. A hot dry wind blew, kicking up dust and grit, and filled the nostrils with the smell of horsehair and manure. Juliane could see a few people's brows break out in a sweat as the artificial sun shone down upon them. A group of men rode by, startling several spectators. Once again, Juliane heard gasps, and she let out the breath she didn't know she had been holding.

The sun was replaced by artificial lights. The desert was replaced by the sterile cleanliness of a room very different from the one they were in. Gone was the smell of livestock, replaced with bleach and bad cologne. The room was filled with rows of large CRT monitors, large buttons, and dials. The image on the monitors showed a rocket firing into space. The operators of the monitors were jumping up and down in celebration, showing glimpses of garish plaid polyester pants on some.

Mission control faded away. They were in a city surrounded by traffic-congested streets. A tower of steel and glass blazed like fire as it reflected the orange hue of the sky at sunset. Nearby, a man-made waterfall cascaded down the sides of a square. Even from this distance, several names could be seen etched into its sides.

A crowd of people nearby cheered as a spire was raised on the tower, which happened to be one of the most recognizable structures of all New York. Its existence was both a reminder of the past and a challenge issued to the future. A challenge to always rise and move forward. A challenge to never be beaten by fear of the unknown.

It was a challenge that Juliane accepted long ago. As a man bolted an etched brass plate into position, Juliane heard someone shout, "Where did they get this footage? That's my grandpa!"

She ached to explain that the simulation had been more than just canned footage and approximations. Her system had homed in on a few individuals within the crowd and cross-referenced their identification badges with historical reference information to create figures based on the composition of identifiable genealogy in the room. The gasps from the crowd had been those individuals either recognizing the event itself from their personal histories or a striking family resemblance.

The display panels turned off, and they were all once again in the Las Vegas Convention Center auditorium. Juliane looked into the shadows where Louis stood. He was frozen in place with his jaw hung open.

She had provided a high-level summary of her plans for the introduction along with her script, but it was one thing to read about what would be on display and quite another to experience it. Meeting her eyes, Louis closed his lips and nodded in appreciation.

Louis stepped onto the dais to thunderous applause. The audience was rapt as Louis painted a picture of a bright future utilizing her technology, one where children could attend school from the safety of their own homes and live history lessons; one where international corporations could trim expenses by conducting meetings without travel, but also without sacrificing senses like touch; one where consumers could sample virtual a products before buying them, reducing the need for stores to carry excessive inventory.

The crowd ate up his every word as he worked them into a fever pitch. If there were any investors in the room, they had to take satisfaction in watching their wallets expand before their eyes.

Louis paused in mid-stride and smiled at Juliane before turning back to the crowd. "We are now at the dawn of a new age, an age where our history can be brought back to life and one where reality can be what we make of it. I give you . . . the Datasphere. And now, I would like to introduce you to the brains behind this amazing advancement. If you haven't already done so, please take off your glasses and put your hands together for Dr. Juliane Faris."

As the lights gradually returned to full brightness, Juliane noticed a woman near the center of the room wipe away a tear as she removed her glasses. Whether the tear was from joy or sorrow Juliane couldn't tell, but really, it didn't matter. That droplet of moisture proved their system was a success. Anyone could manipulate senses such as sight and sound, but that tear proved the scenes had been real enough to produce an emotional response.

Juliane scanned more faces in the crowd. Toward the back, cloaked in near shadow, was a man with hair nearly as black as hers. He was dressed in a dark, expensive, tailored suit. He met her gaze, inclining his head ever so slightly, before handing his glasses back to the small man with the clipboard and exiting the auditorium.

TEN

Juliane waited while the audience finally filed out of the auditorium. Her high from the presentation's success had already transformed into uncertainty about her next steps.

A trio of individuals, two males, one female, continued to orbit around Louis. They were an odd group. One man was desperately trying to hide a balding hairline in the front but appeared to lack the same concern about his backside. The other man, significantly younger, had coated his hair in enough gel that it could likely stop a bullet. The woman, a young blonde, had a smile fixed on her face that never quite reached her eyes. Juliane had the nagging suspicion that she had seen at least two of these three once before.

She watched Louis gesture toward the pillars with his charismatic grin firmly in place, but the motion was an afterthought. Rather than returning his hands to his side, he twirled a pair of glasses while answering the rest of their questions. As impressive as his speech had been, Louis continued to misunderstand where the power behind the technology was housed.

The trio had closed in around him so tightly that she was unable to hear exactly what their questions were, but they looked like they were lapping up whatever he was dishing. The little man with the clipboard hovered impatiently on the fringe of the room. Most likely he would prefer to move the impromptu question-and-answer session out of the room so that he could begin preparations for its next usage, but he was nervous about interrupting such a powerful personage.

As Juliane watched Chad pack up their computing supplies without waiting for instruction, she realized she almost envied Chad's complete lack of personal ambition. He was content to be a drone. Do as instructed, set up equipment, clean up equipment. Repeat. Her next steps were not as clear, yet whatever she did could impact her reputation.

Should she take charge of the cleanup? It might reinforce that she was the expert, but it might make it look like she couldn't handle delegation. Should she inject herself into Louis's conversation? It might potentially jeopardize his media dynamic. Should she continue to play coy? Chad saw her looking at him, shrugged at her unspoken question, and continued with his task.

Juliane considered leaving the auditorium. She could listen to one of the other presentations, but that might ruin the illusion of mystery she was expected to maintain. *Am I still supposed to be mysterious after Louis's introduction?* she wondered.

She could go back to her room, but that would feel like surrender. She could go in search of something to eat but found she had no appetite. Unsatisfied with any option, Juliane decided to continue to wait in the shadows while Louis basked in the glow of the public's adoration. *I've turned into Chad.*

After agonizing minutes, Louis finally looked her way. She captured his focus and returned his attention with a fierce glare, the type of which frequently caused Chad to remember some errand he had to immediately attend to.

She realized she shouldn't have bothered with the effort. Rather than shivering from its icy point, Louis threw his head back in laughter. She was not able to maintain her ire faced with such genuine humor, and her visage softened. He gestured her quite urgently to come to his side.

"Of course, as I said on the dais, none of what you witnessed today could have been made possible without Dr. Juliane Faris, here. You may want to start lining your interviews up now, as she is destined to go down in the history books as one of the great innovators of our generation."

The trio, who had barely registered her presence, turned toward her like children shown candy. "Unfortunately for you, you aren't going to be able to start with those interviews at this moment." The woman pouted. Juliane recognized her then as Melissa Bryant, a field reporter for the Financial Sector Times Network. *The other two must also be part of the press corps*, thought Juliane, although she was not as familiar with either of them. Louis crooked his elbow expectantly. "M'lady?"

Juliane allowed her lips to turn up while taking his arm like an old-fashioned debutante. Together, they departed the auditorium to the relief of Mr. Clipboard. As she glanced back, Mr. Clipboard put his finger to his ear, likely speaking into a wireless headset, as the convention center's version of a SWAT team descended upon the now-vacant room.

Along the way down the hallway, they passed the room where Alan was giving his presentation. He did still have a fair turnout, but Juliane took a nearly indecent pleasure in the knowledge that his crowd was less than her own. The day might not have gone completely as she would have preferred, but at least she had this small triumph.

As she turned to leave, she noticed the same man with a dark suit and hair she'd seen before. He was near the front of Alan's stage, looking out toward the crowd rather than at Alan, and she could tell he had noticed her watching.

The corners of his mouth pulled back in a wolf's grin. As much as she wanted to continue walking, her legs were rooted to the floor. Louis turned to investigate the cause of the delay, and the moment was shattered.

Louis's expression hardened. The man tipped his head in Juliane's direction before turning his attention back to Alan. Juliane jumped when Louis spoke. "I think today's presentation was a success, don't you?" His tone felt forced. However, as quickly as it came, the cloud over his features passed, and Juliane found herself thinking of an eager puppy dog looking at the expression that took its place.

Her early annoyance melted away too. While she might not have been allowed to shine to her fullest, her algorithm had.

"Durham's probably out there getting himself into some trouble," said Louis. "What say we join him?"

She laughed. She had only spent a few hours with Durham but could guess that Louis's jest wasn't far from the truth. Everything Juliane had done since childhood had been done with precision and had gotten her nowhere.

Durham, on the other hand, struck Juliane as one who lived in the moment. And yet he was able to fly in a private jet and party with the rich and famous. Perhaps Alan had been right. Perhaps she should try letting her hair down too. She always did appreciate an intriguing experiment. She nodded at Louis to lead the way.

Louis's private car met them at the door. Although Juliane couldn't see any of the media represented, Louis continued to play the part of the gentleman, waiting by the door as the driver helped her enter the vehicle first. Once inside, he opened the bar compartment while the car departed toward the Vegas strip. It did not take long before Juliane began to feel the alcohol's effects on her empty stomach.

Traffic was still heavy, resulting in a slow procession down the strip. "Would you care for another?" Louis asked.

Juliane finished hers before they arrived at their destination, Club Dareeque. Rather than entering through the main lobby, Louis escorted her through a nondescript side entrance protected by some very large individuals in the standard uniform of black t-shirt and black pants. They made no effort to block their passage. Once inside, an extremely scantily-clad woman offered them more beverages, which Louis and Juliane both accepted with enthusiasm.

The nightlife was alive inside. As Louis predicted, Durham was its heart. He shook his neck and shoulders, loosening his muscles as he halved the distance between them.

Multicolored lights throbbed in time with the blaring music. Conversation was futile as Durham pulled her onto the dance floor. Beverages continued to flow freely. At some point, she must have removed her jacket, but she couldn't recall where it might be. The silky silver camisole she wore underneath shimmered as she twirled and swayed with Durham.

She stretched her arms briefly back into her hair to cool her neck from its weight. She had never felt so alive. A voice inside her head urged her to slow down, warned her of tomorrow's hangover, but she couldn't force herself to care.

She felt a warm hand on her waist. She spun to identify its owner and was pulled toward Louis's muscled chest. A glance back informed her that Durham had already migrated back into the crowd. She could see he was well occupied by another energetic partner.

Time lost its hold. Juliane lost track of how many drinks she had consumed. Others attempted to cut in, but never with long success. Again, and again, Louis pulled her toward him.

She thought she saw the flash of a cell phone camera, and in her inebriated state, she decided to give them a show. She felt the heat of Louis's leg pressed against her thigh as she grinded her body against his. Her skin glistened as she arched her back suggestively.

Her heartbeat pulsed in time with the music. A man—she assumed it was Durham, but her vision had begun to blur—appeared by her side. She closed her eyes, giving herself fully to the moment. A hand pulled at her arm. She wasn't surprised that

Durham wanted to cut in, but she was surprised by how violently she was pulled to the side.

She opened her eyes at the feeling of pain. The hand didn't belong to either Louis or Durham. Instead, Alan had materialized out of nowhere. He grimaced as he pulled her away from the dance floor and into a quieter alcove before unceremoniously shoving her down onto the leather bench.

A glass of water appeared before her. She hadn't even noticed Alan ordering it. It must have taken longer to stumble over to the alcove than she had originally thought. Away from the music, her head began to throb as she tried to estimate how much time had passed since her presentation. *Who'd invited Alan?* Juliane wondered. "Why, Alan, to what do I owe this unexpected pleasure?" she slurred.

"Were you aware that your antics are being broadcast on every gossip rag as we speak?" Alan scowled.

"I thought that what happens in Vegas stays in Vegas?" Juliane chortled at her own joke.

"Apparently when you throw yourself on one of the world's most powerful playboys, people break that little rule."

"I wasn't throwing myself at him; he's the one who keeps coming back to me. Besides, we're just out having some fun. Something, it appears, you need to do more often as well."

"Jules, stop acting like one of these children." Alan gestured toward a small group of females in tight-fitting clothing hovering near the edge of the dance floor. One of the group wore a tiara and sash but very little else.

None of them looked old enough to be making life-changing decisions like marriage, ruling out a bachelorette party, but they were obviously celebrating a major milestone. Juliane suspected it was the woman's twenty-first birthday.

Alan had no right to compare her behavior to theirs. At least half of that party wouldn't have any recollection of tonight's festivities tomorrow. She would remember this evening until her dying day. At least she thought she would. *Where did that jacket go?* she wondered. The room began to spin.

Juliane was distracted by another group, this one comprised of young but significantly more sober males. They also watched the women but were doing so like hyenas lying in wait to take advantage of a weakened gazelle.

One of the men swaggered over to the women with a drink in hand. Within moments, the woman with the sash followed him onto the dance floor. He wasted no time. Juliane could see his hand descend around her buttocks within the first few beats of the song. After losing sight of the couple in the crowd, Juliane returned her attention to the glass of water in her hand. She stared into its depths.

No, her behavior had been nothing like that at all. She had been dancing with Louis and Durham. It wasn't as if she had been letting random strangers grope her.

Juliane savored the feeling of water coursing down her throat. It was not the tap water she was more used to. The liquid tasted delicious on her tongue after the workout she had given her body.

Alan's tone softened. Juliane wondered if he had interpreted her action as a gesture of shame and not just parched thirst. "You are better than that. We are better than that. You and I, we are cut from the same cloth. I understand that it isn't easy for a person like you to work for someone like me. Always in the other's shadow. Always coming up second. But I've always been impressed with you."

If Alan expected a response, Juliane made sure he was left disappointed. He continued, "I wasn't surprised to hear your presentation was a smashing success. I would have demanded nothing else from you. However, I am disappointed that you didn't stick around long enough to allow me to take you out for a celebration. Had you just asked, I would have been more than willing to show you the town. Hasn't anyone ever told you that great things come to those who wait?"

"The music is pretty loud in here, but did you just really say that you would have taken me out if I was only more patient?"

"I did." Alan smiled, resting his hand on her shoulder. "I still would. You have such great potential. In all ways. You just need to learn how to wait."

"And what makes you think I would want to go out with you?"

"Please, Jules. Consider your available options. Sure, he is rich and powerful . . . now. But that womanizer is only going to hurt you. You would be just another plaything. To be used and discarded after you bore him. And you would bore him, assuming he didn't bore you first." Juliane felt her eyebrow rise at the comment. "He wouldn't be able to understand a fraction of what you say, and men like him can't handle feelings of inadequacy. You would be wasting your time with someone like that."

Juliane plucked Alan's hand off her shoulder. "You don't know half as much as you think you do."

Alan sighed. "But I do. People like you and I are extremely rare. You have barely seen the world, but eventually, you will realize that for yourself. You don't have to accept my company today. But believe me when I tell you that spending a night alone in your room would be a better use of your time than what you are doing here."

"Not that I need to justify who I want to spend time with to you, but Louis is not the vapid, spoiled rich guy you think he is, and I am not a child. We were just dancing, but if I wanted to take it further, I could. And again, stop calling me Jules!"

Her attempt at a dramatic exit was ruined when her foot began to slip out from under her as she rose. She felt a searing pain as her ankle twisted in her attempt to remain upright. Alan caught her before she could fall. She fought to push him away even as she attempted to stabilize herself, but he was relentless. "Let me take you back to your hotel. You've had enough."

"I don't need your help!"

"Please, you wouldn't be able to make it to the door on your own."

"I'm not ready to leave anyway. And even if I was, I certainly am not leaving with you." She attempted to hold him back and was surprised to feel iron muscles hidden behind his shirt.

"You are being ridiculous, Jules." Alan pulled her toward him.

"Jules, is it? I did wonder what your nickname might be." Juliane stopped her struggles at the sound of Louis's voice behind Alan. She attempted to draw herself up straight but found she couldn't quite put all her weight on the injured ankle without wincing.

"Ah, Louis, your timing is perfect. Some people just don't know how to respond to rejection." Juliane smirked. Louis appeared immune to the expression of pure hatred that danced across Alan's face.

"Fine, learn your lesson the hard way. Be my guest. Enjoy your time with the common people. You know where to find me when you realize I was only speaking the truth," Alan spat the words as he threw her at Louis, only then storming off toward the club exit.

"Well, I have to say, that is the first time I've ever been referred to as being part of the common people." Louis shrugged, his smile, as usual, in place. "I thought that when you suddenly stopped dancing that you were just in need of some air, but Durham mentioned seeing you leave with 'some guy.' Might I be correct in guessing that it wasn't entirely by choice?" Juliane nodded. "You want to get back to the party?"

Juliane took a step and sucked in her breath as a sharp pain raced up her leg. "Unfortunately, Alan may be half right. I have to call it a night. I must have hurt my ankle more than I originally thought."

Louis knelt beside her, caressing her leg more than was strictly necessary as he examined her injury. She felt her body shiver. She leaned over to inspect her injury herself, using his broad shoulders as support. The skin had begun to develop a purple sheen.

"That is a nasty mark. You've probably sprained it. You need to stay off your feet and keep that ankle elevated." His touch to the damaged flesh was a feather-light touch, but it still caused her to hiss. Within a moment, Louis had scooped her up as if she were the child she so recently protested not being. Only now, she found herself wrapping her arms around his neck.

Juliane stared into his eyes. Alan's parting words played in her ears. There was nothing common about this man. Suddenly she wanted to do something more in her hotel room than ice her ankle. She found herself murmuring, "On second thought, I'm not ready to call it a night after all. I can think of something that can keep my ankle very, very elevated." She trailed her fingers down the side of his neck, making her intention clear.

Louis raised an eyebrow, but the hunger in his eyes mirrored her own as they exited the club. Her vision went black as her eyes adjusted to the bright lights and colors of the Vegas strip. The loss of sight accentuated the crush of his lips on hers as the door closed and the car pulled away.

ELEVEN

The following morning, Juliane stepped out of the bedroom with bleary eyes and a pounding headache. She'd made a mistake. A huge, colossal, career-ending mistake. She'd slept with her boss. *What was I thinking?*

Had she acted the way she did last night only to antagonize Alan, or was it possible that there might be something more between her and Louis? *Our bodies certainly connected*, thought Juliane with a satisfied grin as she exited the bedroom and stumbled over her suitcase.

"Oh, good, you're up," said Louis.

Juliane blushed. "About last night—"

"That was amazing. I asked Durham to take care of your other arrangements," Louis mumbled from behind her. "I'd like you to stay with me for the rest of the weekend." Juliane was troubled that someone had been able to enter the room without notice, but then Louis's hand had begun stroking her thigh and she forgot all about Durham or the thousands of reasons going back into the bedroom was a horrible decision.

After that, she and Louis rarely left his spacious suite; a series of rooms complete with its own bar, kitchenette, and entertainment area. The hours passed in a lust- and endorphin-filled blur.

Feeling adventurous the second afternoon, Juliane decided to try sunbathing in the nude next to the room's private pool. Skin unfamiliar with the effects of sunlight was teased alive by his ministrations. Louis had brought out various exotic fruits and chilled wine which they had sampled together, only to then sample each other once again.

She didn't recognize herself around Louis. It was as if his very proximity silenced rational thought. No one had ever affected her in such a way. She wondered if she could ever go back to the way she was before. Basking in a contented afterglow with Louis sleeping by her side, she allowed herself to wonder, *why would I ever need to?*

Durham arrived on the third morning to take her back to the airport. As she opened the door, Juliane noticed that Durham's eyes were covered by a pair of mirrored sunglasses which he never removed. *He can't still be that hung-over.* She could see Louis approach in their reflection.

Louis's arms encircled her waist as her body melted into his embrace automatically. Louis gently pulled her hair back, caressing her neck with his lips. Juliane wanted nothing more than to spin around and return to their room. She closed her eyes to better enjoy the sensation.

Durham coughed, reminding her that they had an audience. Louis chuckled as he handed a few bills to the bellhop waiting behind Durham. Within the hour, she and Durham were back in the air, and Juliane found herself wondering if the events of the last few days had truly happened.

Shortly after takeoff, Durham had placed a travel pillow around his neck and leaned back in his chair without pressing for a rematch of their chess game. After Louis's warning, Juliane assumed it was probably for the best, but found herself disappointed all the same.

Left to entertain herself, her thoughts returned to the deliciously naughty things she and Louis had done to each other. Could it have been only a few days?

At the airport, Durham lingered only long enough to help load her belongings into her car and sneer at her choice of transport, a fifteen-year-old Tesla purchased for its ability to get from point A to B reliably.

She had barely noticed its dings and rust spots before, but each imperfection must have tripled in size during her stay in Vegas. She thought to herself that its like would never be seen in Louis's collection. Even if he kept a beater vehicle, it surely had to be in better condition.

Though the hour was late, Juliane decided to stop by her office. After spending the past few days with Louis, the idea of going to her empty apartment just felt too isolating. As she walked down the hall, Alan met her at the door. "What? Mr. Wonderful too busy to make sure you got home safely?"

Juliane rolled her eyes. "He has to continue the promotional tour. Surely someone as smart as yourself can comprehend that?"

Alan leaned against the door frame and said, "How convenient for him. Speaking of convenience, did you happen to stop by any of the campus stores on your way here?"

Scattered among the various ACI buildings were several independently owned and operated convenience stores placed to ensure that ACI employees had few reasons to leave the campus. All should have been closed for the evening hours ago. Puzzled, Juliane replied, "No . . ."

"And, I take it, you haven't been home yet either?" Alan asked with a smug smile.

"I came straight here." Alan's smile deepened. "But you probably already knew that. Why don't you go ahead and tell me whatever it is you came here to say? Obviously, you want to."

"Go online. I'm sure you'll find it soon enough."

Hating herself, Juliane pulled out her phone to check the news feed. On the screen were a series of stories, many of which alluded to the presentation. "Looks like my emulator made the front page. Funny, I don't see your presentation anywhere here.

That must be terrible for you. I know how hard you must have worked."

"Oh yes, terrible. Why don't you read the article rather than just scan through the headlines?" Alan might as well have screamed 'I told you so.' The words were clearly written across his features.

Juliane clicked on a link at random. It mentioned the presentation in passing, but the heart of the article centered on speculation of Louis's relationship with a mystery woman. There were a series of photos of the two of them engaged in several suggestive positions. The photos had been taken while they were enjoying themselves in the suite, not just in the dance club. Juliane felt the blood drain from her face. "How? Why?" she whispered in horror.

"I suspect they used a drone just like anyone else. I did try to warn you. You should have listened to me."

Juliane opened another article link. More photos appeared, each worse than the one before. Exactly how many drones had been hovering outside? How could she have possibly been so unaware of her surroundings?

Alan reached out and touched her arm, his smile slipping. "You can't possibly be surprised, Jules. I mean, really? How many times have the media done this to other women in your position? I'm only disappointed that you made it so easy for them. Hotels have drapes for a reason."

She had enough of his smug attitude, even if there was truth in his barb. She would no longer allow him to treat her as his subordinate. They were equals, and it was past time he recognized it. Ice crystals began to permeate her bloodstream as her humiliation was replaced by anger.

Alan took an unconscious step backward into the hallway. She had to take a calming breath before she could trust herself to speak again. Even then, her voice was hard as blue steel and sharp as a blade.

"What I do outside of these walls is my own business. I thought I had made that clear to you before." Juliane's voice took on a dangerous edge, an edge so fine it could cut a diamond.

Alan swiped a hand through his hair, and then back down along the length of his face. "I've been going about this all wrong with you. Jul—I mean, Juliane, you don't understand. I don't think less of you for having a little fun. I just think you can do so much better in your choice of company. You have to admit that you and I, on that last project, made a great team. Together, there would be no one to challenge us."

He clasped his hands around hers. "We wouldn't have to resort to such petty tactics to get noticed, forced to bow down to the powers that be for handouts. Always working under the threat that grant funding is going to dry up before a project is realized. You and I don't need people like Louis Evans."

Alan gestured at Juliane's phone, to images of Louis pushing reporters to the side while casually saying no comment. "He might like to think of himself as a dragon, considering that silly crew team flag he displays everywhere, but people like him are worms. Good for helping fertilize a garden but not much else. People whose only contribution to the world is their family name on a building. We are better than that. You are better than that."

The ice in her veins thawed to a trickle at his words, replaced by pity. She had thought the same things about Louis before she had gotten to know him better—before she had seen that eternal smile, listened to his carefree laugh or wrapped her body alongside his finely defined bulk. Her body began to hum at that last thought so completely she wondered if it might be audible.

"Alan, no, it's you who doesn't understand. I didn't spend the rest of the time in Vegas with him just because of his money or his connections. I did it because I respect him and he respects me, something that you have never demonstrated."

Alan pulled his head back as if he had been slapped. "I've always respected you. Why do you think I asked you to join my team? It's because I respected you that I couldn't make it easy for you."

He slammed a fist into an open palm. "I could have gotten half a dozen girls from one of the lesser departments to stand there and look pretty on a stage if that was all I wanted. Someone just bright enough to keep her mouth shut when she didn't know the answer so as not to embarrass me. But I needed someone with the potential to equal me one day. Only a person like that could challenge me."

"Someone with the potential to equal you . . . one day? Alan, I believe I passed that point quite some time ago." The faint lines on Alan's forehead began to knit. "I can see you are confused. Louis acted as my spokesperson. He may have done most of the talking, but it was my invention. I understand why you don't see it. I didn't recognize what he was doing at first either, but I wasn't the prop this time, he was."

She shook her head. "I'm sorry you didn't get the chance to witness him live in action. He was glorious in the role. He has an air about him, a raw energy you just want to connect with. With his talent and my drive, we could reshape the world."

As the words gushed out of Juliane's mouth, she realized that she meant every word. She suddenly couldn't wait to get back to the privacy of her apartment. She would call up Louis and describe in detail all the wonderfully wicked things she would like to do the next time he visited. So lightheaded in her testimonial, she hardly noticed as Alan's face darkened. "Jul— Juliane, I would be surprised if he saw your relationship quite the same way. He is using you."

"We're using each other."

"You aren't thinking with your brain."

The conversation had gone on entirely too long. She didn't want to hurt him, but he wasn't giving her another choice. "If you had just had the past few days I had, you wouldn't be either."

Alan's shoulders dropped—defeated.

The images that came to mind as she thought back on her time with Louis softened her edge. "I'm sorry. That was cruel. But you and I are never going to have anything other than a professional relationship. He loves me, Alan."

Louis hadn't said the words, precisely, but Juliane thought it best to leave no doubt that she was unavailable. It might not be an exaggeration on her part either. While neither had verbalized their feelings outside of passionate pillow-talk, She and Louis had established a connection that was hard to describe as anything else.

"We're just waiting for the right time to let the rest of the world know." This last part, was true, in that they had agreed it would be best for both of their sakes if they kept their relationship under wraps a while longer. Louis was still establishing himself as the new head of the ACI and while Juliane had made a splash at the Vegas conference, neither of them wanted anyone to think she hadn't earned the right to be on that stage based on what she did outside of the lab.

Alan straightened abruptly. "Don't apologize. I know that sometimes it's better to destroy and rebuild rather than try to salvage something. But you misread my intentions. My interest is purely professional. Alan waved his hands in the air, gesturing at the Internet news still streaming in compromising images. "If you want to pursue this distraction then, as you say, that's your business. I just don't want you losing your focus. Especially not now."

Alan pulled out a slip of paper showing an Internet link. "Your little stunt may have made the front pages here, but there is still real news happening in the world."

Juliane typed in the link on her phone. Her eyebrows rose as she started to scroll down the opening paragraphs. Her anger evaporated as quickly as it had arrived. "Is this saying what I think it is saying?"

"Indeed." Alan once again spoke with the calm authority and confidence that she once had so admired. "Obviously, these so-called journalists aren't half the subject matter experts they think they are. They see this as a more efficient means of altering biochemical bonds, but I thought you would see the bigger implication, and you just proved me right.

He nodded to himself. "With your algorithms at our disposal and my subatomic experience, we can create a device that can manipulate particles as tiny as the Higgs Boson on command. The competition wouldn't stand a chance! We could do this. Together. This is why I came here. I need you on my team, and I need you now."

Juliane thought about Alan's offer for a minute. The article had snapped her out of lust-filled thoughts, and she once again was in a position to weigh the pros and cons. Even so, Juliane knew her decision had been made the moment Alan made his offer. She would take it, even if it meant working with him again. "Fine. But only if you admit we're equals now. Oh, and I get to pick members of the support staff."

Alan released a breath. "Done. I've already started soliciting resumes. I will send their files to your office in the morning."

TWELVE

It had been several weeks since she had accepted Alan's offer, and they were still no closer to identifying a suitable candidate to complete their team. Each day Juliane would find another printed stack of resumes on her desk to review. A matching stack would appear on Alan's desk.

Out of an unspoken agreement, she and Alan interacted at a bare minimum beyond swapping notes. The few times they did speak, Alan seemed humbler and more considerate, but there had been little consensus between the two of them.

A year ago, Alan would not have had the patience to keep his promise and would have hired the candidates from his list regardless of her wishes. In truth, she was a little surprised that he had stayed true to his word for this long. The lack of forward progress had to be chafing on him.

It was chafing her as well. As much as she enjoyed irritating Alan, each day they didn't have their full team gave the competition a chance to reach proof of the concept first.

She and Alan couldn't be the only ones who had seen the report on altering biochemical bonds and realized the scientific advance's greatest potential. Time was running out and they were running out of the option to be choosy.

Louis had been away nearly all of this time. Juliane told herself that was a good thing. She was troubled by how often her intellect left her whenever he was around. However, as much as she knew she shouldn't want distractions right now, she ached for him all the same.

Louis, on the other hand, seemed much more capable of separating business from pleasure. *It's so unfair*, she thought. She fought the urge to dial his number. She reminded herself that he was a newly appointed CEO trying to launch new technology. *Her technology.* If they were going to replace the Internet with the Datasphere one day, he needed to work the media circuit.

His work didn't stop with publicity tours either. He needed to conduct factory audits and negotiate commercial dealings not just for the datasphere access points, but for other technology being developed by the ACI in parallel.

Juliane still hoped that one day she would be able to integrate her algorithm into the biologic network she'd worked on with Alan, which he had dubbed Project Gene Assist. This would eliminate the need for bulkier equipment, but that was still months if not years in the future. The ACI would expect an income stream long before then.

The ACI, on the other hand, didn't mind requiring datasphere users to purchase a headset nearly as much as she did. As a result, approvals for continued investigation into the biologic network had been placed on the ACI's back burner. In its place, several teams focused on developing better, slimmer, and most importantly, more profitable network access gadgets.

Unfortunately. those product development teams needed her insights on a daily, if not hourly basis. The stack of resumes on Juliane's desk were forced to wait as the ACI prioritized its short-term gains.

It also didn't help that Louis had spoken truly regarding the media's reaction to their work and their relationship. She was forced to change her phone number twice before removing it altogether from public records.

Changing her number proved to be the only way to get a minute's work done in between meetings with the product development teams and interview requests. Even the building's hidden entrance was only a moderate obstacle.

She had arrived one morning to find the hallway outside of her office polluted by roving gossip reporters. Juliane had told herself that she would be featured on all the major networks one day; she had just hoped it would be for her work rather than her relationship. Shortly after that morning, she had been moved into a new location offering more privacy.

Determined to prevent a similar occurrence, and to further protect her identity as well as the sensitive nature of her work, she demanded that a fake name be used on the hallway nameplate and directory.

Her day-to-day contacts within the ACI had moaned about accommodating each of these requests, but she didn't hear any complaints about the additional publicity her notoriety had brought to the organization. If anything, she was convinced that they were partially responsible for at least a few tips-offs to the media about where to find her.

Then, just as the frenzy began to die down, Louis would materialize somewhere close to the campus, launching another flurry. The media seemed to know when he was nearby even sooner than she did.

She had told Louis exactly how little she appreciated the interruption these unplanned visits caused to her routine, but if anything, he had made an even greater point of appearing in the most unexpected places. It was almost as if he enjoyed throwing her off balance.

Most unprofessional thoughts about Louis's preferred strategy for working his way back on to her good side filled her thoughts as she arrived at her office. Although she hadn't turned the key, the door swung open without effort. Juliane frowned. She could have sworn that she had secured her office the night before.

She worried for a fleeting moment someone might have stolen sensitive documents. Then she saw him. Louis was comfortably sprawled in her desk chair as if her chair was located in his home rather than her office. His feet rested on top of the stack of applications, and Juliane felt her pulse quicken as she took in the sight.

She tried to maintain an expression of annoyance. This was her place of business. It was her sanctuary. How dare he let himself in like he owned the place? *Okay,* she conceded, *perhaps he did own it, but really?* How hard would it have been to call her first? Louis, as usual, seemed impervious to her displeasure. He stretched even further in the chair as she shut the office door, calling to mind images of other calisthenics they had enjoyed together. Her unruly body tingled with anticipated pleasure.

He wore a well-broken-in pair of jeans as well as a wrinkled button-down shirt. His collar was open at the top, providing a tantalizing hint at the muscular chest beneath.

His chin, darkened with stubble from a missed shave, was a far cry from the tailored man she had first met. Louis must have come directly from his jet to her office.

A sense of smug satisfaction warmed Juliane. "One of these days you should tell me how you manage to sneak in here so easily. Or, let me guess, the company has recently appropriated a teleportation machine." She laughed as she bent over to store her purse in the modest credenza at the back of the room.

"I have access to more technology than you'd ever believe, but appropriate? That hurts. You make it sound like I just go gallivanting around the world stealing other people's ideas," Louis said.

She felt his eyes on her backside as she stood. She was pleased with the knowledge he was also affected by her presence. When she turned, she found Louis standing at full attention behind her.

He placed one hand on her waist and twirled her around the rest of the way until she faced him. His height forced her to stand on her toes to kiss him. However, she kept it chaste. She wouldn't make this too easy on him. He had broken into her office, after all.

Louis growled, "Speaking of travel, I've just crossed the world three times. Is that really how you are going to greet me?" He pulled her closer.

Juliane pushed away from his embrace in mock indignation. "It is if you're going to keep showing up with that stubble. My skin is delicate. Scratches would show on my face for the rest of the day."

"I guess I'll just have to find some spot to kiss you that isn't quite so noticeable." Juliane's senses squealed with excitement as Louis scooped her up and swung her onto the top of the desk. The stack of applications launched into the air like feathers released during a pillow fight.

Juliane gave up any appearance of displeasure. She wrapped her legs around Louis, her skirt hitching up and showing an indecent amount of thigh in the process. She felt like a wanton hussy and didn't care. She dropped her hands back to support herself as she closed her eyes, abandoning all senses but the feel of his lips and his hands on her skin as they laid claim to all of her curves.

"Juliane, I don't believe this is what the ACI signed for when they approved your request for an office space with additional privacy."

Juliane's eyes snapped open. It took a moment for her vision to clear, but when it did, her gaze fixed on Alan standing in the doorway. She had been so lost in the glorious sensation that she hadn't heard the door opening.

Louis returned to an upright position but did so without urgency, making no effort to straighten either of their clothes.

There was no hint of blush on his cheeks, and he left his shirt unbuttoned.

Juliane struggled to emulate his cool demeanor while attempting to stand back up, pull her skirt back down into position, and straighten her blouse. She accomplished none of these things with grace. Her legs felt like rubber, and she swayed while regaining her balance.

"Louis was just stopping by for an update on headset designs," she announced, mentally kicking herself. *You are pathetic*, she thought to herself. It didn't take a genius to see that what they were in the process of doing was anything resembling a progress report. She would have been better off owning the situation and daring Alan to judge her.

Louis's proximity had once again resulted in a surge of hormones at the expense of logic. Perhaps men were not the only victims of blood loss within the brain while aroused.

She caught sight of a wall calendar near Alan. As much as her libido was frustrated, it was a good thing that Louis's business schedule would keep him occupied for the next several weeks; otherwise, she might be as much of a contributing member on the team as Chad had been on the last one.

Alan snorted. "Oh, this is a business meeting then?" He gestured at the papers littering the ground. "Remind me some time to check out your minutes. They are bound to be . . . informative."

Juliane glared at Alan but remained speechless, not trusting her ability to respond with a witty comeback in the present circumstances.

Alan continued, "In any event, I need you to disentangle yourself from your present *conference* for a few minutes. We have some urgent business of our own to discuss."

Juliane looked toward Louis. He answered by shrugging before walking back over to her desk chair, rolling it back into the corner and making himself comfortable once again. "Don't mind me. I'll just wait over here."

Alan scowled. "This doesn't concern you, Mr. Evans," he said, emphasizing the mister as if it was the lowest of insults.

"I believe that the only business you and Dr. Faris have together is your work with the ACI, which makes it very much my concern. Or is there something more to your relationship you haven't shared?" Louis's jovial expression had never left his face, but his eyes grew cold and steely.

Juliane met Alan's gaze when it swung back her way with a smug smile. *What woman wouldn't feel appreciated by the occasional flare of jealousy?* she thought to herself, yearning to resume their 'business meeting.' It had been too long since she had last seen him, and it would be too long again before she would enjoy another of his visits. Her body had no interest in sending him away now.

Alan's nostrils flared. The clash of wills in the room was nearly tangible. Outnumbered and outranked, Alan would have no choice but to concede defeat.

"Fine." Alan walked over to her desk, making no effort to avoid the stray papers on the ground. "I had come here this morning to discuss the progress, or lack thereof, that we've made in our team's selection. I shouldn't have to remind you that while you've been otherwise . . . distracted, we've fallen further behind." He glared daggers at Louis. Louis raised an eyebrow but did not contest the statement.

"I know that I promised that you would have a say in the creation of the team, but I can't continue to wait for you to become bored with the little games you are playing. You can bring Chad on if you want. He understands your style, but I've made the remaining selection. She's already been notified." He slapped a folder onto Juliane's desk.

Opening the folder and scanning its contents, Juliane looked for a reason to reject the applicant and found none. She had to admit that had she been given time to research the candidate on her own, she would have recommended her selection as well. It struck her that there were many similarities between the applicant's academic and professional trajectory and her own, albeit via a different course of study.

She glanced down at the paperwork strewn about the room and saw its copy lying among the others. It had partially slipped under the desk. If she hadn't been looking for it, she most likely would not have seen it for days. As much as she hated to admit that Alan was right, she had lost her focus.

She looked back at Louis. His body continued to call to her for attention. He leaned back in the chair, rocking it slightly, the movement causing his hips to thrust ever so slowly. She felt her pulse quicken again and fought her most basic urges.

She closed her eyes, preventing Louis's body from discouraging logical thought. "I look forward to meeting her."

When she opened her eyes, she had halfway expected Alan to gloat over his victory. Instead, he nodded. "Excellent. Now that this matter is settled, allow me to get to the point of my visit this morning. We are going to need an edge to make up for time lost if we are going to remain relevant. I've decided to move forward with trials. Would you like to join me?"

Louis spoke up from the back of the room. His voice, the low rumble of a tiger, equal parts purr and threat, tempted her once again to shove Alan out of the office. "Trials? For what exactly?"

Juliane snapped back to full attention, mentally berating herself from allowing her mind to wander once again.

"The human variety. You might recall the little project that Dr. Faris and I were working on ahead of your . . . eh . . . more active involvement. Well, I haven't been twiddling my thumbs here and can tell you with absolute certainty, the process is no longer theoretical."

Juliane nearly broke the sound barrier as she twisted back toward Alan, his words registering in her brain. "You've achieved live imprinting?"

"I believe that is what I just said. You weren't the only one with a side project. While you've been otherwise occupied, I secured approval to conduct small animal trials. Of course, they were a resounding success."

"Why didn't I hear about this?" asked Louis.

"The study was so far along and the risk so small, I am not surprised your signature wasn't required." His cheek twitched. "However, the study results have been sent to legal for review, if you feel the need to second guess the process."

Alan turned his attention back to Juliane. "Juliane, I am confident the process works and would like you to be a part of proving it once and for all. As one of the first subjects. Think about it. This is our opportunity to evolve!"

Juliane hesitated, not sure how to respond. Alan was suggesting moving to human trials before the ink dried on the patent filings. Without those patents, the ACI would not authorize the publication of the study's results. There would be no chance for peer review. Could Alan have really gotten the necessary approvals to move forward? Even if he had, who would they find willing to participate in the study under those conditions?

"Won't you join me?"

Juliane's eyes widened as she realized what Alan wasn't saying. He was moving forward with Project Gene Assist, with or without her. Alan's smile deepened, but there was nothing soft about his expression. The paperwork in her hand sent another clear message. If she missed this opportunity, it would not come again, nor would future collaborations. Alan wasn't just looking for a person to fill out their immediate team, he was actively searching for her replacement.

If the process worked, she would be forever changed, but all the combined knowledge of the world would be open to her. She would be able to access any server anywhere with just a thought. She had no doubt it would work. To be among the first was the opportunity of a lifetime. The process wouldn't just give their team an edge on this particular project; it would blow rival companies out of the water.

Louis came over to her side, placing a hand possessively on her waist. "Well, I'm game. Lead the way."

THIRTEEN

When they arrived in Alan's lab, a young woman was already seated at the desk. "Ah, good. I do so appreciate it when people arrive on time," Alan quipped. "Dr. Faris, I would like to introduce you to Dr. Elizabeth Omondt."

The woman rose and extended her hand in greeting. "It is so nice to meet you, at least formally. You saved my behind that day with Dr. Than."

If she hadn't been the only other person in the room, Juliane might never have noticed her. Her features were only striking in their averageness, and it was as if the woman wanted to blend into the crowd.

She wore her brown hair in a braid that stretched down just beneath her shoulders—a hairdo that did nothing to soften her sharp beak-like nose. Her clothes hung over her frame like a bag, and her brown eyes were hidden behind a pair of over-sized glasses.

She could not have looked more like the stereotypical researcher had she tried. *Who still wears glasses?* Juliane thought. She fidgeted as if aware of the nature of Juliane's scrutiny.

"Um, maybe you don't remember me. I was trying out contacts that day, and well, let's just say they aren't for me, but the leg is all healed. Oh, and I have my doctorate now." She bit her lip. "Of course, I have my doctorate. I wouldn't be here if didn't have it."

Juliane took the offered hand and shook it, hoping the other doctor hadn't picked up on her initial reaction to her physical appearance. The woman's shoulders slumped in relief.

"Anyway, I know that you and Dr. Dronigh must have been buried under applications. I can't tell you how excited I am to be able to join this team. Getting to work with you both at the same time is truly an honor. Please, call me Betty."

"And you can call me Alan," he practically purred out the phrase.

Juliane did a double-take; it almost sounded like he was attracted to the woman. Betty's cheeks reddened as she pulled off the glasses. Juliane had to admit, the blush was a charming effect with her complexion. Perhaps she had misjudged Alan's earlier intentions after all.

"I took the liberty of calibrating the equipment. The system is warmed up, and we can proceed whenever you are ready."

"Well, Jul—Juliane, which is it to be? Age before beauty or ladies first?" Alan bowed while gesturing to a nearby gurney.

"I'll go first," Louis spoke up before Juliane had a chance to respond. Betty seemed to jump a foot off the ground.

She wasn't prepared for company, thought Juliane as she watched Betty try to figure out how to react to Louis's unexpected presence. *She and Chad will get along splendidly.* Juliane couldn't blame Betty for being surprised. Louis moved like a panther. Silently. Dangerously.

Juliane shook her head to clear her thoughts. Now was not the time to get lost in daydreams. Aloud, Juliane asked Louis, "You're not considering being a test subject, are you? We don't know for certain that Alan's process is entirely stable."

"Are you planning on participating?"

"Well, yes, of course."

"Then I've no reason to worry, do I?"

Juliane chewed her lip. "Er . . . I don't imagine the board will be all that thrilled with your risk-taking, that's all."

Louis leaned in and whispered conspiratorially, "Well, then I guess I just won't tell them. Besides, you just said there isn't any reason to worry."

A short time later, Betty had him strapped to a chair. Alan looked positively gleeful as he adjusted instruments.

Juliane silenced her misgivings by imagining tying Louis down in a very different manner. Louis leered at her, and she knew he had been thinking along the same lines.

I've made my choice. I just hope, this time, it's the right one. Time to evolve.

Juliane woke with no concept of how much time might have passed since she'd been given the injection. She remembered that after freeing herself from the straps, she'd collapsed on the cold laboratory floor.

However, at some point, she must have been moved to one of the temporary cots that were hidden away in various nooks and crannies throughout the building. It was common for staffers to conduct tests and experiments over several days, and the ACI had decided that it was cheaper to purchase the beds than take on the liability of researchers driving home with only a couple hours of sleep.

Louis. Her gaze darted around. Louis had been slumped in the chair the last time she'd seen him. Alan hadn't warned him of the risk. Alan hadn't warned either of them. *I'm such an idiot,* she thought. *I should have demanded to see evidence the process was safe with my own eyes before agreeing to let that man come anywhere close to me with a needle. What was I thinking?*

She groaned. *You weren't thinking at all,* she reminded herself. She'd warned Chad that Alan knew how to manipulate people into doing what he wanted, but hadn't followed her own advice.

He'd dangled a chance to be a part of something greater than herself and once again she'd taken the bait.

However, it had been one thing to risk her life for science. It was quite another to risk Louis's. *Had he survived?* Doubt settled into her gut. Would he blame her for putting his life in danger?

Betty sat near the head of the second cot, dabbing the occupant's forehead with a moist cloth. She must have pulled together a full tray of the happy homemakers' basic flu remedies. Juliane could smell the chicken soup from where she lay. Her stomach turned in protest as she struggled to pull herself upright.

"What happened? How long was I out?"

Betty wrinkled her brow in thought. "I guess it's been close to eight hours. Quite impressive really. I looked over Alan's notes after you all started to collapse. According to his observations, the transition in animals tended to take much longer."

"Out of curiosity, how long was Alan's transition?"

"About thirty minutes less than yours." Alan's muffled voice came from the direction of the cot.

"But I thought you injected yourself yesterday. Why would it only affect you now?" Juliane asked as she scanned the room. There were no other cots in the room. Where was Louis?

"I didn't say that I injected myself yesterday."

"Yes, you did." Juliane distinctly remembered saying as much right after he admitted that the procedure wasn't as safe as he'd implied in her office.

"No, I asked if you would feel better if I said that, and you did. See? I told you that you had nothing to worry about." Alan's voice sounded weaker than it had this morning. He might have known what to expect, but the process had taken some toll on him as well.

Her gaze continued to dart around the room, but Louis was nowhere to be seen. She fought the desire to panic. *Betty wouldn't be acting so nonchalant if something had gone wrong.* "Where is Louis?" she finally allowed herself to ask.

Betty said, "Oh, Mr. Evan's people called probably an hour after you fell. They didn't seem at all surprised to find him out cold, but were fairly annoyed that he wasn't where he said he would be."

The news was good, but not enough to dismiss Juliane's concerns. "Has anyone checked on him since then? Did he make it through the transition?"

Betty shrugged. "I wouldn't worry too much. If he suffered any worse than you did, I am sure we would have heard about it by now. He may not have even woken up yet." She turned toward Alan. "At least you'd better hope he's okay. I'd prefer to have not killed the big boss on my first assignment."

Juliane fumbled around until she located her phone and dialed Louis. The call went straight to voicemail. Panic mixed with disappointment. Louis's impromptu appearance in her office this morning had allowed her to hope they might be able to spend a little more time with each other. As memorable as his last visits had been, they were far too brief.

She pushed the feelings deep down. *Provided we survive this, we'll soon have all the time in the world together.* Until he returned her call, there was little she could do. "All right, Alan, we're upgraded. Now what?"

"Animals operating on raw instinct really are beautifully simple. All I had to do to prime the system was hack into their biologic network, but I believe the process for humans will be a bit more complicated. We build up so many walls, you see. You'll have to figure out a way to open the data exchange yourself."

"And how, pray tell, do you suggest I do that?"

"You just have to focus your intent; the neurons should do the rest. It should be similar to how you control that emulator system you were so proudly showing off at the conference."

"Except my emulator doesn't have the risk of knocking you out cold. You could have warned us about the side effects."

"You should have asked."

"Do I need to prepare for any other unpleasant surprises?"

"Oh no, the only surprises from here should be pleasant, quite pleasant. It's a brave new world, Jules."

Juliane attempted to clear her mind and ignore Alan's use of the nickname for the time being. Nothing happened. "Any other brilliant suggestions?"

"All my suggestions are brilliant. Try relaxing. Think of something pleasant."

Juliane smiled as she thought of how the sunlight played upon Louis's face in the early morning, making him appear more youthful than his business dealings let on.

"Something a little less personal perhaps. Maybe a flower blooming, the warm glow of a fireplace."

Juliane raised an eyebrow. She was going to need to double her effort to school her features. Alan noticed too much. She visualized a stream.

"Now stop. Visualize making a connection."

Juliane's mind went blank. It was as if a dam burst behind her eyes as the stream became torrents of data rushing through her mind. She had access to the full breadth of the Internet. She had always lived for the pursuit of knowledge, and now it surrounded her. She pictured herself dipping an arm into the raging current of bits. The ones and zeros pulsed against her senses. She dipped deeper, wondering just how far she could reach.

Then, she was flying through the air. She could see a forest of trees beneath her and rooftops in the distance. The setting sun behind her created a blurred shadow on the ground below. She could just make out the shape of animal remains beneath her just as her body began a rapid descent back downward. When she landed, she could not tell what the animal used to be, as it had already begun to be picked over.

Another wave of nausea took over and broke her focus. She shook her head and was back in the lab atop the cot.

"What was that?" she exclaimed.

"What was what?"

"I started accessing data, but then I was flying. And not just accessing satellite feeds. I mean, truly flying. Then I saw some roadkill and I was back here."

"A few days ago, some of my early test subjects, a few rats and birds, went missing. It occasionally happens. Animal rights activists." Alan sighed. "They never worry about what they might be unleashing on the public with these 'liberations.' But until now, I haven't been overly concerned. The virus isn't transmittable after all. It wasn't worth reporting."

Alan's eyes shone. "You must have been able to access one of the subject's vision as if they were just another node on the network. Did it act as if it was aware of your presence?"

"I can't be sure, but I don't believe so."

"Do you think you can access mine?"

Juliane opened herself once again to the stream of data. She focused her intent upon Alan, but all she could see was him staring back at her. She shook her head.

"Excellent. I visualized putting up a firewall. It must have been successful. Fascinating. Absolutely fascinating."

Juliane focused her intent on locating Louis. She shifted through the data stream until she found the location of his jet's departure log.

Betty was correct. Louis's people must have been in a panic to reach him. It was a wonder he had taken the time to visit her at all. His jet took off immediately following his transportation from the campus to the airport.

She was able to access some security camera footage which showed him being wheeled to the craft, but nothing that would indicate that he was in serious condition. While the log had given her the basic time of departure, it had not provided any further information such as where he was going or what time he might arrive at his destination.

It was as if there was no formal flight plan filed. *How was he able to get away with that?* she wondered. She was unable to access any of his physical senses as she had with the bird. She couldn't be sure if that was due to distance, his lack of consciousness, or his natural self-preservation instinct. Juliane decided she would try again once she knew for sure that he was safe and well.

She returned her attention to Alan as he attempted to pull himself off the cot using an eager Betty for support. It occurred to Juliane that Alan might be similarly testing his ability. Alan had too much control of her life as it was; allowing him in her head would be disastrous.

She visualized slamming a wall down within her mind. The datastream raged against her interference. She felt her eyes well up as its pressure surged against her insides. She changed the mental image, softening the wall, allowing the current to flow but only as directed. The pressure eased, and she could once again see clearly. She hoped it was enough. Alan did nothing to indicate he noticed her effort.

"Betty, would you mind running down the hall and fetching us a little more coffee? I don't think we will be sleeping again for a long while."

Betty frowned and looked as if she would like to refuse. Juliane hadn't seen Betty leave Alan's side since she woke; however, Alan's gaze hadn't left Juliane since the firewall test.

He finally turned toward Betty when she did not immediately jump at his command. Juliane could not see what look must have passed between them, but it was enough to cause Betty to purse her lips and exit without protest.

Alan came over to Juliane's side, each step surer than the last. He began to speak, but Juliane couldn't understand the words. A thought struck her, and she cocked her head, listening to the frequency of the sounds passing his lips.

Her mind began to match the sounds to a database of language, and within a moment, she could understand Alan as if the language he was speaking was her mother tongue.

"I assume that you've just discovered that there is no such thing as a dead language anymore."

"Possibly, but the database is only as good as the information within it. What we are saying is only based on speculation as to what Sanskrit might sound like. If that database was lost, then it truly would be lost again."

"Always the pessimist, aren't you? There would be nothing to prevent us from replacing it with whatever we wanted. Who would know but us?"

Juliane rolled her eyes at Alan's rationale. "Have you always been this willing to rewrite history?"

Alan smiled in response as if he was a three-year-old who knew he had been up to no good and was determined to try getting out of the situation by being as cute as possible. Juliane chose not to point out that it was the exact expression that Louis so frequently used.

Betty returned to the lab with mugs of steaming coffee and Chad in tow. Chad rushed to Juliane's side. "Are you okay? I am sorry I wasn't here sooner, but Nadia and I were taking a little day trip. I don't think Nadia's going to forgive me for a while, but I made us turn around and come back as soon as I got Betty's call."

"Nadia will forgive you. In fact, I suspect she might just respect you more for putting your foot down." Juliane also realized that if Chad was just arriving, it meant that Betty had been forced to care for both her and Alan all by herself. Juliane wasn't sure how the woman had been able to move them both to the cots. She must be quite a bit stronger than she appeared.

Betty handed her one of the cups, and Juliane sighed in contentment as the warm liquid settled in her belly. At least there was someone else on the team who appreciated the importance of a good cup of coffee. "It would seem that I need to thank you, Betty. I had no idea that the process would have that side effect. I'm sure Alan and I can come up with a gentler method in the future."

"I'd prefer not to wait if it is all the same," Betty stated.

"Alan wasn't upfront with me on the risk. As you saw, the process still has some pretty significant flaws. You need to have a strong will and self-control." *For a few minutes, I lost myself in a bird. A bird,* Juliane thought.

She didn't know this woman at all. *Who knows what could happen to the casual user?* Juliane no longer shared Alan's belief that the process was ready for human use. *Why hadn't Louis reached out to her yet?* Aloud, she continued, "We'd have no way of guessing how you might respond to the procedure."

"I am well aware of the risks. I was here while you were out cold on the floor. Alan mentioned something about having confidence in your success from your experience with some emulator device. If it would help ease your conscience, I would be happy to prove myself using that program first."

Juliane looked toward Chad. "I suppose you would like to be upgraded as well?"

Chad looked like a gazelle spotting a lion. "Absolutely not. We both know how I've done in the emulator. I think I can wait until the process is a little more proven, but I can go fire up the chamber for Betty if you'd like."

Juliane's lips twisted as she engaged in another mental debate. "I think that is a great idea, Betty," interjected Alan. "Juliane, it's not our place to deny evolution, especially not to such a brave volunteer. Take her to your chamber and truly do your worst. I am confident that if she can survive you, she can survive my little procedure."

FOURTEEN

Not entirely confident on her feet, Juliane leaned on Betty for support as they made their way back to her old lab space which still housed the original emulator. Chad had run ahead to ensure that the system was online before they got there.

"All right, Betty, just enter the chamber and the test will begin. The system will be monitoring your brain pattern and will be creating a whole world for you. You will need to maintain control of the environment at all times." Juliane's fingers danced across the keyboard. "I'm going to put you in three situations. In each case, you will need to find a way out of the simulation; otherwise, I will not allow Alan to administer the serum. Are you ready?"

Rather than answer, Betty attached the earpiece and microphone. She stepped through the glowing arches with her head held high while Juliane continued to fume behind her screen.

If something happened to Louis because of her need to establish herself at any cost . . . *I'm not going to let Betty undergo the procedure as blindly as I did.* Who knew if Louis was ever going to wake up, and if he did, would he wake up as the same person?

Juliane squashed the thought before it could undo her and focused on the newest member of her team. What was done was done. There was no turning back, but she could make sure Betty was more prepared for the risk than she had been. If that meant helping her find her breaking point, so be it.

The simulation appeared on the display. Realizing her upgrade meant she no longer had to watch the test unfold on a monitor, Juliane created a mental connection with her program. Her vision was replaced with the image from the screen. Even before the scene came into focus, Juliane's nose twitched from the smell of heavy application of bleach.

A bedroom appeared. Bits of yellow paint could be seen behind movie posters and photo collages. A mountain of stuffed animals covered a slim white daybed positioned along the length of the far wall.

The bed coverings themselves were wrinkled, tucked in with hospital corners. A desk made out of particle board sat on the other side of the room. The desk was immaculately organized, with paper in a neat stack. Pens and pencils were sorted by type and color filling black plastic containers with the same excess as the room's other decorations.

The bedroom door opened, and a middle-aged woman entered. The floorboards creaked over the sounds of a TV playing down the hall. The house must be decades old to produce such a sound as the woman couldn't have weighed more than a child. "Mom?" Juliane could hear unshed tears in Betty's voice.

"Were you expecting someone else?"

Betty ran over to the woman and crushed her in a hug. "I know you aren't real, but it is so good to see you!" Juliane could feel the woman's graying hair tickle her skin as if she was standing there instead of Betty.

"What do you mean I'm not real?" The woman's hand caressed Betty's cheek, and to Juliane, her touch felt like lace. Betty jumped backward. The woman's hand hung in the air for a moment where Betty's face had been. Then, as gently as an autumn leaf, it fell back to her side. The woman's brow knit in confusion.

"You're just a simulation. You may look like her, sound like her, and even smell like her, but you aren't my mom. She died years ago, and this isn't my room. Dad had to sell the house to pay off the medical bills."

"Oh, Betty dear, have you been up late studying again? You always have those crazy stress dreams whenever you fall asleep at your desk. You know your father and I are so proud of you, but you work too hard. I don't know that I want you to go to that fancy college if this is what it's going to do to you. I know, how about we spend the day together and relax, just you and me? We can go shopping and then end the day with pedicures. Won't that be fun? Why are you crying, Betty?"

"I would give up anything to be able to go back and spend more time with my real mom, but you're just a computer program. I reject you."

Betty's mother looked crestfallen. "Betty, honey, you are starting to worry me. I have been feeling a little under the weather, but I didn't die, and I definitely haven't run up any medical bills." She held her arms out wide. "I'm right here. Your dad and I haven't gone anywhere. Sweetie, you look so pale. Let me feel your forehead." Betty's mother took steps forward, eliminating the distance Betty had put between them. Betty leaned her brow against the back of her mother's outstretched hand—

Betty reeled back again as if struck by a snake. "No. As much as I want this to be real, it is not, and I have to go." Betty walked toward her bedroom door with determined strides, giving her mother a wide berth as if another touch would break her resolve. She didn't risk looking back, but paused in the doorway long enough to whisper, "I love you, Mom."

The scene faded to black as Betty crossed through the bedroom doorway. "I wasn't expecting you to make it easy, but I didn't expect you to be cruel."

Juliane had wanted to challenge Betty but hadn't expected the simulation to take that turn either. She released a breath she hadn't known she held. The scene would have gone much differently had Juliane's past been put on display. While she and Betty might have had a similar career trajectory on paper, it was clear they had vastly different backgrounds.

Juliane's stomach knotted as she buried a surge of resentment. As the next test began, Juliane reduced her connection with the program, limiting its impact on her senses. Betty was the one whose self-control was supposed to be tested. Not hers.

Spray from an ocean wave crashing against the side of a small boat slapped Betty's face as the vessel appeared beneath her feet. Betty collapsed against the side railing as the floor rocked with the motion. Another wave pounded the craft as Betty struggled to regain her balance. After a few more failed attempts, Betty abandoned efforts to remain upright, and instead, leaned against the gunwale while the boat heaved up and down.

A strong wind turned Betty's hair into miniature whips as steel-gray clouds took over the portion of the horizon not consumed by water. Electricity began to pulse through the sky, providing shadowy evidence of shark-shaped creatures hidden beneath the surface.

Betty glanced around, but there was nothing in the boat that could come to her assistance and no sign of land as far as the eye could see. Another wave struck the side of the boat, and its wooden boards groaned in response to the abuse. Betty grabbed the side of the vessel once again, her knuckles white.

The change in the boat's weight combined with the rising waves caused it to lean over precariously. A slick dark body briefly crested near Betty's fingers before dropping back into the surrounding depths.

Betty pulled back into the center of the dinghy, but not before the dinghy began to take on water. As if the water had merely been waiting for the initial invitation, more waves followed suit, soaking through Betty's clothing and filling the base of the hull.

Boards snapped from their fastenings. The little boat would not protect Betty from either storm or ocean inhabitants much longer. The boards near her feet echoed with thunks as something large came into contact. Betty screamed, but the sound was muted beneath the weight of the storm.

Another large wave, at least twice as large as the last, began its approach. It would close in fast and when it hit, the little boat would not be able to withstand its onslaught. Betty curled her body, bracing for impact. Another splash of water briefly sent the boat underwater.

Juliane watched as Betty stood fully erect. The boat continued its plummet toward its inevitable demise, but as it dropped down, Betty remained in place, hovering in the air. Upon impact with the rogue wave, the boat splintered into hundreds of shards.

The destruction of the boat did little to halt the progress of the storm. The debris, now lethal stakes, churned in reckless abandon as a new wave came closer, but Betty's face no longer showed signs of distress. Her lips thinned into a small line as her arms dropped down by her sides and she squared her shoulders.

"This is a computer program. That is not the ocean, and this is not real. I reject it all!" Betty shouted into the wind.

The wave slammed into an invisible surface directly in front of Betty, and her entire vision was consumed by a wall of water. What hadn't hit the wall flowed under her, but her shoes no longer showed signs of being wet. The undulation ceased, and the dark water became the floor beneath her feet. The wind's howls became a mere whimper before ceasing altogether.

Once again, Betty was surrounded by darkness.

"I nearly drowned once when I was just a child and avoided the ocean for years. Your system is good, but no amount of simulation can compare to the real thing." Betty's fists remained white and closed, while her breathing remained labored.

A sliver of light penetrated the darkness of the chamber, and Alan rushed in. "Betty, I could hear you screaming from down the hall. Is everything all right in here? What have you done to her, Juliane?!"

"I'm fine, really. Nothing I couldn't handle," Betty sputtered as if still battling against the onslaught of the wind and waves.

"You are positively shaking. Juliane, I think you've sent her into shock! What is wrong with you?!" Alan shouted.

"No, really. I'll be okay. I just need a couple of minutes to catch my breath. Dr. Faris is just doing what you asked her to do—her worst." Betty glared as if she could see Juliane through the curtain. "I hope that I've now proven that I am just as capable of handling the effects of the procedure as she is."

"You don't have to prove anything to me. I knew from the minute that we met that you were perfect just the way you are." Alan wrapped Betty in his arms, pulling her close.

"You mean I will be perfect once I've had the procedure like you and Dr. Faris."

"That can wait for another day. You don't have to rush into anything. I don't want to risk losing you." He brushed his hand against the side of her cheek.

"But what about the project? Surely you need all of us on the team to be able to contribute at our highest levels?"

"I don't know about you, but I am exhausted from earlier. I doubt that Juliane or I would be able to accomplish all that much in the next few hours anyway. Why don't we call it a day?"

Betty pulled back from Alan, although not so much as to break away from his embrace. "I've read through some of your previous project notes, and I did my own background search on you. I know a little thing like a stomach bug isn't going to hold you back for long. Weren't you the one to go for four nights without sleep just to prove a point?"

Alan smiled, urging Betty's face toward his own with another caress of his hand. "I do so love a woman who does her research. I'm sure Juliane won't mind locking up, will you Juliane? Come with me, Betty. You know I can make waiting worth your while." Alan closed his eyes, leaning his head in toward Betty's lips.

For a moment, Betty looked as if she would meet Alan's advance, but then shoved him away. "No! You aren't real. This is just another one of her tests!"

"No, Betty. This is no test! I heard you scream and made her turn the device off. This is real. You and I are real." Alan reached toward Betty; she took another step back.

"You said you love a woman who does her research, and I did. Everyone knows you call Dr. Faris 'Jules' because it drives her crazy."

"What are you talking about? What does that have to do with anything?"

"You've called her Juliane repeatedly just now."

"So?"

"I've heard the jokes around the building and the two of you talking. I know that even when you do call her Juliane, you still always stretch out the last syllable as if you are making a point to call attention to how considerate you're being."

"Now I am seriously concerned. Dr. Faris's testing has put a strain on you. I wouldn't approve subjecting you to the procedure now, regardless of how well or not well you've done in her test chamber. Betty, I know that we haven't known each other long, but I feel as if I've known you all my life. We have a connection. One that I would like to develop more. You need some rest. Please, I am begging you. Come with me." Alan reached his arm out to Betty once again.

"Alan doesn't beg. This is not real. I reject you." Betty's eyes welled up with tears as she spoke the words. "Dr. Faris, I believe we are done here."

Alan faded away as Juliane drew back the curtain surrounding the pillars. "Yes, Betty, I would agree. I'll call upstairs and have Alan prep for another upgrade."

FIFTEEN

When Betty and Juliane arrived back at the medical lab housing the Gene Assist serum samples, Alan was not there. Juliane, grateful that her mind was much clearer than before, used the time while they waited for his return to look over Alan's procedure notes, all of which were handwritten in nearly indecipherable scratch.

"I probably would have saved myself a few hours of terror after you all collapsed if he would have stored his work online like most other people," muttered Betty.

Juliane, not looking up from the page, remembered her early struggles with Alan's script. "It took me a while to figure out the trick of it myself. Alan has trust issues."

Betty grumbled something in response that sounded like, "I wonder why." The following silence between them was an oppressive wall. Juliane found herself looking forward to Alan's return if only so that he might help break it down. Betty appeared shaken by the results of the test. *Does Betty think that I would share any of that?* Juliane didn't think any less of her. If anything, she now had greater respect for the woman's drive.

"Betty, I know you think I am an awful person for putting you through those tests, but I had to be sure that you were going to be able to handle the upgrade."

"I understand." Betty's voice was clipped in anger. "I didn't realize that the system could see quite so clearly into my head."

"Those thoughts weren't as hard to find as you might believe. I had the system home in on your greatest fears, wants, and regrets to ensure that you were able to stay focused."

Betty made a harrumphing sound. "Well, what's done is done. You now know everything you need to know about me. I trust I won't have to go in there again." Betty was being childish.

"You were the one that insisted on being tested." Juliane tried to remain calm and composed, but Betty was completely overreacting. Juliane wondered if perhaps it was due to being exposed to all three strong emotions in such short order. It might be something worth incorporating into her algorithm. Her mind immediately began framing the problem in terms of variables.

Three strong emotions. Three-X. Juliane stopped turning the pages of Alan's notes. Could the solution be so simple? "Betty, I believe that Alan's dosing equation is off—however, this is not my area of expertise. Would you care to take a look?" The question was more of an olive branch, as Juliane was confident enough in her assessment. Whether or not Betty chose to accept it would tell Juliane much about her character.

Betty seemed grateful for the distraction and hurried over to look at the page. "Well, I understand why he would have come up with this equation. It is definitely the most expedient method of uploading the data, but you're right. He didn't consider the subject's natural health response. By modifying the frequency and dose rate, we can reduce the risk factor by at least a multiple of three, if not ten."

"And decrease the subject's potential strength as a result." Both women were startled by the comment as Alan returned to the lab. As the door closed behind him, Juliane could see that Alan was accompanied by another man with dark hair; whoever he was, the man did not follow Alan through the doorway. "And yes, I did take the subject's health response into consideration. However, I felt the payoff worth a little extra risk."

There is no possible way that the procedure would have been approved based on this equation. "Alan, you didn't get approved for human trials based on this information, did you? She still hadn't heard from Louis. Juliane fought to keep her anger in check. If something happened to him, Alan might be the only one who would know what to do. They couldn't afford to put him on the defensive; he could leave the room and never come back.

"Especially when the alternative is so obvious!" added Betty.

"Ah, good. The heat must be back on. When I first opened the door, it felt freezing in here. I assume then that your testing went well?"

"I have no further concerns."

"Well then, if you both are so confident your way is better, how about we go ahead and update Betty using your recommendations?"

Juliane knit her eyebrows. As Betty had pointed out, the alternative had been extremely obvious, almost as if he had planned for one of them to stumble across it, but she still had expected more of a fight from Alan.

Before she could ask if Alan had some master plan he wasn't sharing, Betty launched herself onto the procedure bed. "I am ready to begin whenever you are."

"Your wish is my command. It is so nice to see some enthusiasm around here. You'll not regret it. Ready, Juliane?" asked Alan.

He did stretch out the last syllable. Juliane sighed, closing her eyes. Data flowed in her veins, warming her and making her more aware of the world like only a good cup of coffee could. Alan was right. The payoff was proving to be worth the risk. She had survived, and she had to believe that Louis would wake soon. How could she deny anyone else the same opportunity?

"Right, let's begin." Alan made a show of bringing the equipment around. While he might not compare to Louis for showmanship, occasionally Alan did have a flair for the dramatic. "Betty dear, you may feel a little pinch."

SIXTEEN

As they anticipated, Betty's reaction to the treatment was less severe than what Juliane, Louis, or even Alan had experienced. She had still grown pale and feverish, but overall, the difference was like a slight cold compared to an extreme case of pneumonia. More importantly, she never once lost consciousness.

Louis finally made contact while Betty practiced mastering her focus. He had woken up in the air hours ago. Other than the fever and blacking out for a few hours, he hadn't suffered too many ill effects. Juliane had wanted to tell him about her experience with the bird, but before she could bring up the subject, the call was disconnected.

He must have traveled into a cellular dead zone. It has to be why he didn't call sooner. Juliane had returned her attention to Betty. Within hours, Betty too was accessing information across the globe as if she had been born with the ability, albeit not quite as powerfully as Juliane.

As the weeks passed, Chad continued to abstain from the procedure himself, even after seeing how well Betty responded, preferring instead to support the team by running errands. Even with only the three of them online, they were able to compile data with record speed. Juliane reveled in her ability to access massive amounts of computing power by mere thought.

A supercomputer is limited in that it can only respond to the parameters of its programming. It was one of the major challenges in the development of artificial intelligence, but they had no similar limitation.

Seemingly unconnected data points were correlated together for no logic-based reason, yet they fit together perfectly. Soon the team developed a basic working equation that would serve as the backbone for the rest of their next experiment.

The team then set up a collaborative online platform using Juliane's virtual reality software. They could then access the virtual world Louis had named the datasphere and manipulate objects and materials without the need for additional programming as easily as modeling clay in the real world. Except, there was a lot less clean up required.

If it were up to Juliane, they would conduct all their work in the virtual world, but that would limit Chad's involvement, leaving her feeling outnumbered. Except for that first day, Betty didn't act like she still held a grudge against Juliane, but she did tend to side with Alan whenever a topic came up for a vote.

As Juliane left the datasphere for another day of face-to-face meetings and office work, she clenched her teeth. There had been no further negative side effects. Juliane couldn't understand Chad's continued reluctance to upgrade. Chad was only able to enter by donning bulky gear kept on the campus, which meant their meetings were in person. *I could be in the comfort of my home right now.* If it hadn't been for Chad, she wouldn't have to deal with Alan in the flesh.

At least she had Louis. Juliane closed her eyes and accessed her email server. There were no new messages since the last time she checked it ten minutes ago. Her text feeds remained equally empty. It felt like it had been ages since he'd last visited.

Juliane knew she shouldn't complain though. He more than made up for his absence when his schedule did allow for an occasional check-in. She reminded herself he was still trying to strengthen his position in the company as much as she was.

Think of the positives, she told herself. The media frenzy surrounding their relationship had finally died down—and this time stayed down. Without the media's constant interruptions, Juliane had been able to pay more attention to her work.

It also meant they no longer had to be as secretive about their rendezvous. This was unfortunate as Juliane had found she rather enjoyed the added element of stealth. It made their lovemaking seem all the more dangerous and forbidden.

She'd also discovered her body now associated the flash of the camera with the anticipation and afterglow of time spent during those clandestine meetings. As a result, she now experienced a Pavlovian reaction whenever she spotted nearby reporters and reason to reason to avoid the gossip outlets. *Unless Louis was in town*, she amended to her thoughts. Then, it was quite a different experience.

Lost in her delicious thoughts, Juliane did not hear the door to her office open. As if summoned by magic, there stood the object of her daydreams.

"You never call. You never write," Juliane said with a smile on her face as she ran to him.

"You know I can't risk putting anything about what we do in writing, at least not yet, and I'm always in meetings." Louis pulled her close, lifting Juliane in his embrace while using his back to close the door. Returning Juliane to the ground but only unwrapping one-half of his embrace, he reached behind and turned the lock with an audible click.

"I can't stay long." He looked into her eyes. His eyes shone with hunger. Louis pivoted his heel, bringing Juliane with him, pinning her to the wall near the door.

"You never stay long." Juliane pouted.

Louis leaned in, nuzzling her neck.

Juliane tilted her head to the side, giving him more access. Having him here, in person, was always so much better than any of her imaginings.

"Louis?"

"Mmm," he answered, not halting from his ministrations. One of his hands began similar strokes along her thighs.

"I know I said I wanted to keep up the mystery act, but you could take me with you sometimes."

Louis stopped what he was doing. Juliane's body ached in protest. He pulled back and looked at her. "And take you away from your work? When you are so close? You'd never forgive me."

Louis was right. She wouldn't. She needed to see this project through, but it was so difficult to remain focused on the future when her immediate needs were demanding an altogether different form of satisfaction. "I know. It's just that I miss you so much when you aren't around." Juliane bit her lip. She could see his body tense up as if to further pull away. She shifted her hips, where his hand still lay frozen. "There's just so much more I'd like to do to you and never enough time."

Louis smiled and leaned back toward her. "Is that so?" His hand once again began its exploration. "Why don't you tell me more? What would you do?" His voice dropped into the husky baritone that she associated with some of their more enjoyable phone calls. If only the feeling of his lips upon her could be as easily transmitted over distances. She could do such wicked things to him if only she could be two places at once.

The thought brought her up short. "What if we established a private network?"

Louis muttered, "I must not be doing something right. You sound like you just switched into work mode."

"I'm serious. You've been upgraded. I've been upgraded. It's just a matter of manipulating data. We could do it."

"Do what?" Louis asked.

Juliane threaded her fingers through his hair. "We could set up a network between us, and no one would ever know. No risk of public leaks. We would be able to not just tell each other what we'd like to do, but show each other," she murmured. "Explicitly." She felt his hand slip behind her waistband as she once again lost her grip on logical thought.

SEVENTEEN

Juliane attempted to straighten a few of the books on her office shelf which had become jostled when Louis had sought better leverage. She smiled and shook her head when her eyes spotted her solitary picture frame. Perhaps she would add a few more photos one of these days. "You never did answer me."

"About what?" Louis asked while straightening his clothes.

"About the idea of establishing a private network between the two of us."

Louis wrinkled his forehead in thought. "Do you think that is necessary?" he asked as he walked over and unlocked the door.

"It could be the perfect solution to our problem." Juliane turned to face Louis. "Your father sure could have used it."

Louis's face darkened. "My father made mistakes. I don't want to discuss him. Ever. Is that clear?"

She took a step toward him. "I'm sorry. I didn't mean to sound judgmental." She took another step and helped adjust his tie. "If you ask me, the girl was asking for trouble, even if she wasn't a princess. I am sorry that your father was sent away and how hard it's become for you to travel in the open without looking over your shoulder. But think of it this way, if they hadn't made those choices, you and I may never have met."

Louis's eyes softened as he lowered his head to kiss her forehead. "That's true. Fine. If you think this will make you happy, let's try it."

Juliane closed her eyes and focused. She could see the datastream flowing through Louis. She visualized reaching out to him, her own data stream branching out to him in a line separated from the flow of the rest of the network. As the connection was made, she was flooded with additional sensations. As a test, she projected her feelings of euphoria resulting from the aftermath of their passion. She opened her eyes in time to see his smile deepen.

"It was good for you then?" Louis asked with a smirk.

The corners of his eyes tightened, and Juliane suddenly felt a warmth travel down her torso, the same path that had so recently been traveled by his hands. Her breath quickened. He didn't move from where he stood, but Juliane found that she could feel his lips press against her nether regions. She fought the urge to moan.

"This may have been your best idea yet," gloated Louis.

Louis's phone rang, shattering their concentration, and the sensation dissipated, leaving Juliane aching for satisfaction.

"It's time, sir," the voice on the other end of the line announced.

"I'll be right there," advised Louis. Hanging up the phone, he said to Juliane, "I have to go, but don't worry. We'll finish this later."

After taking a few minutes to regain her equilibrium, Juliane joined the rest of the team in Alan's lab. She was deep into programming when her vision of the room was replaced with an image of herself in a compromising position. Along with the image, she received a sense of Louis's hunger and arousal. She blinked, clearing the image, and looked about the room. None of her colleagues noticed anything unusual.

Once again, she felt the sensation of his body on hers. Her breath became shallow.

Betty looked up from her workspace. "Is everything all right?"

"I'm fine." Juliane gritted through her teeth, biting off the moan that threatened to escape from her lips.

"Are you sure? You look flushed."

Alan turned around and scanned her face. "Your eyes are glazed," he announced. "You aren't coming down with something?" he asked.

"Coming down?" Juliane advised. Spiraling out of control maybe, dancing the fine line between torture and ecstasy definitely, but sick? "No. I feel wonderful."

Alan frowned. "Good. We can't afford to lose our momentum now."

Juliane visualized smacking Louis on the buttocks and received back a sense of unapologetic mirth. She must have gotten her point across because the rest of the sensations faded away immediately, allowing her to continue work uninterrupted.

Back in the privacy of her apartment, Juliane tried to find Louis. For some reason, she still was not able to pinpoint his exact location even with her advanced abilities. When asked about it, Louis had only shrugged and told her that he had equipped his phone with some additional security since his father had made some enemies.

Why Louis would need the same level of security as his father was a little unclear to Juliane. It was more than a little paranoid in her opinion. She guessed Louis must have his reasons, but he could be so frustrating at times.

She searched until she believed she had identified his whereabouts to within an approximate ten-mile radius. He was on the West Coast and likely in a meeting with some very influential business leaders. Juliane's lips turned up in a coy smile. Perfect. She projected her desire across their network and waited for a response. When none immediately followed, she imagined the feel of his chest beneath her hands and pushed. Still nothing.

Disappointed, she sent a message through their private network. No response. She sent another message through the public network. This time, Louis sent a message back. He was sorry to report he hadn't felt a thing but was looking forward to chatting with her soon.

Juliane contemplated sending Louis an invitation to meet her in the datasphere but thought better of it. She didn't trust that Alan wouldn't be using the virtual world, and the last thing she wanted would be for him to find them there for any reason outside of pure research.

More days passed, and Juliane hadn't found the source of the issue. It was as if Louis was blocking her transmissions for some reason. He, on the other hand, did not seem to have the same problem.

He had also remained uncharacteristically in one place for all of this time, and the time difference had placed her at a distinct disadvantage. There had been a few occasions when she had been forced to excuse herself from the lab before she embarrassed herself due to his preferred manner of wishing her a good morning. The team had begun to take notice.

As enjoyable as those moments were, the private network overall was rapidly losing its appeal. At least in Juliane's opinion. For Louis, well, Juliane didn't quite know what Louis thought about it. His recent calendar allowed for little time to talk. And even less time for the kind of talk that didn't first involve play.

After facing yet another morning of her team's glares and wrinkled foreheads, Juliane decided it was time to disable the network. *So much for being spontaneous. Louis will understand,* she told herself. *He probably won't even notice it is gone.* She really had to put her full attention into the task at hand; otherwise, when he eventually did have time for some well-deserved rest and relaxation, she wouldn't be able to join him. *He is bound to be back soon. I'll explain it to him later.*

Juliane isolated the network link in her mind and severed the connection. Immediately, her body felt cold as if she were physically bleeding out. It was as if, without the link, she was suddenly less whole, less alive. Even her vision was affected. The world looked grayer. *How would someone go about cauterizing a virtual wound?* she wondered.

Juliane slogged toward the lab. She felt a desperate need to be surrounded by other people, yet she wanted to lock herself away in her office until the end of time. Her body felt foreign. Wrong and alien. Something had gone very, very wrong.

EIGHTEEN

Juliane glanced at a clock only to realize that several minutes had passed of which she had no memory and minimal accomplishment. Most of the last several weeks had passed in a similar state of fog. The fact that Juliane was able to focus long enough to complete anything at all had become her daily victory.

"Have you completed the next simulation profile? Juliane? Juliane? Earth to Dr. Faris?" Betty's voice cut through Juliane's thoughts.

"I'm sorry, Betty. Yes, the simulation profile is ready. Would you care to go online with me to view it?"

"Excellent, Alan should already be there waiting for us."

Juliane attempted to glance around the room without Betty noticing. Until Betty had spoken, Juliane hadn't realized that Alan wasn't still in the room. *How long have I been out this time?*

"Is the meeting in the same place as before?"

"It seemed appropriate enough."

Juliane closed her eyes and imagined entering the virtual reality universe they had selected. It was a process that had grown routine. Not that she was complaining. Even if she was only going through the motions, she was at least going forward. Her avatar appeared outside of the CERN reactor laboratory.

As Betty had advised, Alan was already there, rendered in full lab coat complete with safety goggles and clipboard. The corner of Juliane's lip twitched as if she wanted to smirk but just couldn't remember exactly how. "You certainly seem to enjoy looking the part in here."

He smiled as he answered, "As they say, 'When in Rome.' I'd hate to see the dry-cleaning bill on the outfit you are wearing in real life."

Juliane looked down. She hadn't given a thought to how her avatar should dress when she entered the virtual world. As a result, her subconscious had chosen for her. Her outfit was a version of the same iceberg white suit from the symposium; only here it was made with a fabric that could be described as being a modern take on samite. Her loose hair swayed in a breeze that she alone could feel. *I must look like an ice princess*, she thought.

The virtual Betty, on the other hand, appeared exactly as she did in real life. Juliane couldn't be sure if that was by choice. Betty did not seem to be able to perform more than a handful of actions at a time in the datasphere. Alan had speculated that the safer procedure would have such an effect, and Betty's performance would suggest he was right.

"Have you uploaded the latest equations?" Alan asked.

"Chad should be processing Juliane's portion now," answered Betty.

Betty disappeared and then re-appeared by Alan's side. Chad had shared a rumor that the two were dating outside of work. At the time, Juliane wasn't able to muster the energy to scold Chad for spreading gossip.

She told herself it wasn't any of her business. What did it matter if Betty and Alan chose to have a romantic relationship in addition to a professional one? She'd be the last person at the ACI who could pass judgment. But today, seeing them so close together, she couldn't help wondering if there was any truth to the story. It was like trying to ignore a scab that refused to heal.

Alan had mellowed since she'd severed her connection with Louis as if he could sense something different about her. He'd even stopped calling her 'Jules.' The corner of Betty's lips turned up as Alan's virtual hand hovered near hers for a moment.

Juliane realized how badly she wanted what they appeared to share, and she cursed the shadow of her former self she had allowed herself to become. The next time Louis was in town, she would re-establish the link if only to feel whole once again. Then, they would find some way to make it, and their relationship work properly out in the public.

She wondered for the thousandth time how he must be coping with the connection's loss. She hoped for his sake that whatever had been limiting its effectiveness on his side had in some way shielded him from its loss. She was afraid it hadn't. Her calls and messages had thus far gone unanswered.

"Ah, Juliane? You were fading out just then. There isn't anything wrong with the simulation?" Betty asked.

"No, nothing is wrong. I was momentarily distracted, but I am back now."

Juliane forced herself to forget about everything but the simulation. A series of components began to appear before her and gradually assembled themselves into shape. Juliane reached over and pressed a small switch. "Now this is based on available components found today. I would suspect that once we have a workable tool, much smaller, more commercially-available substitutes will be on the market, and we will be able to offer a version greatly refined in size and shape."

The device began to hum. Juliane waved her hand, and the floor around Betty and Alan became a pool of water, which remained even after Juliane switched the device off.

"And you are one hundred percent sure that you did not create that pool purely by thought?" Alan asked. "Accidents can happen here if you aren't careful."

As if she didn't know that. "I am positive. I had keyed in a program restriction just to be sure." Juliane nodded, emphasizing her point. It was one of the few things she was sure about.

"Well then, I will begin the requisition process for the materials in real life."

"Do we have a budget for that? Isn't the board going to need more proof of concept?" Betty asked.

Alan laughed. The sound seemed eerie and wrong in Juliane's ears. "You let me worry about that."

"Alan has had the board eating out of his hand for years," elaborated Juliane. "I don't know exactly what he has over them, but he's always been able to get them to sign off on whatever he needs to be successful." Juliane's jaw ached. She may have spoken more today than she had in days.

Alan did not offer any additional comment other than a smirk.

With childlike glee, Betty clasped her hands, beaming with pride at their accomplishment. "I guess that's all we can do for now. Alan, will you be coming by later? Er . . . you too, Juliane? I feel like celebrating."

Alan turned to her. "Not right away. Juliane makes it sound like all I have to do is snap my fingers. I'm good, it's true, but there is a certain amount of paperwork required first."

"Oh yes, of course, there is. How about you, Juliane? You've been working so hard over the last few weeks. Would you like to go out for a celebratory toast?"

Juliane sighed. "Thank you for the offer, Betty, but I'd prefer not to celebrate, at least not yet. Chad? Would you work up the remaining task list? I'll start work on the costing proposal. Alan can explain it later. If that's all, I am going to sign off."

Before either could respond, Juliane opened her eyes back in the real world. Betty's blank expression was evidence that she lingered in the virtual space. Chad would be still tethered to the machines. Alan was nowhere to be seen in the lab. Juliane found herself wondering where Alan might have disappeared to, but was grateful for his absence.

Had he been there, Betty might have returned promptly as well and then she would have been forced to listen to more of Betty's bubbly happiness. It was more than she could take.

She took a step and was momentarily blinded by a splitting headache. Juliane reached out to stabilize herself as the room spun and her legs buckled. The entire episode lasted less than a minute while Betty continued to sit like a doll in her chair. While vertigo may have left, Juliane still felt weak. The lab walls felt oppressive. She had to get out of the room.

Juliane made it as far as her office before she had to rest once again. Reaching into her desk drawer, she frantically tried to find her phone before remembering that she had stopped carrying it some time ago. While her head no longer felt as if it was being puréed in a blender, she was unable to focus, leaving her with no access to the network and no other means of locating Louis. She didn't have his private line programmed into the desk phone. She had never needed it.

"Dr. Faris! Are you all right?" Chad stood in the office doorway, but she had trouble focusing on him. "When was the last time you slept?"

Juliane wasn't able to form the words of a witty retort, so she settled on a futile attempt of waving Chad away. Chad ignored the gesture. He came to Juliane's side and reached out as if to hold her hand, but froze in mid-movement as if afraid of her reaction.

"Migraine. I need to talk to Louis," Juliane whispered. The sound of her voice created aftershocks of stabbing pain. Blinking rapidly did not help her vision, but she still noted Chad blanch, and he took a step back.

"Er . . . hmm . . . well . . ."

"Chad, I can barely stand my own voice. If you've nothing to say, then don't." Each word was like a miniature ice pick in her brain. "I don't have my phone. Find his number and call him. Now."

"Um . . ."

"Now, Chad."

"Well, I'm not sure that is such a good idea . . ."

"I don't remember asking you for your opinion." Inundated by another wave of pain and nausea, Juliane was forced to rest her head back down on the desk.

The staccato melody of Chad's phone ringing played across her ears like a jackhammer. As she was taken over by blissful darkness, the last sound she heard was something that sounded much like Chad saying, "I don't know if she's heard yet or not."

NINETEEN

When her eyes fluttered open again, her head was wedged in between the pillows of her bed. The warm pale light on the wall suggested early morning. *How did I get here?* she wondered.

Chad must have moved her after her collapse in the office. But how would he have gotten into her apartment? He must have rooted around in her purse to find the key.

She wouldn't have thought he would possess the nerve. She risked a glance down and was relieved to see she was still in the same attire that she had worn before. It was stiff and wrinkled, but otherwise all there. Juliane's lips inched upward a fraction. At least there had been some limits to Chad's caregiving.

Juliane pinged Louis's location with her next breath. Her fists tightened on their own accord as she realized that not only was he in transit, he was moving in an easterly direction. *Finally.* He had to be coming this way. He must have heard about her collapse and dropped everything for her.

Once he got here, she would explain everything. They would debug the private link issue, and everything would be just as it should be. Juliane closed her eyes, displacing the threatening tears.

Juliane's lips settled back into a fine line. Now she just had to summon the energy to get herself out of bed. It felt like trying to open her car door in the dead of winter. She filled her lungs in anticipation of the effort and nearly gagged. *Is that smell coming from me?* Juliane rubbed her fingers over her temples. Her skin felt cool to the touch, more like it belonged to a porcelain doll than a person.

She pulled herself upright only by a supreme act of will. Stumbling, Juliane made her way to the shower. As the water began to flow, she could feel the impact of each droplet on her body like hailstones. Juliane began to worry that she might shatter under the assault.

Emerging from the shower, she did not recognize the face in the mirror. Her normally alabaster skin was tarnished by dark lines, giving her skin the appearance of veined marble. Her dark hair, still wet, clung to her neck and shoulders. The dryer, a dead weight in her hand. Chad was right. She had been working herself too hard. She would go into the office, finalize the remaining tasks, and then insist on some time off.

She went through the rest of her morning ritual on autopilot. Every step she took was a small victory. Each time she felt like giving up, Juliane reminded herself that everything would be better soon. Following the success in Vegas, Juliane's paychecks had increased. After paying back Durham, she'd splurged on her clothing, making sure everything was tailored. If she was going to be featured in the tabloids, she wanted the picture to look good.

Dress for the job you want, she told herself as she paid for the extra service. Fine suits became her armor, but she noticed that her clothing no longer fit her to perfection. *When did that happen?* Juliane realized she couldn't recall the last real meal she had enjoyed.

As she put on her shoes, the entry door opened. Juliane immediately stopped struggling to line up her foot with an errant shoe. Pulling on its pair had taken several minutes. "Louis," she whispered. She lost her grip on the shoe.

As it clattered on the floor, Juliane's vision once again blurred. A shadow came toward her. She felt a hand on her arm, pulling her upward. Juliane realized she must have fallen along with the footwear.

The figure's face came into focus. She had expected to see Louis's wickedly sexy smile. Instead, she was greeted by Chad's look of concern. There was something else though about his expression. Something she couldn't quite place. It was the same look that had met her at the door of each foster family. *Pity*. She recoiled from the sight.

"What are you doing here, Chad?" she asked, fighting back the tears threatening to consume her. No one pitied her now. She had come too far. Chad must have forgotten who was in charge. She would have to be careful not to show any more weakness in front of him.

"Oh, thank goodness you're moving around! I worried that it might be time to call the emergency room!"

"It was just a migraine, nothing to get that worked up about. Definitely not worth going to the hospital over. I am grateful that you got me back home. It was much nicer to be able to wake up after a day like that in my own bed."

"Umm . . . it's been more than a day."

"What? Two?" Juliane sniffed.

"Er . . . more like a week."

"A week. How could it possibly have been a week?" she demanded.

Chad frowned. "You don't remember." Never letting go of her arm, Chad walked her to a chair. Even after she was seated, he did not completely release his grip as if he was afraid she might fall again.

Juliane pushed him off, straightening her back. "Remember what?" she asked.

"When I brought you back here, you were awake, but in a daze. The following morning you drank some water when I came by to check on you but demanded I leave you alone. We were beginning to worry you might not be willing to come back.

Nadia wanted to call the doctors right away, but I . . ." Chad trailed off.

"You what?"

"I couldn't help worrying what could happen when they started treating you without knowing what effect that procedure might have done to your systems. I didn't want to be the reason if you got worse."

Chad's face was flushed brilliant red. Juliane took a deep breath as if the added weight in her lungs would somehow help anchor her back into the land of the living. "Well, I feel fine now," Juliane responded as if the words being spoken out loud would make them true. "At least you were able to get through to Louis. How about the project? Was Betty able to help Alan finish up the requisition process?"

"Oh yes, I've never seen anything like it. I don't know what he did or said, but everything we asked for was in the lab the next day. The final assembly should be taking place today. If you think you are up for it, we could go together for the trial." Chad glanced down at his phone. "But we all understand if you would prefer to stay away one more day."

"Nonsense. I told you I am fine. There is no reason I would miss this." Juliane waved Chad toward the door, determined to rise and make her way on her own.

Arriving at the lab, Chad hovered behind as if she might break into a thousand pieces at any given moment. True to his report, when she opened the lab door, she was met by a large metallic device. It was a near-replica of the simulated one she had created in the virtual world, only missing a side panel. Betty and Alan were crouched over a corner desk examining the remaining electrical components and wire harnesses like puzzle pieces.

"Branching out to new fields of study, are we?"

Although Alan did not glance up as Juliane and Chad entered, Juliane watched as he slowly returned the component he had been holding back to the table.

Juliane had been building circuits almost as long as she had been programming, but Alan had never quite mastered the skill. There was a certain amount of artistry involved by tapping into an innate skill that just couldn't be taught. It was a talent Alan lacked, and they both knew it. Juliane knew it had to gall him that there was something he wasn't the best at.

Betty, on the other hand, immediately jumped up and ran over to them. She reached out to touch Juliane as if she needed reassurance that the real Juliane was in front of her and not just a virtual simulation.

"Thank goodness! We were streaming soldering for dummies, but I think even the dummies have more experience with electronics than I do. I am so relieved you're back on your feet. I am so, so sorry that I wasn't there for you. Why didn't you tell anyone you were feeling ill?"

"You and Alan seemed to have other things on your mind. Besides it was only a little headache, nothing at all to concern yourself about."

"A little headache doesn't keep you from our work for over a week," Alan spoke up. "I'm glad you're feeling well and rested now, but you could not have picked a worse time to have a breakdown."

"I'll try to make sure to schedule the next one at a more convenient time."

"See that you do."

Juliane scanned the workbench and the supplies strewn about it. Random silver blobs appeared in between twisted wires and broken chips. Her nostrils detected the smell of metal and burnt fabric. "Your iron is too hot and the sponge is too dry, but you haven't done too much damage yet. Chad? Can you please bring me my tools? I should be able to get us back on track in no time."

Juliane soon lost herself in the work at hand. She was aware that Betty was speaking, but her voice was like white noise. It wasn't until a distracted Alan suffered a burn from an ill-placed soldering iron that she returned to the present. Alan glared at Betty as he moved to take over the mechanical portion of the assembly. Juliane realized that hours had slipped by, but unlike before, she wasn't troubled by their unnoted passage. She almost felt alive again.

Finally, the last bolt was tightened. The device was just as Juliane had designed it in the simulation, a series of interlocking tubes surrounding a grouping of transformers and power generators.

"Well, I guess that's everything," stated Chad. "Who gets the honors of flipping the switch?"

"Should the rest of us go behind a screen or something?" Betty asked, eyeballing the device. Juliane took a deep breath, calming her racing heart. She told herself she had no doubt about the device's performance. They had logged hundreds of hours in the simulation environment for just this moment. Did Betty think that time spent had been merely for fun?

Juliane spotted Alan as he took a step forward placing him in between Betty and the device. Betty appeared to relax as if his presence was all the reassurance she needed. Betty might interpret the gesture as heroic, but Juliane wasn't convinced his motivation was as selfless as it seemed. *I miss a few days and Alan immediately thinks he has been in charge this whole time*, she thought.

Juliane realized that she was frowning and forced her features back into a neutral expression. If Alan and Betty were in a relationship, it meant she was well and truly outnumbered. Chad would shy away at the first sign of tension. Of course, if

Louis were here, there would be no question as to who should take the honors.

Thinking of Louis again, Juliane's eyebrows knit in confusion. Where was he anyway? When she had last tracked him, his trajectory had suggested that he would be in the general area by now. Juliane tried to get another reading on his location and was shocked to discover that she could no longer locate him at all.

It was as if he were no longer on the grid. Her pulse quickened. Had something awful happened to him in transit? His jet was safer than most, but accidents still happened.

Lost in her concern, she did not protest as Chad led her back into an observation room along with Betty. Alan moved to the center of the room, the twinkle in his eyes blurred by the oversized safety goggles he wore.

Alan paced around the perimeter of the device as if this last inspection might find some undetected design defect. Juliane snorted at Alan's attempt at showmanship. Out of the corner of her vision, Betty's chest swelled with pride. *No doubt about it, they are definitely in a relationship.* It was everything she could do not to roll her eyes.

"I feel as if I should have prepared some formal statement," said Alan, "as this moment will go down in the history books for sure."

"What? You didn't prepare for this moment? Here I was hoping to be inspired." Juliane might have spoken with more venom a year ago, but she had to admit that Alan's childlike glee was infectious. It couldn't cut through all of the fog from the loss of the link, but it softened the fog's effect.

"I am sure that Juliane and Chad will agree to sign off on whatever speech you want to claim you made in the final report," said Betty. "The suspense is killing me! Say the magic word or something, and turn it on."

Alan laughed. "What a marvelous suggestion! Chad, make sure you are recording this. Three . . . two . . . one . . . Abracadabra!"

The device lit up as it came online indicating that all systems were functioning normally. Even in the other room, Juliane thought she felt the barest tingle on her skin. A layer of water materialized on the lab floor, just as it had in her simulation.

Chad took a step back. "We've done it," Chad whispered before correcting himself. "You've done it . . ."

"Glad to know you never doubted us, Chad." Alan's voice vibrated as if his teeth were chattering. Juliane broke her gaze away from the growing puddle to really look at him. Alan saw the light of the sun about as often as she did, but could he be paler than he was just moments ago?

"No arguing with me this time, Juliane. It's time to celebrate!" Betty ran over to the small cooler in the back of the lab and pulled out a bottle of champagne. When Juliane looked back at Alan, whatever she thought she had seen in his expression was gone; if anything, Alan's cheeks now looked flushed as he swung Betty up into an embrace with uncharacteristic abandon.

"You did consider the increase on my insurance premiums and made sure to install appropriate drainage in this room before this little experiment, correct?" a voice she hadn't heard in weeks spoke up from the lab doorway.

The bottle crashed to the ground, sending fizzing spray across the room. The sound barely registered in Juliane's ears. She spun toward the doorway, not bothering to watch for broken glass on the ground as she leaped toward Louis. Only then did she notice that there was something off about his expression. Juliane realized then what was missing was his characteristic smile. Without it, he looked older, less forgiving. She pulled up short.

He hadn't made any move toward her. His posture was formal, matching the tailored suit he wore. Juliane detected a figure in the shadows behind him. Louis turned, and the smile she missed bloomed once again on his face, only this time it wasn't directed at her.

"I received a call that the project was nearing finalization and thought it was time to schedule an impromptu inspection. Had I realized that you were already preparing for the trial, I wouldn't have dawdled at the airport." His voice was pure business, only softening with a hint of mirth when he mentioned being delayed at the airport.

Juliane was confused. Why wasn't he rushing to meet her? Why wasn't he pulling her into one of his crushing embraces? Hadn't he worried about her? She looked at her teammates. Chad's eyes immediately dropped to the floor. Had any of them even tried to reach him about her health? If he didn't know she had been out of commission for a week, it would explain why he didn't arrive sooner, but why wasn't he making eye contact?

A female voice spoke up behind him. "Are you going to make me stand here in this hallway all evening?"

"Where are my manners? Dr. Dronigh, Dr. Faris, I would like to introduce you to Elena." A delicate-looking woman stepped into the lab light. She had long blonde hair that flowed down her back in soft curls, blue eyes, and flawless skin. Juliane's eyes darted between Louis and the woman like a hummingbird seeking sustenance. A wave of hot blood hit her ears in a futile attempt to block out Louis's next words. "My wife."

TWENTY

Although Louis had always spoken with a slight accent, it was as if he now spoke a different language. Each syllable leaving his lips blended as if the words fought against the forward movement of time. Though Juliane clearly saw the woman standing next to him, a double vision of her entering the lab and Louis encircling her waist with his arm played over and over again in Juliane's mind's eye.

She looked to Chad in a desperate attempt to find someone who could make sense of the situation. His gaze was at least off the floor, but his expression lacked the sense of shock she felt. Juliane began to question whether she had heard Louis's introduction correctly. None of the others had made any attempt at greeting the new arrival either. *Is this a bad dream?* No, the pain of crawling out of bed was much too real to be a dream. *Am I hallucinating?* Juliane wondered. *Is that woman even there?*

Juliane closed her eyes and took a deep breath in an attempt to calm her nerves. When she opened them, the woman was still there, Louis's hand continued to rest upon the small of her back, and Louis's smile still had an idiotic dreamlike quality to it.

Chad's eyes met hers and softened. *Pity.* A quick glance showed a similar reaction on Betty. This couldn't be happening. The taste of copper filled her mouth as she bit her tongue to keep from screaming.

She felt as shattered on the inside as the broken glass that marred the lab floor, but drew herself up like an empress. She would not shed tears. Not in front of this woman. Not in front of Louis. Not in front of anyone.

Alan's voice cut the awkward pause. "Rest assured, Evans, we are more than equipped to deal with a little water here. As you can see, it is already finding its way to the drainage system."

"I don't understand. What is all the fuss about a little water?" the woman, Elena, asked.

"The fuss, as you so put, is not about the water, but where the water came from." Alan launched into his lecturing tone. "I will try to keep this to the high-level concepts. Nearly half a century ago, researchers were able to finally confirm the existence of a particle, dubbed the Higgs Boson."

Elena glanced up at Louis, who nodded for Alan to continue.

"This particle is important because it is what gives an object mass. Without it, you and everything with mass around you would merely be raw energy instead of what you see today." Alan tapped on a countertop to illustrate his point.

"There have been several attempts to study the power of the Higgs Boson over the years through various experiments, but until today, no one has been successfully able to control its power and modify the particle's bonds at will with such a small and deployable mechanism." Alan splashed the water with the toe of his shoe. "What we have done here today is, well, you could effectively call it magic. In simple terms, the water you see here was created out of thin air."

When Elena did not immediately respond with gushing praise, Alan sighed. "I am sure your husband can explain this all to you while you travel to wherever it is you are going next." He waved toward the door.

When neither of the pair moved, Alan added, "Mr. Evans, as you can see, we've had a rather eventful day, and while I can't speak for the others, I am exhausted. I'll issue our formal report at the end of the week along with a demonstration. You would be welcome to attend, or if you would prefer, you can have your people contact me to schedule a more convenient time."

Without waiting for a response, Alan began collecting his things. Betty fidgeted nervously in the corner of the room as she attempted to pick up the shards of glass from the broken bottle. "Er . . . yes, it has been an extremely busy few days. We can celebrate after the formal report . . . unless any of you would like to come out with me after this mess is cleaned up. Juliane? Chad?"

"I'm supposed to meet Nadia in the next thirty minutes or so . . . so . . ." Chad continued to look at Juliane, his shoulders slumped in apology.

Juliane said, "No, Alan's right. There is still quite a bit of work to do, and I've been away from the office for far too long as it is." The image of Betty's pitying gaze burnt in her memory. She had to get back to her office where things still made sense. "Betty, if you can take care of the rest of the cleanup, I believe I'll head that way to get started on some paperwork."

Juliane began walking toward the door directly into the path of Louis and Elena, frowning when it became clear that neither was moving out of her way. Whether Elena's vacant expression was a result of not understanding Alan's explanation about their work over the last several months, or if she truly had come into the room without any thought to what her reception might be, Juliane saw no point in wasting her breath asking either of them to stand aside.

Juliane glared at Louis. His grin slipped, but Louis appeared more irritated at Alan's borderline insubordination than ashamed of his actions. As she continued her approach, Louis raised the arm not currently attached to Elena's waist briefly. Juliane arched an eyebrow in disbelief. *At least a part of him acknowledged our past connection,* Juliane thought to herself. Immediately, his arm dropped back to his side.

Louis moved first, but only to take a step closer to Elena. Juliane briefly paused on the threshold, taking another deep breath before taking the first step into the hallway. A large part of her wanted Louis to say something to break her professional demeanor, anything that would explain this sudden change in their relationship.

As she walked away, she heard Elena barely whisper to Louis, "Did Dr. Dronigh call her Betty? I thought you said Dr. Faris's name was Juliane?"

"Juliane was the one who just left, but don't worry about keeping the names straight. Alan Dronigh is the only name that really matters."

Juliane stopped and stared at the hallway lighting fixture in an attempt to regain her equilibrium. She envisioned funneling the tempest of her anger and hurling it into the light. She imagined that the LED bulb pulsed in response.

The lab door had not entirely closed, and Juliane heard Betty exclaim, "Alan, did you turn the generator back on? We've got a situation. Everyone get back! I don't know what's happening here!"

Juliane found herself back in her office, although she didn't remember making the trip. She debated going back to see what the commotion was about, but that would mean coming back into contact with *that* woman again and Betty's pitying eyes. *No.* She wouldn't go back. She couldn't go back. Only forward. Just then, Alan entered the room.

"You missed all the fun, Juliane."

"What fun would that be?"

"Well, just after you left, there was an energy surge, and the generator came online by itself."

"I guess it's possible that some of the capacitance didn't fully discharge." Juliane leaned over the papers on her desk again. They were surrounded by technology, but the ACI had still never fully embraced going paperless. She could access all the documents in the world digitally, yet her inbox remained full. Normally, she hated paperwork, but right now, she was grateful for the distraction caused by the waste. "You can ask Chad to take another look at the groundings."

"Ah, but I haven't told you what happened next."

"I'm on pins and needles." She continued to move papers from one pile on her desk to another, adding the occasional signature.

"Well, it seems that there must be an error in at least one of your equations."

Unable to ignore such a statement, Juliane put her pen down. She folded her arms and gave Alan her full attention. "I didn't make any mistakes. You saw the results of the simulation. Everything went exactly as I had anticipated."

"Well, then, how would you explain the lack of stability in the resulting water?"

"What lack of stability? When I left, the water was draining exactly as it should." Her forehead knit in confusion. Juliane knew she was being led along, and she wondered what grand point Alan was trying to make.

"Yes, when you left, it was, but almost as soon as the door closed, the outer perimeter of the pool ignited. Then boom!" Alan spread his fingers wide like a child describing simple fireworks. "The floor is completely damaged, and poor Mrs. Evans"—Juliane's lips tighten at his casual use of the name—"may have gotten herself a little singed. It's a wonder the entire room didn't explode." He casually examined his fingernails as if the nail beds might still show evidence of ash. "I dare say, neither of the Evans left impressed. We may have just lost our funding."

Juliane felt a flutter of panic. She could not understand why Alan seemed pleased to deliver such devastating news. They both had leveraged much of their reputation on this project. Such a failure could set them back years within the ranks of the ACI. "No, I can't believe Louis would do that to us. This is only a mild setback." The words rang false even to her ears.

"Right. And Louis has proven how loyal he can be. If he could toss you aside so easily, why wouldn't he do the same with our funding? As far as he is concerned, you and our project were merely distractions. Now that he's occupied elsewhere, we will all be forgotten."

Juliane slouched in defeat. "I just don't understand. What did I do wrong?"

"Don't take it personally. I suspect some of the hydrogen and oxygen bonds began to break down. Then, with all that pure oxygen floating about, it wouldn't take much, maybe just the spark from some static cling or some preservative in the champagne to ignite the hydrogen. Fairly basic chemistry." Alan shrugged. The smile plastered to his face told Juliane that he was purposely misinterpreting her question.

Juliane closed her eyes and took a calming breath to center her emotions. Had Chad or Betty been in front of her, she might not have had the strength to continue, but she would not break down and cry in front of Alan. "You know what I mean, Alan. None of you were surprised when Elena," Juliane spat the name, "entered the lab. What did you know? What happened while I was ill?"

The smile dropped from Alan's lips. "You really had no idea at all? After all that moping around the lab over the last few weeks, I thought for sure you were reading those rumor rags Betty so enjoys. You seemed to be paying them a lot of attention when you were featured in them every other day."

"I admit it. I read the occasional article about myself. I'm only human, but the magazines aren't exactly high on my daily reading list." As she had started to fade from being a regular feature in the tabloids, other more farcical stories had taken her place. Stories about athletes rumored to be shooting up with extremely experimental performance-enhancing drugs, giving them competitive edges, but the drugs had monstrous side effects, such as fingernails hardening into claws and gums that receded, making teeth look like tusks. Ridiculous stuff.

"Then, I am sorry you had to find out the way you did. You were so calm in there—I mean, I could tell you were rightfully pissed, but overall calm. I thought you had to have heard the rumors even if you didn't know for sure." Alan ran his hand through his hair, taking a few steps closer to her.

"I still don't know. What are these rumors you keep referring to?" Juliane pushed her seat back, wanting to keep the distance between them constant. Alan recognized the move and stopped his forward progress.

"You may need to talk to Betty. She's the one who told me, but what people are saying is that Louis suffered a nervous breakdown, anxiety attack, or something like that about a month ago, and this Elena person saw him wandering the street. Supposedly, she had no clue who he was and no idea about his fame or wealth or anything. The magazines say she took him back to her home where she nursed him back to health. They got married by the end of the week. Betty tells me it is being portrayed as quite the fairy tale romance."

The timing of his 'attack' would have put it around the time when Juliane first severed the bond. While she was here trying to fill the void with her work and feeling miserable, Louis was off getting played by wannabe Florence Nightingale.

Juliane felt a coldness settle into her heart. "Idiot." Juliane wasn't sure if she was referring to Louis or herself. "He should have called me. I could have explained everything."

"Could you?" Alan asked. "Because I would like to know what the hell has been going on with you lately. If you didn't already know about the rumors, then what is your excuse for the last few weeks? And what really happened today with the generator?"

Juliane ground her teeth together before answering. "The generator surged and the hydrogen ignited. You just finished telling me that."

Alan closed the remaining distance to the desk and leaned on it. "You and I both know you don't make mistakes. Something or someone sent a command to the generator. It wasn't Betty, and even I didn't know it was capable of doing anything like that." Alan leaned over further. Juliane could see her stunned face reflected in the safety glasses he still wore. "I believe it is your turn to do some explaining."

TWENTY-ONE

Juliane bowed her head. "I didn't know. I swear. I didn't mean for anything like that to happen. I overheard him tell her that I was nothing. I was so angry, but it couldn't possibly . . . I never would . . ." Juliane chewed her lip as she played the scene back in her memory. Louis's words. Elena's smug smile. Her shoulders slumped. "I haven't been myself ever since I disabled the private network."

"What private network?"

"The one I established with Louis. I thought we would be able to have a deeper connection, only it never worked right. I broke it off thinking we could just fix it later, but I think I did even more damage and now, now . . ."

Alan stepped around the desk and put his hand on her shoulder. Juliane decided to ignore that it was Alan offering comfort. She was tired of fighting. There was no point. She was never strong enough. Never good enough. Nothing had gone according to plan. Juliane admitted to herself that at that moment she needed someone. Anyone. Even Alan. Juliane leaned into the gesture, whispering, "I don't know what's happening to me."

"You are evolving. We are evolving." Juliane looked up from her seat. The way Alan stood above her allowed for the glow from the overhead lights to reflect on the surface of his eyes, giving them a near fiery appearance. He was confidence manifested.

Juliane pulled away as if burned. Alan was too confident. He might not have had his heart torn inside out, but his career was equally affected by the accident. "Tell me you saw this coming and that everything is going according to your grand plan."

Alan snorted. "Juliane, after all this time we've been together, how can you even doubt it? Everything is going according to my grand plan. Everything."

"But what about our project? What should we do?"

"I think it may be time to introduce you to my other benefactor." Alan smiled, but it was a wolf's grin.

Alan arranged for all their transportation to his mysterious benefactor. He hadn't elaborated other than to say that the office was a mere ninety minutes away from campus, in Worcester. When the car arrived, Alan opened the door for her as he held a quick exchange with the driver. Juliane was deaf to whatever passed between the two of them.

As they left the campus, Juliane turned off her newsfeed filters. *Gossip news be damned,* she thought. Immediately, she was bombarded with articles featuring Louis. Pictures leaked from the private ceremony adorned several magazine covers, and interviews by the friends of the new Mrs. Evans filled the feed.

Other, more insidious rumors began to weave their way into the conversation. Juliane saw her name appear in the feed summaries. She clicked on a few links. The articles speculated that she had only been a paid cover to divert the media's attention from the real relationship.

Reporters and celebrity profilers alike dissected every detail about Louis and her relationship, looking for the telltale sign that things hadn't been what they had seemed. What did their body language say? Where was she during high profile events? Where was Elena at the same time? The reporters even attempted to estimate how much she might have made in such an arrangement.

Unfortunately, once her filter program was turned off, it was incredibly difficult to turn back on, especially now that her name was involved. As all media continued to stream directly to her brain, there was little she could do to escape its onslaught as the car sped toward their destination.

The car pulled up in front of one of the several towers in the heart of the city. It had been constructed out of sandstone and glass. It was easily the tallest building in the area. A mountainous pillar of beige and blue scraping the sky. And yet it almost appeared natural, as if it had been carved directly out of solid rock by the elements rather than man-made.

The top of the tower consisted of only a moderate slope and lacked many of the gaudier finishing touches so prevalent on the tallest buildings found in other locations. At least Juliane thought it did. It was difficult to tell for sure from the base of the building. A plaque next to the door announced it housed a group called Apex.

The interior was elegant, yet minimal. Juliane's heels clicked on the floor as she and Alan crossed the cavernous lobby toward the elevator doors. A guard looked up as they passed but appeared to recognize Alan and allowed them to continue unchallenged.

Alan walked past the first three elevator doors before stopping in front of a fourth, set slightly out of sight. He held his thumb on the call button for an unusual length of time. Alan noticed her look of curiosity; he leaned over and whispered, "Biometric security."

Within minutes, the elevator doors opened, and they ascended in silence made even more notable by the lack of easy listening music or sound of whirling gears or turning belts.

The lobby at their only stop mirrored the one below, with a few small differences. High-end pieces of artwork hung on the walls, although none of them were by any artist Juliane recognized. Juliane judged that they were most likely originals rather than reproductions.

The woman at the front desk smiled as they approached. "Alan, how nice to see you. I hear that congratulations are in order."

Juliane shot Alan a quick glance. "I thought we were supposed to keep our research under wraps."

The woman tilted her head in Juliane's direction. "Ah, you must be Dr. Faris. Rest assured; he's never shared any of what you do over in Meriden with me. I was congratulating him on his engagement, of course."

"Engagement? You and Betty are engaged?" Juliane couldn't prevent the depth of her disbelief from entering her tone.

"Jealous?" Alan asked with a smile.

"No. I am just surprised, that's all. When did this happen?"

"Oh, a few days before your . . . recent personal days. It isn't relevant to our work, so we didn't think it worth mentioning." Alan paused as if considering to deliver his next words. Juliane readied herself for a biting retort.

"Betty also seemed to think you wouldn't react to the news well under the . . . ah . . . circumstances," Alan murmured.

Juliane felt a blush begin to bloom on her cheeks and fought it back with icy determination.

"I suspect now she was right."

The woman at the front desk continued to stare at Juliane. Her eyes momentarily widened, and Juliane knew she had made the connection between her name and the various news stories. Then, Juliane saw it. The softening of the woman's face. *Pity.* Pity from this stranger. Another blast of ice water hit her veins.

She had made a mistake letting her guard down with Alan back at the office. She would not show weakness again.

"Well, let me also extend my congratulations to you both." Turning back, Juliane arched her back and held her head straight. She looked down at the woman without lowering her chin. "Now I don't believe we came all this way to exchange gossip and pleasantries. I believe we have an appointment?"

The woman blushed. "Yes, of course, right this way. Mr. Knightley is expecting you. Can I get you anything? Coffee, tea, water?" She scurried around the desk and toward a large pair of double doors.

"Juliane, was that tone necessary? She was just trying to be friendly."

"I didn't come all this way to make new friends."

"That may be, but that's a quick way to make enemies, and you don't want to be on Sarah's bad side. Besides, Damien has been a good friend to me for some time. He's been quite eager to finally meet you."

The room behind the double doors continued with the minimalist theme except for a large water feature that took up a portion of one wall. The water trickled down a series of slate stones and emptied into a narrow pool at its base. Scattered around the base and throughout the pool were a series of flames. Juliane couldn't tell if the flames were gas-powered or merely simulated. In either case, the effect was captivating.

Juliane didn't realize how mesmerized she was until a voice spoke up from the center of the room. "I see you appreciate my serenity wall."

She broke her gaze from the fountain as she realized that she recognized the voice's owner.

It was the same man she had noticed in the corner of the Vegas auditorium. The same man who she spotted later near Alan's platform. She vaguely remembered that Louis had appeared to recognize him, but did not seem particularly happy to see him.

The man Juliane presumed was Damien Knightley walked over to the serenity wall where Juliane stood. Just like in Vegas, he wore a finely tailored suit and not a hair was out of place.

"It is very peaceful," Juliane said.

"It only looks that way from a distance. If you were smaller and positioned on one of those rocks, I am sure the view would be quite terrifying. Everything comes down to a perspective, don't you think?"

Juliane raised her eyebrows in quick salute of his observation.

"I must say I have looked forward to meeting you for quite some time," Damien Knightley continued. "I can't say most people would describe me as a patient man, but he kept telling me that you weren't ready yet. I was beginning to worry that Alan here intended to keep you to himself until the end of time."

Juliane risked a glance at Alan, whose teeth shone brightly in the room's lighting.

"I'm sorry, ready for what? Alan's not told me anything about why we are here," Juliane said. Her hand tightened into a fist on its own accord. More secrets.

"Really, Alan? You know, one of these days, your little flair for the dramatic is going to backfire on you." Damien attempted to scowl at Alan, but his eyes didn't quite commit to the gesture.

"It's your program. I thought you might prefer to tell her all about it yourself."

The man clicked his tongue, then paused. "I suppose you are right. Now let us start over. I may have heard about you, but obviously, Alan was not polite enough to reciprocate the favor. My name, as you probably have already guessed, is Damien Knightley." He paused as if he was expecting Juliane to recognize it. She didn't. He shrugged after a second and continued, "I happen to head up a fairly discreet group made up of individuals who believe that there needs to be an alternative to the ACI. A group not afraid to take bold initiatives for the greater good, rather than just for profit."

Juliane relaxed, unclenching her fist. She looked again at Alan as another thought took her. "You've been working for the competition. All this time? What does that make you, a corporate spy?"

"Labels," Alan snorted. "I saw an opportunity and I took it."

"But what about your contract? Couldn't you get into serious trouble for violating your non-disclosure agreement?" Juliane asked, alarmed.

"What non-disclosure agreement? I certainly have never signed anything of the sort. At least, not anything legally binding." He smirked.

Juliane's gaze darted about the room. She took a step back.

"Oh, come on, Juliane," Alan sighed. "We both know that you've been willing to bend a rule or two when it helped you get ahead."

"Bending the rules is one thing. You've been doing much worse."

"You've been as much a part of this as I've been," Alan countered, taking a step toward her.

"I most certainly have not." Juliane drew her head up, refusing to be intimidated.

"Think about all those projects we've worked together on. The ones that needed quick funding. You never once wondered where the extra money came from?"

"I just thought you knew ways to fast-track approval."

Alan grinned. "And I did." He swung his arms out, emphasizing the lavish room. "I do."

Juliane turned her attention to Damien. "I don't understand. Isn't the ACI the competition? Why would you be writing checks for its projects?"

Damien shrugged. "Business is rarely black and white. I invest when and where I see potential."

"So why did you bring me here? Alan might think he can get around his contract with the ACI, but I have no interest in participating in corporate espionage."

Damien's eyes softened. "No. Unfortunately, you would have little value for my organization in that capacity. Especially not after recent events."

Juliane felt her shoulders slump. Damien was right. The explosion in the lab would ensure she would never be granted access to sensitive projects ever again. If she was Louis's wife and had been on the receiving end of that explosion, she would have made sure of that. "Then why?" she whispered.

"I told you, I invest when and wherever I see potential. You are that potential. I want to invest in you," Damien said.

Juliane blinked as she tried to make sense of Damien's words.

He laughed. "For being made up of a number of geniuses, the ACI has still not learned how to fully capitalize on its assets. If you don't mind me saying so, you are the complete package: ambition, brains, and beauty. So often we only encounter people with one or two of those traits."

Damien began to stroll around the perimeter of the room. "Sign with me and you would get to pursue whatever you fancy, as long as there's a business case for it." Damien's voice softened into the quiet tone of a concerned parent. "My group may not be as large as the ACI, but we are comprised of the very best in their fields, the most promising individuals of our time. I allow those who sign with me the freedom to pursue their interests as they see fit, provided we all work together toward the group's benefit."

Damien stopped behind his desk. "By accepting my offer, you would, however, need to sever any remaining ties to the ACI." He paused to scan her face for a reaction. "But am I wrong in thinking that this might not be a large request?"

"I didn't know what to expect when Alan invited me out here, and I don't know anything about you or your firm." Reaching the pinnacle of respect and success within the ACI had been her goal for so long, it was difficult to consider anything else. If she stayed with the ACI, she would likely have to grovel before Louis or worse Elena with every proposal. The thought was unbearable.

Starting anywhere new, especially if the lab accident came to light, would mean clawing her way back up from the bottom. Although Juliane was uneasy with the arrangement Alan had with Damien, Damien was at least offering her a chance to start at the top.

Damien smiled. "Of course. It just so happens your timing today is excellent. I have a meeting scheduled in just an hour with several of my other key players in the organization. Why don't you and Alan go and enjoy a cup of coffee and then join us in the large conference room on the sixteenth floor?"

"How much does the rest of the group know about me?" Juliane caught herself asking. She didn't know if she would be able to stand more looks of pity.

"Oh, they are aware of most of the work produced within their fields but are not always as tied into the history of specific individuals. As a group, we tend to be too busy to pay attention to gossip. Alan has only discussed you in detail with me. But I haven't felt the need to pass your information along to the rest of the group. Besides"—Damien directed a pointed glance at

Alan—"I wasn't sure if Alan was ever going to arrange a meeting."

"If I do agree to join your team, I would like to have a fresh start. Would you be able to offer that?"

"I can understand the desire to rebuild your reputation in private considering your present, er . . . celebrity," Damien said the word as if it was a delicate piece of china. "As I mentioned, we pride ourselves on our discretion here. If you would like me to introduce you under a different name or gloss over your most recent background, I would be happy to do so, although I can't promise that they won't eventually make the connection. Would that suffice?"

Juliane considered his offer. Shaking her head, she said, "No, I don't think that will fool anyone. They might not recognize me right away, but someone would be bound to connect me with the woman on the news."

"What if they didn't see you in the flesh regularly? Would that satisfy you?"

"What do you mean?"

"Several of our group prefer to maintain their primary offices elsewhere. I would be more than happy to grant you the same privilege. Thanks to that upgrade of yours, you might not even have to physically step through these doors again after today. Would that offer you enough of a fresh start?"

Juliane chewed her lip. Damien's suggestion would give her more freedom than she previously had with the ACI. She could make her avatar look however she wanted. She could blur its features or change its look, and none would be the wiser provided she limited her face-to-face visits. Then, even if someone did make the connection to her name, they might think it was just some unlucky coincidence. His idea could work.

Damien glanced down at his watch. "I don't want you to feel as if I am rushing you into a decision, but I do need to make a call. Why don't you think about my offer over the next hour?"

Juliane nodded. "One hour."

As if by magic, the office doors opened. Either Damien had a secret call button or his assistant had been listening to the entire conversation. Juliane's stomach tightened. Perhaps she had, as Alan suggested, made a tactical mistake by being rude to her.

"Until then."

TWENTY-TWO

As the elevator doors opened, Alan took a sharp left, directing her to a coffee shop located just outside the lobby. Gesturing for Juliane to take a seat, he ordered for the both of them, not bothering to ask how she liked hers.

The steaming mug was thrust under her face. The swirling dark liquid smelled and looked perfect. Juliane tipped the cup back in ready anticipation of the first sip. As she did so, it occurred to her that Damien's offer meant it was unlikely she would have to suffer Chad's coffee-turned-sludge ever again. She sputtered, setting the cup down on a table. *Wow, that's bitter*, she thought. They must have over-roasted the beans.

Alan settled into a chair covered in plush purple fabric in prime view of other shop patrons. As he drank from his mug, he looked very much like a medieval lord surveying his court. *He doesn't have a care in the world*, Juliane thought. *And why should he? Everything always works out for him.* Her eyes tightened, and she turned away.

She tried to imagine what life would be like, being equally respected and appreciated through Damien's firm. She realized then that her subconscious had already decided to take him up on his offer.

Lost in her thoughts, she was startled when Alan placed his hand on her shoulder, a finger coming into contact with her skin along her neckline. "Are you ready to meet the others?"

As she stood, the anxiety and remorse of the last hours was replaced with a feeling of confidence and calm. Starting over. She had a lifetime's experience starting over. She would not be weak. She would not be pitied. She had a sudden vision of herself as a newly-crowned queen being escorted to the balcony to greet her subjects for the first time. "Lead the way."

Alan must have sensed some of her state of mind because he bowed slightly at her words.

When they arrived on the designated floor, she followed Alan into a large conference room shaped like a piece of honeycomb. He hadn't needed to stop for any directions, so he must have attended a few meetings in the room. She wondered how long Alan had been working for both sides.

Ten members of the board were in the room already, seated at a large U-shaped mahogany table. Juliane didn't look at any of them. Her gaze was instead caught by the room's interior. The walls were decorated with large canvases of paint splatter. At first glance, each piece looked as if the artist had thrown colors against the surface at random. She was startled then to realize that if you scanned your eyes over all the pieces together, the chaos they individually represented was transformed into a beautiful landscape. It was breathtaking work.

"Your timing is excellent." Damien's voice brought her attention back to the table and the meeting in progress. "Everyone, we have a special guest visiting us today." He nodded to an empty seat. "But perhaps you would prefer to make your own introduction?"

"I'm Juliane Faris." She wouldn't hide. She was done pretending to be anything but who or what she was—a capable woman who deserved to be recognized for her own merits. "My experience to date has been in augmented reality and bioprocessing, and I look forward to joining the team."

Damien grinned. "Short and to the point. Maybe you will rub off on some of the rest of us." He directed a glance at Alan. "Well, then I would like to introduce you to Camille Nadal, who has thus far led all our efforts within the general health and wellness space as well as applications that touch on behavioral science. There are so many advances being made in biotechnology. I expect she is eager to get some of that work off her plate.

"Next to her is Eithan Yuan, our resident expert on genetics and gene therapy. Lillian O'Rail heads up finance. Rhett Mossel leads our political advocacy. Alan, of course, helps us with market intelligence, research, and the occasional talent acquisition." Damien smiled at his joke. Each team member had inclined their head as they were introduced.

The door to the office opened again, and the woman from Damien's front office entered, carrying a stack of papers, which she distributed. "Ah, yes, this is Sarah, my assistant, whom you've already met. Don't let her friendly manner fool you. In addition to keeping me on schedule, she handles most of the day-to-day management of the support staff. I hear she can be quite the taskmaster."

Sarah's lips turned up as if she was well used to her boss' accolades, but the smile never reached her eyes. Juliane suspected Sarah was the type who could hold a grudge. When all the papers had been distributed, Sarah took a seat to his right at the base of the U.

"Finally, last but not least is one of our newest team members, only joining us a couple of months ago. I will admit that I was overjoyed when he reached out to us, as he is quite the steal. Heading our legal department is Durham Ladensham."

Juliane started. A smile crept on her lips. *So that explains where he disappeared to.* She hadn't seen Durham since they'd left Vegas or heard from him since sending him a check. However, a friendly face would make the transition to the Apex team much easier. The smile slipped from her face. *He's Louis's friend. He'll be able to report back everything I do. Is there no escape from that man?*

He turned in his chair. While there was a shine in his eyes, there was no warmth radiating from him in response to Damien's words. *Or maybe he won't.* Juliane was startled to realize there was no sign of recognition at all. *How does he not recognize me? Did Louis ask Durham to entertain so many women that we all blended together?*

Perhaps she should feel grateful for Durham's lack of recognition rather than irritated. But they'd spent hours together. how could Durham not recognize her?

Juliane forced her hands to unclench. If he wanted to act as if they'd never met before, that was fine by her. She had already announced she was joining the team, so there was no going back now.

She focused her thoughts, accessing the datasphere and her simulation software. Several scenarios played out in her mind's eye at a fraction of a second. There was nothing he could say or do now that she wasn't prepared for.

Decision made, she stepped toward the empty chair as Alan took a seat near Sarah with a cocky and amused expression on his face. Shoulders straight, Juliane looked Durham squarely in the eye. She was Juliane Faris, and this time, he would remember her, but for the reasons she wanted. She would make sure they all did.

TWENTY-THREE

Less than five years had passed since that first day in the conference room, but already her contributions since joining Damien's group could be seen attached to the ears and around the necks of individuals in every major city and many small towns as well.

She launched a line of slim devices made to look like jewelry but also encapsulated nano-processors and sensor packets in various form factors. Louis and the ACI might have the headset market locked, but overall, she thought her solution was far more elegant.

True to his word, Juliane had been free to launch a company around her technology provided she occasionally reported into the main office. She'd named it Fair Use—a nod to her name as well as the fact her devices ensured the ACI couldn't achieve a monopoly on access to *her* datasphere.

One of her products was an ear clip which sent a signal into the brain, allowing a wearer to interface with the virtual world simply by closing their eyes and opening their mind. It wasn't as fast or as powerful of a solution as genetic imprinting. However, the Gene Assist serum was not something she could replicate without wasting millions in patent litigation. As a result, it was an option available only to those who never had to ask how much something cost and offered exclusively through the ACI.

The pendant version was an entry-level model for those even less risk-averse and budget-conscious. She'd put everything she had into the launch. Framed images of models wearing her products as they walked down the runway hung along one of her office walls.

Even though Betty still worked for the ACI, and certainly didn't need the access point, she had worn one of Juliane's earliest product releases at her wedding to Alan. The device caught the light at just the right moment in one of the photographer's shots and the product had gone viral. Early product reviews and press releases covered the other wall. Her company's more recent news was much less frame-worthy.

"There was another suicide reported last night." Juliane glanced up from her desk as her assistant, Stuart, added another stack of documentation to the top of the increasingly unstable pile.

"You are positive it was a suicide?"

Juliane sighed. It was the fourth reported death at her manufacturing partner's factory. Her only chance to get her product into the hands of enough of the population to revolutionize society was through a low-cost production facility.

That meant long hours in locations not known for high wages. There was always a risk that the demands might eventually take their toll on individual technicians employed at these sites. Eyes wide open to the risks, she had toured numerous locations all boasting programs for their workers designed to maintain, if not increase, worker morale, and she had ultimately selected what she believed, at the time, was a quality partner.

"An investigation is underway, but it appears that way."

"Well, at least we don't have to worry about a murderer being on the loose." Juliane knew as soon as the words were out of her mouth that she was being insensitive, but another investigation would only further delay their next launch.

First, all work would stop while the root cause was investigated. The worker's friends and family would be interviewed. New processes, procedures, and safety nets would be installed. Each of those things took time to implement, as necessary as they were, and it cost money she might have spent elsewhere.

An alert scrolled by her vision. A research center in Southern California speculated that there could be a link to cancer from the overuse of her ear clips. She ran a quick cross-reference. The center's proximity to Elena's hometown should have thrown the validity of the research into question, but the media always seemed to latch on to potential issues with her products, or her partners, with far more glee than they did with Louis's . . . especially after the ACI announced that it had found a way to embed nano-generators into roadways, building materials, and even some fabrics.

Almost overnight, everything was self-powered. All you had to do was pay a royalty to the ACI, and the world was grateful for the privilege.

Politicians and pundits raved about how generous the ACI was with their cheap energy. Juliane grimaced. *If they only knew what technology the ACI held back.*

People in developing nations were still dying of dehydration and illnesses spread through contaminated water. The ACI could have been giving them instant clean water if only they hadn't shelved the matter generator project after the accident.

It's all Elena's fault. If that wasn't irresponsible enough, tens of thousands of people were put out of work as power plants were taken offline, replaced by the ACI's nanos.

Does anyone care? No. Everyone loved the ACI, especially Louis, and why? Because their little electronic toys were powered indefinitely just by standing near the street.

Meanwhile, she and her company were at risk of being made to look like a monster. Juliane crumpled a piece of paper that she hadn't even realized she had picked up from the stack on her desk.

"I'll arrange a conference call with the production facility manager," her assistant said, already backing out of Juliane's office.

"And go ahead and start working up the press release. We may need to get out ahead of this one."

Juliane had ensured that all of her production heads were equipped with functioning ear clips or pendants as part of their manufacturing agreement, so at least she wasn't going to have to squeeze in an international flight. They all wore them constantly per their agreement, which came in handy for meetings like the one she needed now.

Juliane closed her eyes and sent a meeting command. You really could not get a sense that people understood the gravity of the situation on a conference call, but thanks to her virtual world, she could make sure those that worked for her did. All she had to do was create the correct motivation.

TWENTY-FOUR

Nets, he said. Juliane's lips curled in displeasure. *Nets.* Nets would only prevent tragic landings. They did nothing to address why a person would jump from the facility in the first place.

The conversation with her initial contact had been a waste of her time. As she listened as the man detailed the list of fees and upgrades the facility would need, she wished she had the luxury of shifting the entire production line, but that wasn't an option. At least not now.

Signing off, Juliane decided she needed to discuss strategy with Damien. Surely some of his connections had found reliable manufacturing partners who could provide volume manufacturing at a reasonable cost without devaluing human life.

Her office door burst open to a very pale Betty. Upon first glance, the years had not been kind. Betty's eyes were sunken and her skin shone with a waxy hue. Juliane couldn't quite remember the last time she had seen the woman in the flesh. She had always looked the same as she had the day they first met whenever they corresponded in the virtual world.

"I hope you don't mind that I let myself in. Your assistant wasn't at his desk."

"Yes, we have a situation that I need to attend to."

"Oh." Betty froze, glancing furtively at the door. "Am I keeping you from something?"

"Well, I might not be able to give you a whole lot of time, but I can spare a few minutes. Unfortunately, we have gained some experience dealing with these sorts of things."

Papers positioned next to the chameleon paperweight on Juliane's desk fluttered from the breeze caused by Betty's sigh of relief. Juliane caught sight of the lizard's grin and scowled. It was designed for one job. One.

"I appreciate it." Betty's voice was hardly more than a whisper. "I hate to bother you at the office. I know how busy you always are."

Juliane nodded in acknowledgment as she attempted to gather up a few of the files she would need for the next hours' worth of meetings.

"Betty, you know I would love to be able to spend more time after hours with you if I could . . ."

"That's not why I am here—"

"Don't apologize. What can I do for you?" Until the factory was held accountable, each minute wasted was putting more lives at risk.

Betty moved like a cuckoo bird, only one that had lost its voice. "I don't know where to start."

"Well, trying usually goes a long way." Juliane had meant the comment as a joke, but her present mood made the words terser than she intended. She looked away, only to have her gaze catch on the only framed image on her office wall not featuring a Fair Use product—a pair of dogs. There was no time to consult with Damien. She knew what she had to do to get through to these people.

When she had entered the room, Betty's face had been somewhat yellowed; the subsequent blush made her resemble rotting fruit. "You're right, but of course you are always right, aren't you?" Betty chuckled at her joke, but the laughter was forced. "It's Stevie."

"Your son? He's what, two now?"

"Four, actually."

"Has it been so long?"

"He's seeing things."

"It's perfectly normal for a boy his age to have an overactive imagination."

"I wouldn't be here if it was an imaginary friend. What he is seeing is much worse."

"Could he have stumbled across some of your and Alan's work? Images of the human body dissected can be quite traumatic to a young boy."

"Alan and I . . . we aren't working together anymore . . ." Betty's voice trailed off. Juliane had to strain her ears to make out Betty's last word.

"Oh?" Juliane didn't expect a response but took Betty's silence as confirmation. "That's a shame. You both seemed to be quite the team."

Juliane mentally checked her internal clock. Stuart likely had notified the majority of the remaining production heads by now. If she could wrap this up in the next couple of minutes, she might still have time to pour a cup of coffee before beginning the interrogation. "As nice as it is to see you, I'm the last person you should be coming to with family problems. Perhaps you might want to talk to someone like a—"

Betty interrupted, "I don't know how much more time he has!"

Juliane returned her attention to the woman in her office, taking in the dark circles under her eyes. With a thought, she sent a message to her assistant informing him that she would be delayed for a few more minutes but to start arranging the next call.

"What do you mean? What's going on?"

"It began several months ago. Stevie started telling us fantastic stories about places we'd never been to and about awful people we've never met. At first, we thought what you did, he had just started to create imaginary friends."

Juliane nodded in encouragement.

"But then he described seeing some place that sounded like a torture chamber with people being transformed into monsters. Alan and I had a huge fight about it." Betty twisted her shirt. "I accused him of allowing Stevie to watch inappropriate movies. Then it got worse."

"Stevie would start screaming for no determinable reason, only to go catatonic immediately afterward. I tried everything to snap him out of it, but nothing worked." Betty's eyes shone. "He just wasn't there. The episodes started getting more frequent, and he would be gone longer and longer."

"I've had to stop working—one of us had to be home with him at all times." She grumbled. "Now I'm afraid to even sleep, terrified that one of these days he won't wake up at all."

Tears flowed freely down Betty's cheeks as Juliane took a nervous step before freezing in place. Juliane was completely out of her element and at a loss as to what might be expected from her after such a revelation.

"Where is he now?"

"There's a children's clinic here. He is there for observation, but no one seems to know anything."

Juliane crossed the remaining distance until she was at Betty's side, placing an awkward hand on the woman's shoulder. "Well, I am sure that they will be able to figure out what is the issue. You look exhausted. Did you come here to ask to take a nap on my couch while you wait for the results?"

"I would have slept at the hospital if I just wanted a nap," Betty snapped.

"Sorry—I just don't understand then. What does Alan think is the matter? I would advise you if I could, but I'm not a medical doctor. My studies were purely theoretical. I don't have any experience with what you described."

"Yes, you do." Juliane pulled her hand back as Betty spun with violence to face her. "You and Alan have more experience than anyone." Gone was any appearance of nicety from Betty's expression. "The doctors aren't going to find anything. They don't know yet what they're looking for, but I do. I was there. I saw what it did to you and Alan." Betty's shoulders sagged under the weight of her pronouncement.

"You think Alan performed the procedure on your son? He takes incredible risks, but I can't imagine he would risk a child's well-being." Juliane considered what she knew about Alan. "Well, perhaps he would with other people's kids, but never his own! What did Alan say when you asked him about it?"

Betty's shoulders slumped as the fight left her body as quickly as it had arrived. "He denied everything of course."

Juliane was out of her depth and racked her brain to find a way to defuse the situation. Pressure expanded behind her temple like a thunderhead. Her virtual vision flashed with another headline.

There was no time for distraction. She had to get back to the business at hand. "Alan and I don't see eye to eye very often, but I would be inclined to believe him. There has to be another explanation."

Betty raised an eyebrow at Juliane's statement but did not challenge her further. "Alan may not have strapped him to a chair and stuck him with needles, but he's wrong about not being responsible."

Juliane's forehead knit. "What are you suggesting?"

"If he didn't have the procedure, then there is another fairly basic explanation. He was simply born with the upgrade, but doesn't have the mental maturity to control it."

"But that's not possible. The serum—"

"Required a virus to work. Viruses mutate. You of all people should understand how survival depends on adaptation. Now, unless I can figure out a way to help him control it, I expect the energy drain is killing him."

The room took on a temporary red hue, and Betty's features blurred as a meeting notice flared within Juliane's mind. Stuart must have successfully gotten everyone online.

Betty was under a lot of stress. That much was clear to see. Her marriage was suffering as was her child, but she had to be grasping at straws. There was simply no way Alan would have allowed the virus to escape his control. Juliane knew him too well.

The minute hand on her internal clock shifted again. By now, her first contact would have briefed his colleagues on their earlier conversation. If she was going to be able to bring them around to her way of thinking, she needed to make sure this time they understood exactly how displeased she was, and each second was more time for them to agree on some lip service statement. Her legacy, as well as several lives, were potentially at stake.

As much as she wanted to help her friend, there was nothing she could do better than the care he was already receiving at the clinic. While Juliane had debated her options, Betty had wiped her tears away, but her skin remained smeared with moisture. Clearly, she was looking for some form of comfort, but Juliane was still unsure of what she could offer.

"What did Alan say when you talked to him about this possibility?" Juliane began moving toward the door, hopeful that the motion might encourage Betty to follow.

"At first he tried to convince me it was something like night terrors or epilepsy—like I wouldn't have already ruled those out. When I didn't agree, he practically accused me of hiding a genetic defect in my family history." Betty's lips drew thin. "As if our son's condition couldn't possibly be a result of something from his side of the family tree." Once again, Betty's cheeks flared with pent-up anger.

Juliane could almost see the remaining evidence of tears evaporate when exposed to the fire of Betty's expression. She had never seen her friend look so fierce.

Pulling the door open for Betty, Juliane commented, "I know too well how Alan can be at times, but he is one of the most brilliant minds alive today. I am sure that if he just has time to look at the problem, he'll be able to figure it out."

Betty refused to budge.

Juliane continued as if Betty wasn't like a land mine posed to go off with a single misstep. "Until then, I am sure the doctors are going to take great care of your son."

Betty remained where she stood.

Looking at the open door, Juliane wondered if it might be easier to join the call from a nearby conference room. "You are still more than welcome to stay and get some rest here before heading back to the hospital."

Betty chewed her lip as she took a small step toward the open door. Her voice dropped to a dull monotone when she next spoke. Her shoulders shifted not unlike a lioness readying herself for a strike. "I don't believe you realize how close you came to dying in the labs while you adjusted to the change."

Betty pivoted and began strolling along the side of the room, running her finger along the wall. "If Chad and I hadn't made sure you were cared for, you wouldn't be in this fancy office today."

Stopping near Juliane's desk, she picked up Juliane's paperweight and held it as if studying its living counterpart. "You always thought yourself so much better than the rest of us . . ."

Betty returned the metal lizard to its resting place. "Remember how concerned you had been about my ability to handle the upgrade? You didn't think I could. Now, imagine what it must be like for my son. He's only a child."

Betty wrung her hands. She looked at Juliane. "All I am asking is for you to help me take care of him. There is no one in this world as experienced as you to guide him through the process." Betty's eyes shone with unshed tears. "Please, Jules. I am begging you."

Juliane winced. She recognized that the woman was a desperate mother, but if Alan suspected the child's condition was caused by epilepsy, then it probably was, and no amount of mentoring would change that. Juliane shook her head. There was nothing she could do.

Betty's nostrils flared. "I see. I came here looking for a friend. But I see now, I never had one here. The next time you need help, and you will don't look to me to bail you out," she spat.

The room flared red again. Juliane drew herself up. She had never asked for Betty's help. She had managed for years without anyone. She didn't need anyone. Relationships just got in the way. Juliane sighed as her headache began to ease. Perhaps it was better this way. She'd keep it professional, but perhaps it was time for them all to focus on the bigger picture.

Juliane mentally summoned Stuart back to the office. He must have returned to his desk as he was instantly inside the room. "Dr. Dronigh has had a tiring past few weeks. Can you please make sure that she has something cool to drink while I attend this meeting and arrange for a car to take her back to St. James Hospital?"

Her assistant's eyes closed as he began to make the requested arrangements, but Betty interrupted them, "There is no need. I am perfectly capable of finding my own way back."

Before either of them could say a word, Betty made her way out of the office door, her every step like that of a death row prisoner resigned to her fate.

TWENTY-FIVE

"**D**r. Dronigh's just under a great deal of stress," Juliane explained to Stuart as Betty exited the office. "Even if she won't accept our help, can you please make sure that someone follows her back to the hospital to ensure she makes it there safely?"

Juliane paused in thought. Betty wouldn't appreciate the gesture, not after Juliane's refusal. "But have them hang back a few feet. I am not sure that she would recognize it as kindness in her present state."

"Right away." Stuart turned, following Betty's path. Juliane forced Betty out of her thoughts; she could not allow herself to be distracted, especially not in the virtual world.

She closed her eyes and focused on accessing her domain. The virtual image resolved into a well-furnished conference room, mirroring an office space located on the other side of the planet. A trio of individuals sat around the table.

Her first point of contact was seated on the end and lacked the degree of command over his virtual appearance displayed by the others. His clothes alternated between power suit and armor. A woman appeared on the other end of the table. While her appearance remained constant, her body was as translucent as a ghost. The third, another man, appeared solid from the waist up but had neglected to visualize his feet.

Juliane frowned. Their lack of competency in the virtual world should have been an indicator of their competency in the real world.

"Let's get started. I've called you here today because I just received word that there has been another incident reported. I trust that you have already initiated the required counseling for his roommates? Who would like to tell me more about the unfortunate worker and what is being done to prevent a recurrence?"

The man in the center of the trio began to answer, but Juliane couldn't understand the words. She bit down on a curse. While caught up with Betty's dramatic visit, she had neglected to turn on her translation program. It really did not take up that much processing power; she decided that once she finished this meeting, she would just keep it running in the background continuously.

The words began to flow into English as the translation tool took effect.

". . . not been able to identify any family or next of kin. We acted very efficiently in response. The body has already been sent to the furnace for incineration." Juliane pursed her lips. The translation program's only failing was it occasionally substituted an incorrect word, especially with languages that contained multiple dialects. *It couldn't have translated that last bit right.*

Juliane felt a tug on her senses. *What now?* she thought. Turning back to the trio across from her, she said, "It would seem that I need to cut this meeting short."

It was time to make a lasting impression. "These sorts of incidents cannot continue." The conference room transformed into a wilderness. "I shouldn't even have to use the plural of that word." She willed her avatar to grow in size until she could easily grind them under her shoe like bugs.

"I need you to make significant changes, and I need you to do so now. We may not have to worry about a family coming around, making demands, or talking to the media this time, but we cannot afford for there to be a next time."

Storm clouds rolled in, filling the artificial sky. Creatures with disjointed limbs, razor teeth, and gray-scaled skin slithered toward her audience. The translucent woman tried to stand and run away. Juliane exerted her will, rendering her incapable of movement.

"Consider this your number one priority. I don't want you to sleep or eat unless you first bring me a more permanent corrective action. If you do not, you can believe I will reprogram your brains so that all food tastes of ash and only nightmares find you when you close your eyes."

She shifted her focus to the man in the suit of armor. The metal plates became red hot under her gaze. His lack of experience with the virtual world was apparent as he struggled to physically remove the suit rather than just wishing it away. She stopped only when he stood naked before her.

The third paled when she turned her attention his way but did not attempt to fight or flee. There might be hope for at least one of the sorry group after all. "I believe I've made my point. Now go. I expect a full report, and I expected it yesterday." All three disappeared like soap bubbles popping the instant she released them.

"And you tease me about my flair for the dramatic." Alan strode into view on the virtual landscape as she shrank herself back to her regular size. Alan gestured in the direction where the trio had been. "At least one of them is now trying to explain the loss of bladder control without losing face."

Two Dronighs in one day? Juliane shook her head. Her meeting was supposed to have been set up in the datasphere with private access controls. "Eavesdropping again?"

Alan shrugged. "It's not my fault you don't take better precautions."

Juliane ground her teeth. Stuart must have been lax in setting the meeting up. She'd have to have a word with him later.

"But now I am curious," said Alan. "Would you go through with it?"

"Through with what?"

"Reprogramming their minds?"

Juliane sniffed. "Of course not. That would be cruel as well as against every law on the books."

Alan cocked his head the way he did whenever he wanted to engage in a conversation that seemed to have no point other than cause her blood to boil. Juliane took a breath and reminded herself that the Dronighs were in a bad place. "I'm sorry to hear about Stevie."

Alan sighed and glanced at the framed photograph on her wall. "You know, it's always seemed odd to me that you'd have a picture of dogs framed. Childhood pets I assume based on the image quality." He scanned the contents of her office. "You don't have any other family photos."

"My mother wasn't exactly the family portrait type." Juliane pressed her lips together. "And the dogs weren't pets. They belonged to one of my mom's boyfriends. Troy."

"Why then do you have their picture?"

"It's a reminder." Juliane bit her lip, debating whether to tell him more. She didn't owe him an explanation. She didn't owe anyone. However, Betty's parting words still stung. Betty and Alan might be going through issues, but he was her husband. Perhaps if she made more of an effort to be nice, Betty might eventually cool off and forgive her.

"I used to be so envious of those dogs. I wasn't allowed to make a sound. My mom told me that after working all day my voice gave Troy a headache, but the dogs could jump and bark, and no one seemed to mind." Juliane's eyes tightened as the memory came back.

"My mom doted on those animals." She nodded at the photograph. I think she thought Troy would love her more for it. I would be starving, and she would make sure they had a piece of steak from the table."

Juliane's eyes tightened. Explaining the why behind the photograph was harder than she anticipated. "Then they would laugh about the dogs having a job while I didn't."

She pressed her lips together. "I didn't know what that meant until I saw a few bills drop to the floor as Troy came inside stinking of cigars and wet dog. I realized then that Troy was betting on the animals."

"I could have turned him into the police. I could have turned them both in. But I didn't. No, I thought if I could prove I was just as tough as those dogs, maybe then I wouldn't be treated as just some kid who got in the way." Juliane sighed at the memory of her misguided self. Not having witnessed a dog fight firsthand, she didn't then realize what a horrible practice it was. Troy's dogs never showed a hint of injury.

"And I regret to say my plan worked," she continued, "Once Troy figured out I knew what was going on, he stopped trying to hide it. He started to tell me about how well his dogs did, more specifically, what they had done to the losers." Juliane grimaced.

"I suspect the idea was to make me cry, but I found that if I focused on the statistics of the fights instead of the gorier details, I could forget we were talking about living things. That's when I started to notice patterns." She waved at the picture. "Those became my first theorem, and I used it one night, to tell Troy how to place his next bet."

"It didn't take him long to recognize I wasn't just some airhead." Juliane's mouth twitched. "Suddenly, I was served steak, and Mom, the leftovers."

Juliane took a breath and turned her back to the wall. "Unfortunately, my mom couldn't handle not being the center of attention, so we left but not before Troy taught me one last lesson. When it comes to gaining respect, love is a nice concept, but sometimes a good healthy dose of fear works even better."

The smug look, normally plastered to Alan's face, had softened as she told her story. He shook his head as if he realized he'd let his empathy show.

"I've no doubt you managed to be permanently etched in all three of those workers' memories," Alan said, once again himself. "I just wonder how many of them are going to change their ways because it is the right thing to do, versus how many of them are going to do as instructed just because they are terrified of you."

Juliane tilt her head. "Does it really matter what their motivation is? I'm saving lives."

Alan's eyebrows rose with the corner of his lips. "I'm sure you know how to deal with your people best."

Juliane smiled at Alan's acknowledgment. "Indeed. So, what can I help you with? I assume you didn't come here just to discuss my lack of a childhood."

Alan placed his hand against his heart. "You wound me. I always look forward to our little get-togethers."

"So much so that I haven't seen you for nearly a year, yet you show up uninvited on the same day that Betty visits. I am sorry, but I can't believe it is entirely coincidental."

The smile left Alan's face, and his avatar instantly aged several years. "Ah, Betty has already been here then?"

"She's the one who told me about Stevie."

It was the first time that Juliane could recall Alan appearing to be anything but in control of the situation. "Well . . . that is"—his tongue flicked out as the words escaped like a serpent sampling the air—"regrettable. I am afraid that the last few months have not been exactly kind to my wife. The combination of stress and parenthood may be getting to her."

"She needs sleep. Maybe you two should take some time off."

"She needs more than just a weekend getaway."

Juliane fought the blush from showing on her cheeks. "I didn't mean to suggest . . ."

Alan waved the words away with a flick of his hand. "No need to apologize. She and I will work through this time just like any other problem we've faced. I am only sorry that she chose to share our personal life with you."

"For what it is worth, I am sorry that he is going through this—that you all are going through this."

Alan shrugged again. "The boy will survive or he won't."

Juliane fought the urge to rub her arms to fight the coldness of Alan's words. It was no wonder that Betty was seeking help if that was the support she was getting at home. "How can you say that? He's your son."

"That came out harsher than I intended. What I meant is you shouldn't be concerned about Stephen."

"I shouldn't? Betty said—does that mean you think he is going to be okay?"

Alan pressed his lips together. "I'm a number of things, but a pediatric specialist is not one of them. I'm letting *qualified* doctors make that analysis. Something I wish Betty would do too. No one enjoys being second-guessed when they're trying to do their job—as I am sure you know." He shook his head.

Juliane exhaled her relief. His son's condition couldn't be as dire as Betty had led on if he was acting that calm about it. "If you aren't here about Betty or Stevie, what brings you today to my world?"

The smile was immediately back on Alan's face as his avatar transformed back into the confident individual she remembered back from their time together.

"Damien offered me a pair of box tickets to see the Sharks play this weekend. Betty can't make it, for obvious reasons, so I wondered if you might like to go with me instead?"

Juliane's brow wrinkled. "You're as much a sporting type as I am a dog person."

"It's not about the game. It's about the experience. Or so I've been told. Frankly, I don't exactly see what the appeal is, but they are perfectly good tickets and I would hate to see them go to waste. Come with me. We can laugh together at the ridiculous commentary."

"I'm not sure . . ." *Now that the conference call is over, I really should go to the hospital if only for moral support.* She pressed her lips together. Then again, if Alan was right and Betty was simply being paranoid, she might interpret a visit as validation. "I don't follow any of the teams."

Alan dropped down onto his knees. Juliane scrunched her face further. "Nor do I. I'm begging you. Please don't make me make small talk with some random wannabe jock that Damien might find. I'd much rather go with a friend."

Friend. She would never have used that word to describe their relationship, but he hadn't attempted to insert himself into her business dealings over the years, nor had he ridiculed her for her upbringing just now. Perhaps Betty there was hope for him yet. Juliane looked back out to the field, which so recently played host to her little drama with the production heads as her head began to ache again. *It might be nice to spend some time out of the office,* she thought.

When she did not immediately respond, Alan stood. While the corners of his lips remained turned upright, the line of his mouth had thinned. "I wasn't supposed to say anything, but Damien specifically requested I bring you."

She lifted an eyebrow. So much for thinking this was his way of extending an olive branch. The invitation became far less interesting—and yet, if it was Damien's idea, the tickets were also harder to refuse. "Why in the world would he make that suggestion? He knows too well what pressure I've been under."

"I think that is the point. From all reports, you've been locked away up here for months."

"Don't be ridiculous. Of course, I leave the office. I travel to any number of places."

"I don't mean leaving here just to go to another meeting. When was the last time you saw the inside of your home?"

"I took my lunch there just this afternoon."

"I am not one of your employees, Juliane. Seeing the inside of your home via a virtual interface is not the same as physically being among your own things."

"But I am among my own things. Don't you see? Everything you see in this office is mine. Every scrap of paper, every piece of furniture, every detail on the wall is mine. This"—she spun around with her arms outstretched—"is my domain. I am more at home here than I could be anyplace else."

"It's not healthy for you personally or for your company. What you are doing within the virtual world is truly impressive, but things are happening in the real world that you need to be a part of. Life is moving on without you."

"Are you getting philosophical on me?"

"Perhaps, but I've had a lot of time to think recently, without you or Betty around to interrupt me in the lab," said Alan with a laugh that sounded forced.

He is worried. He just doesn't want anyone to know, thought Juliane. "Why don't you install a mirror in there? Then you'd have the assistant you've always wanted," she joked. If the way he needed to cope with his family's situation was to pretend everything was fine, she'd let him.

Alan threw his head back as he laughed. "Oh, how I've missed our talks. Don't think I haven't already considered that option."

Juliane snorted. "Fine." She would call Betty after the game and apologize. Then, after everything with the factory was resolved, she'd even offer to watch Stevie so Betty and Alan might then take a night off. It was a perfect plan. "You can report back to Damien, like a good little errand boy, that I'll go with you. I imagine there are team colors or the like that I should find to wear."

"I've already taken care of that for you. I have a whole outfit here for you made up of licensed apparel. Damien is a part-owner of the team, after all. It wouldn't do for you to be seen wearing anything else."

Juliane shook her head. "Saying no was never an option, was it?"

"You always have a choice; I was just tasked with helping you to make the right one."

"Send the bag over. Stuart will ensure that it gets to me in time."

"It's already here, Juliane."

Juliane glanced about. There was nothing on the field remotely resembling a bag of clothing, and she was puzzled how he intended to transfer the bag from the virtual world to the physical world.

"Juliane," he sighed. "That's exactly my point. The bag is here in your office because I am here in your office. I've been standing just a few feet from you this entire time. We've practically been touching."

Juliane blinked, and the field was instantly replaced by her solid office walls. Just as he said, Alan stood on the other side a of the room, a plastic bag with the Sharks' emblem on its side resting next to his foot. She had seen about as little of Alan in the flesh as she had seen Betty over the years.

Unlike Betty, Alan didn't appear to have aged more than a day. In fact, he almost looked younger than he had when they first began working together. Obviously, he hadn't been losing the same amount of sleep over his son's condition than his wife had.

It was further evidence that Alan had to whole-heartedly believe his son's condition was treatable, unless he was a monster of a parent. She felt the last of the guilt from turning Betty away melt from her shoulders.

"What is that expression on your face, Juliane? If a person didn't know you better, it would almost look like you were happy to see me."

Immediately, she forced the grin from her lips. "We can't have that sort of rumor start, now can we? I'm just shocked to see how great you look, that's all."

"You say that as if you expected anything else." Alan swiped his hair back as he struck a pose normally found on a fashion runway.

"Betty just looked so . . . um . . ." Juliane bit her tongue, hoping Alan would not hear her unspoken words.

"She looks drained. I'm well aware of it. If you listen to her, you might think that being a mother and spouse is sucking the life right out of her body."

"Er . . . I didn't mean to suggest . . ."

Alan interrupted her by holding up his hand. "No need to apologize for speaking the truth. It is hard on me, seeing her like that, but she's fully embraced the idea of being a martyr. She's much like you in that regard. Once she has decided on a course of action, there is little that anyone can do to change her mind."

He bent down at the waist, blocking his face from her view. He paused with his hand on the bag's plastic handle, and Juliane saw the rise of his back as he took a deep breath before returning upright.

A message scrolled across her vision. "We briefly lost visual on Dr. Dronigh, but the visitor's log confirmed she did make it to the hospital without incident. Our associate is heading back to the office now."

Juliane blinked the message away. Alan locked his eyes onto hers while handing over the bag. His gaze was so intent that she briefly wondered if he could somehow see the text over her vision, but then she shook her head. It wasn't as if there was a lens over her eye physically displaying the information.

"You, though, haven't changed a bit over the years either. Frankly, I prefer the real you. Your avatar doesn't do you justice."

Gesturing to the bag, he added, "I took a chance on your size and am confident I got it right." Alan started to turn to the door. "Before I forget, Damien mentioned that while he wasn't going to be able to stay through the entire game, he and a few others might stop by. I trust that won't scare you off. It will be nice to have a chance to swap some war stories, don't you think?"

TWENTY-SIX

The football stadium referred to by the fans as the Reef, and its surrounding parking lot was already packed by the time they arrived. By the sounds blaring from inside, it was close to kick-off time. Juliane was thankful they had a professional driver as the car maneuvered around stumbling fans on their way to the gates.

"That one over there sure has started early. I wonder if he will remember any of the game," observed Juliane as she watched one man regain his footing. The man would have been flattened by the passing traffic had he not been pulled to safety by his more sober companions at the last second.

Alan glanced in the direction Juliane gestured and shrugged. "Sometimes the tailgating experience is the best part of the game. The Sharks aren't the division favorite at the moment." Alan looked just as ridiculous in the oversized team jersey as she felt; however, he didn't seem to be nearly as aware of his appearance as she was. It was probably the first article of clothing she had worn in years that wasn't designed for either the boardroom or bedroom.

"No? Well, I can't imagine Damien is happy with that."

Alan chuckled before answering. "You don't know the half of it. Why do you think he has to force the likes of you and me to fill the seats? He keeps saying that his team is on the brink of greatness, but just like any other fan would say, it is always next year."

"How many seasons has it been?"

"The team isn't all that old. It was one of the more recent expansion teams, but they've not exactly exceeded expectations since the day he signed the check. You should bring it up sometime. I am sure he'd love to go over his team's record with you. Maybe you could help him draft more winners." Alan eased himself back into the comfort of the leather interior.

"Well, if it's that sore of a subject with him, what is he doing about it?"

"What he has to, I'm sure."

The car finally pulled up to a VIP entrance tunnel. Alan sprang out of his side without waiting for the driver to open the door.

"It doesn't look like you were forced to be here."

"When Damien first offered the tickets, I was just as hesitant to accept as you were. I know this might shock you, but I was never really the athletic type growing up. Frankly, I didn't see what the big deal was, but then I started studying up on the subject." Alan raised a finger as if an idea had just struck him. "Much like you did with the dogs."

He beamed and pointed at the entrance. "You'll see what I mean. When the game starts, don't bother watching the individual plays. Instead, try to see if you can decipher the strategy behind the coach's game plan. It's almost like watching generals test out battle plans but without the ammunition. Absolutely fascinating."

Juliane raised one manicured eyebrow.

"Doubt me if you want to, but it's good to develop an appreciation of well-executed tactics whenever you see them. You never know when you might need to apply them."

"I'll keep that in mind the next time I find myself deep in enemy territory trying to execute a counter run play."

Alan roared with laughter. "And here I thought you weren't interested."

"I looked up one or two things on the way here." She nodded. "I'll admit, you might have a point."

"I knew you'd come around to my thinking . . . eventually."

Juliane attempted to twist her lips into a scowl, but Alan's laughter was contagious.

They arrived at a set of elevator doors guarded by a pair of men in ill-fitting ticket handler's smocks who examined their credentials without speaking a word. The movement from one floor to the next was seamless. Juliane had just begun wondering if the elevator was broken, as she could feel no movement when the doors opened on the mid-level deck.

Several other people were mingling in the lobby, but Juliane could tell by the way they held themselves that these individuals were an entirely different sort of fan than the ones they had passed on their way into the parking lot.

A pale light in the corner of her vision caught her attention. When she turned, the light seemed to encapsulate a nearby woman like the glow from an aura. Within a second, the glow faded out, and Juliane was left wondering if there had been anything there in the first place.

"Everything okay, Juliane?" Alan touched her arm. "Supposedly someone will come by once we are in the box to take our order, but we can grab something now if you'd like."

Juliane shook her head. Out of the corner of her eye, she thought she spotted an additional glow from other people in the room, but those faded out just as quickly. *It must be the way the lighting of the room is designed*, thought Juliane. Audibly she said, "No, sorry, just taking it all in. It's not quite what I imagined. I guess I expected a little more . . ." Juliane frowned. What had she expected?

"A little more grunge, a little less sophistication?" Alan suggested.

"Perhaps."

"I am sure we'll see more than enough of the less desirable before the day is through."

"Our seats are this way?" She pointed and walked with purpose toward one of the doorways. She needed to get out of the room before the effect gave her a headache.

Their box was just one of several nestled within the end zone of the stadium. While the majority of each unit was walled off, providing occupants with a degree of privacy, the outside wall and the adjacent quarter of each side was a sheet of glass, including a portion of the floor. Juliane was rather glad that she had chosen not to wear a skirt as she toured the room from end to end.

"You don't have to worry. It's one-way glass."

Juliane looked at Alan in curiosity.

"Admit it. You were worried that someone might be sneaking a peek at you just then."

"I was simply pitying the people below us who must feel like a crowd of people are going to come crashing down on their heads if this so much as cracks."

"If that glass cracks, then they have larger issues to worry about."

"Speaking of worries. Have you heard anything more from your son's doctors? Are they made any progress?"

"He is still under observation. How is your factory's investigation coming along?"

Juliane sucked in her breath.

"Listen, I know you mean well, but I'd rather not discuss it more than we already have. Can we at least pretend to have a carefree life, if only for a few hours?"

At a loss for a response, Juliane looked out toward the sea of humanity below her, placing her hand on the glass. She was surprised to feel it vibrate. "Is it supposed to buzz like that?"

"Well, it's slightly more advanced than your standard window. I am given to understand there is a control panel around here." Alan scanned the back of the room. "It's more force field than glass. Supposedly, by just adjusting a few settings, we can make it so that the fresh air and noise from outside can pass through, or keep it in its current privacy mode."

Locating the control panel, Alan adjusted a dial, and Juliane was surrounded by the roar of the crowd and the metallic smell of smoke from used fireworks as the players took the field.

Juliane was struck by how enormous the players were. Even knowing that some of their bulk was made up of pads and other protective gear, they appeared unnatural in proportion. One could almost describe them as ogres. The opposing team looked like fragile dolls in comparison.

Without taking her eyes off the advancing players, Juliane asked, "And you say the Sharks aren't winning this season?"

"Damien pushed for some organizational changes. They must have gone along with his suggestions. I heard the news that they are heavily favored to win this one."

"I would think so. The other team doesn't even look like it is in the same league."

"Well, that might have something to do with their ownership philosophy."

"How so?"

"Let's just say that some teams are blinder than others to their players' efforts to improve their competitive edge through the wonders of modern science."

"Damien lets the Sharks cheat?"

"Damien doesn't have time to be involved in every detail managing the team. That's why he hires other people. Besides, the Sharks are hardly the only ones looking for an edge. It's a violent sport; muscles tear and bones break. A person who depends on their physical performance for their livelihood can hardly be blamed for wanting to go under the knife if the surgery minimizes the potential for career-ending injuries."

Alan shrugged. "They found out that artificial muscle made up of spider silk was over fifty times stronger than natural muscle. It was only a matter of time before athletes found a way to trade up. Heck, even I am considering that one."

The monitor showed a close-up of a player attaching his helmet before running from the sideline to the field. His nose was broad but flattened, and as he ran, his nostrils flared, making him appear goat-like.

"Now that is a face only a mother could love."

"The man makes several million dollars per season. I know for a fact he's not suffering in that department. He's dated five supermodels in the last year alone. Rumors have it that he intentionally altered his nose so that he has increased airflow. Supposedly, it makes him faster and able to make quicker decisions on the field."

Juliane grimaced. "What some people will do to get ahead." The camera panned to another man who could have passed for a werewolf in a horror film.

Alan raised his eyebrows with a quick laugh. "Indeed."

The snap of the football sent the crowd into a frenzy, preventing further conversation through the first half. Alan had been right when he suggested that she focus on the coaches' strategies rather than the individual plays. Even though the Sharks had a significant size advantage, the other team was nimble and their trick plays proved remarkably successful. When the clock ran out, the Sharks were down by fourteen, and the majority of the crowd had been silenced.

Alan stood up and rolled his shoulders. "I don't know about you, but I think my legs could use a stretch. Would you like to come with me?"

"Why not? I could use some refreshments."

As they returned to the central lobby, a man's voice came from the direction of one of the other boxes. His words were slurred, but that didn't prevent him from doing his best to ensure they carried throughout the area.

"What incompetence! I think I am going to have to have a word with the management."

Juliane froze and scanned the crowd for the source. An opening broke through the sea of people. At first, Juliane only saw a slim woman with blonde hair laughing in response, but then the woman stepped back. Standing with his arm wrapped around the woman's waist, his face flushed, was Louis.

Juliane sucked in her breath as Louis looked her way. He looked as if he had gained a little weight around his waist over the years but was mostly unchanged. Juliane screamed to herself, *No, no, no!* as he began walking toward them with the woman, who had to be Elena, in tow.

Juliane looked to Alan as she tried to come up with a way to avoid the situation, but Alan appeared oblivious to Juliane's distress. If anything, he looked pleased to see the pair.

Louis, dressed in the opposing team's colors swayed from side to side as he walked. "Juliane! I never expected to see you here. Visiting old friends? We should catch up. How long are you in town?"

Juliane felt a pressure build behind her eyes at Louis's easy manner. He smiled boldly as he approached as if greeting a long-absent friend. His body showed little of the discomfort she felt at seeing him so unexpectedly. Juliane ground her teeth. *He still doesn't regret how he treated me at all,* she thought.

Louis leaned into his wife and whispered something in her ear. Elena looked at Juliane and let out a quiet, musical laugh. Juliane's muscles tensed as she steeled her nerves. She reminded herself that she had grown in multiple ways since he had so casually tossed her aside. Factories filled with enough people to populate small cities cowered in fear of her displeasure. She was a force into herself and needn't shy away from anyone. *Even Louis.* She drew up her back like a queen.

"I never left, as I am sure you know."

Louis stumbled, and the grin momentarily dropped from his face. His eyebrows wrinkled together as if he had trouble deciphering her words.

"Actually, I didn't. I am sorry to admit that I haven't exactly been following your status updates since you left the ACI. For some reason, Elena tends to look down upon that sort of thing. Don't you, my dear?" He attempted to nuzzle Elena's neck, but in his state, he slightly missed the mark, leaving a mark of saliva on her shirt collar. Elena didn't seem to mind, giggling at his gesture.

"If you aren't aware of what Jules here has been up to, it's no wonder we are losing our competitive edge," said Alan without humor in his voice.

Louis glanced at a passerby rubbing a delicate ear clip. "Ah. Yes. That's your work then?"

"Yes, and has been for some time now."

"Alan, I'd hardly call her little trinkets a serious threat, but you are right. I should know the faces behind the competition."

"Honey, the game is going to start up again, and I am still thirsty. Why don't we let these two get back to enjoying their date?" Elena patted her husband's arm, breaking the tension.

Louis rubbed his free hand over his face. Juliane watched as his eyes widened as his gaze darted between their faces. A sly grin crept back onto his face. "Tsk, tsk, Alan. Sneaking behind your wife's back? Surely, Betty deserves better."

Juliane did not need to look in Alan's direction to feel the heat generated by Louis's words. *You're one to talk.*

Louis, on the other hand, was either blind or too drunk to care about how his words were interpreted. He continued, "Well,

I can't say I am entirely surprised. I always thought there was something between you two. Ah look, Elena, Jules is blushing!"

"It's Juliane," she said through clenched teeth.

Louis swayed, falling onto Juliane while pulling on his wife's waist. Elena had been holding a cup; the sudden movement sent a portion of the contents spraying onto Juliane's shoe.

Juliane struggled to maintain her composure as the liquid spread its stain. It took every ounce of her will not to run back to their seats.

Louis smiled at his wife. "It can't be that great of a date. Those two are much too serious." Alan pushed him upright as Louis continued, "Aren't these games supposed to be the great American pastime? You should be relaxing and having some fun." At least that was what Juliane thought she heard him say. His accent combined with his inebriated state made the words swim together.

"You are thinking about baseball." Alan using a clipped tone that reminded Juliane of her old professors.

"Well, aren't you a fountain of information? I bet you are a blast at parties." Louis suddenly leaned in, nearly bringing his wife down with him. "Speaking of party tricks, you two should appreciate this." Louis removed his arm from Elena's waist to block the room's light from one hand with the other. He cupped the hand in the shadows while Elena leaned back to sip her drink.

Just as Juliane began to wonder if Louis had forgotten what he was going to say, his shadowed palm began to glow. "I sometimes forget which house I am in and couldn't find a light switch anywhere. After I stubbed my toe for the hundredth time, all I could do was think of how badly I wanted a light, and then, the next thing I know, poof! I'm glowing. If Edison could only see me now . . ."

Louis glanced back at Elena, who grinned as she enjoyed another sip. As he straightened and returned his arm around her waist, she handed him the cup. He finished its contents with one large swig before crumpling the plastic and tossing it into a nearby garbage bin. "Well, my dear, it looks as if I may have stumbled across yet another unanticipated discovery. Alan, isn't that what am I paying you to do?"

The pair lurched back toward the concession stand, but before they had taken more than a few steps, Louis turned back. "On that note, I think, Alan, seeing you fraternizing with the competition, makes me think you may not have the ACI's best interests in mind. Consider yourself a free agent."

"I always have," whispered Alan as Louis and Elena walked away. He sniffed. He turned his head toward Juliane. "Now, how about I get you that drink."

Juliane watched Louis order and consume another round of drinks. Instead of stopping him or urging him to cut back, Elena just stood there, enabling him. Juliane was disgusted. "I'm suddenly not thirsty anymore." Spinning on her heel, Juliane walked back to their seats.

The box was no longer vacant when they returned. Damien stood near the back of the room deep in conversation with Eithan Yuan. Apparently, she wasn't the only Apex board member to be invited to tonight's game. Juliane glanced around to see if Durham was around, but if he had a ticket, he hadn't arrived yet.

At their entrance, Eithan cocked his head, acknowledging their presence. He then bowed to Damien and departed.

"Damien, did you know that Louis would be here when you asked Alan to bring me today?" asked Juliane.

Damien's eyebrows rose as he answered. "I assumed he likely would be. He does own the Suns, after all, but I wouldn't have expected him on this side of the stadium. Perhaps, they cut him off at the concessions closer to his box." Damien shrugged.

"In any event, I hope he didn't cause too much of a problem for you."

Juliane drew herself up straight. "Nothing I couldn't handle."

"I never doubted it. You are the mother of enhanced reality. The ACI should never have let you go. He should never have let you go. You are single-handedly going to bring his company to its knees."

Juliane smiled at the pep talk.

Alan produced a sound that was a cross between a laugh and a gag. "Well, Damien, as long as we are talking about bringing down the competition and launching a whole new world order, I should mention that I will no longer be able to serve in my current capacity."

"No?"

"It seems that our dear friend Louis has decided to make a few organizational changes of his own."

"That is a pity, but that can only mean that he is feeling scared, which means we must be doing something right. I think it may be time to start upping the ante."

"Exactly what I was thinking."

Juliane waited for Damien to elaborate on his plans, but there was no further explanation.

The stadium began rocking as speakers blasted music and the crowd regained its roar. Walking up to the edge of the glass, Juliane stared at the players as they returned to the field. They seemed different from the first half. She gazed at the monitor. "The team looks even larger than they did before halftime."

When Damien spoke up, he was directly behind her ear. "I decided to stop by the locker room to give them a little pep talk before heading up this way."

The enormous scoreboard flashed to the interior of the visiting owner's box. Louis and Elena waved to fans as the players lined up below. As they represented the opposing team,

Juliane expected to hear some boos but instead heard some applause.

Just before the camera panned away, Juliane saw Louis's hand creep up the side of Elena's blouse. "I would never have anticipated that they would still be together after all these years, especially after such a short courtship period." Damien must also have noticed their display of affection. "It is enough to make you wonder if there might be some truth to those rumors."

"Down in front!" Alan shouted, bringing Juliane's attention to the movement on the field.

"Do you think we have a chance in beating the Suns?"

"His team may have speed and agility, but just like their namesake, they will eventually burn out. My team, on the other hand, has strength and stamina. They won't just beat the Suns— they will rip them to shreds."

"Juliane?" Damien asked.

Juliane realized that she had allowed her eyes to drift back toward the opposing owner's box.

"I think you've hidden in that office of yours long enough."

"I haven't been hiding. I've just been busy."

"I know you have, but I have plans, and I'd like to know you can be counted on to play a big part in them. Don't you think it's past the time the world recognized you? I mean the real you."

TWENTY-SEVEN

The second half began with a kick-off return for a touchdown, and the Suns never regained the momentum. As Juliane and the others left the stadium, the car's newsfeeds were alight with stories about broken records and interviews with several of the most outstanding players of the game.

The interviews blended together—many of the players were products of multi-generational dynasties and thanked their parents as well as their coaches—and Juliane tuned the noise out. It had begun to sound more like an animal breeder announcing their fine pedigrees than news.

The following morning, Juliane awoke completely disoriented. It took a few seconds before she realized that she had fallen asleep in her own bed rather than the couch in her office. As she regained her bearings, she stretched her fingers out against the surrounding fabric. Her sheets were still nearly as crisp as they were upon initial purchase, even though she hadn't updated her furnishings in close to a year.

Her feet screamed in protest as she stood. She must have walked more yesterday than she had originally thought. After being sheathed so long in heels, her arches ached as she padded flat-footed across the room.

Doing her best to ignore the pain, she entered into the kitchen and its promise of coffee on demand. Juliane allowed herself a smile as she placed a coffee pod into the machine.

One of the first things she had done after leaving the ACI was to buy a French press. However, she never was able to get it right and mug after mug contained floating grounds. She'd thought of Chad after each failed attempt. Perhaps she'd been too hard on him. Coffee from the machine might not be as good, but it was the proper temperature.

The various gears whirled as the machine came online and the liquid began to drip into her cup. A message indicator flashed in her vision, signifying that her inbox had been working overtime while she slept. Alan was right; it had been too long since she enjoyed the convenience of her home. She ignored the alert. It could wait until after she had eaten some breakfast.

The message indicator flashed again. Juliane disabled the alert with a thought. Another indicator flashed informing her that someone was trying to place a call. Juliane disabled that alert as well.

Once her stomach had been satisfied by a quick breakfast, she returned to the living room. As much as she had enjoyed her morning's peace, Juliane knew that she could not afford to be off the grid for much longer. With a sigh, she re-engaged her messaging protocols as she scanned the newsfeed.

Juliane sank into her couch. Her breakfast felt like an anchor as her feed was filled with hundreds of variations of the same headline. Louis had been involved in an accident after the game. Images of his automobile accompanied many of the stories. It was hard to imagine that crumpled ball of bent metal and shattered glass could have carried anyone from one place to another.

No one seemed to have firm details as to the cause of the crash or the conditions of the victims, but all the reporters were free with their individual speculation. There was no mention of who drove the car when it happened—nor did alcohol appear to be a factor.

Louis must have arranged for a driver, especially after consuming as much as he had, thought Juliane. *Or Elena had.* Juliane read further.

The reports morphed into nothing more than gossip. Reporters were reaching out to anyone, regardless as to how tenuous the connection to Louis might be, for their comments and initial reaction.

By mid-morning, additional details had been gathered, although there was still some doubt as to the authenticity of the sources. According to an individual who wished to remain anonymous, there hadn't been a driver. Instead, Louis had been at the wheel at the time of the accident. He had been driving at excessive speeds when he lost control of the vehicle. The reporter commented that Louis had been lucky. He had been thrown from the car just before it ignited into a fiery inferno. His condition was listed as extremely serious. His wife, however, was not as fortunate.

Lacking any further comments from hospitals, friends, or family, many of the outlets chose to cobble together featurettes on the charitable contributions of the late Mrs. Evans. Previously submitted press photography showed her caressing children's faces in their hospital beds, feeding children in developing nations, or otherwise looking angelic.

One might think Elena was on her way to canonization by the way the stories were positioned. Juliane pressed her lips together as she read more interviews. Everyone, it seemed, bemoaned how the world was made a little bit darker by Elena's loss.

Then, the stories began to rehash the details of Elena and Louis's whirlwind romance. They described Elena as Louis's true partner and love of his life. Juliane felt her eyes tighten as reporters reminded their audience of the rumors regarding those days and how early their relationship truly started. Juliane even saw her own image and old name referenced in a couple of stories.

Juliane's phone alert flashed once again. She glanced at the identification code in the corner of the screen and accepted the call.

"Durham. I'm surprised you are up this early."

"Good morning to you too, Juliane. We need to talk," said Durham.

"About what?" Juliane frowned. He wouldn't be calling her about Louis, would he? Durham hadn't mentioned Vegas once over the last five years. As far as she could tell, he'd never recognized her from the time when she and Louis were together at all.

She suppressed a groan as the other reason Apex's legal consultant might be calling. *The factory.* If he was calling about her factory, that could only mean that the news had leaked to the media, and she still didn't have a satisfactory report from the production heads.

"About last night."

"Last night? Was there another . . . look, my people at the factory are still conducting their investigation. I'll forward the report to you as soon as I get it." She frowned.

"You were at the game last night."

"Yes, with Alan."

"Not just with Alan."

"No, you're right. Damien and several other thousand people were there too."

"Like Louis and Elena."

Juliane rolled her shoulders. He was calling about Louis after all. She couldn't decide if that was a good thing or not. "Yes . . . they were there too."

"There are witnesses who saw you together, claiming that there was a somewhat heated exchange."

"Louis made a fool of himself and terminated Alan, but it was hardly a heated exchange. If anything, Alan acted happy about it. We walked away and watched the Sharks beat the Suns in the second half. That's all. What are you implying?"

"I'm not implying anything. I am merely trying to understand the facts so that I can get out ahead of any rumors that might come out of this."

"Rumors? What kind of rumors could there be? If you ask me, the real story I'd like to see investigated further is how the ACI managed to keep alcohol out of the press. Louis was practically a bottle of antiseptic; he had so much in him."

"Unfortunately, you just confirmed the stories I've been hearing that Alan was fired. Not only that, but fired very publicly. And what about you?"

"What about me?"

"You haven't been seen in public in years, and then, the first time you are, you just happened to run into your ex-boyfriend? Some people might question anyone's mental stability in the situation."

Juliane bit back a quick retort as Durham's words registered. "You recognized me after all?"

"Juliane, I am not an idiot. Of course, I recognized you. All of us did. Well, at least most of us," Durham amended.

"Why didn't you say anything?"

"Damien told us before the meeting began that you wanted a fresh start, and after what Louis did to you, I chose to respect your wishes." Durham paused. More softly he said, "I'd hoped . . . After all . . ." His voice trailed off.

"After all what?"

Juliane could hear him inhale over the phone. "Didn't you ever wonder why I left the ACI?"

Juliane looked out her window. "I assumed because Damien paid you better." The day had started with brilliant clear skies, but clouds were beginning to roll in. She realized she had been pacing around the room's perimeter.

It was one of the rare times she wished she still maintained a separate phone device. She had read some classic novels over the years and finally believed she understood why the characters would waste time twirling cords.

The silence stretched. Then Durham's voice all business again. "So, back to last night. Is there anything, anything that I should know about what happened at the Reef?"

"I went to the game. We saw Louis and his wife during halftime. The Sharks came back in the second half to win. I was dropped off here. Nothing else."

"And you stayed in your condo all night?"

"That is what I said."

"I meant that once home, you didn't log into your virtual reality program?"

Juliane frowned. Durham had undergone a version of the upgrade procedure too, the same as all of Damien's high-level officials. If he hadn't recognized her program's benefits yet, he likely never would. Some people were just blind.

"No, I had promised Alan that I would take a night off. But it is beginning to sound like I shouldn't have. Are you satisfied yet?"

"It is better I ask these sorts of questions than the police."

"I still don't understand why in the world the police would be involved in the first place. Louis was obviously under the influence. I don't see why any investigation would need to look any further."

"Well, that's an interesting thing. There's not a single report which would suggest Louis was intoxicated at the time of the accident."

Juliane found herself shaking her head before remembering that Durham wouldn't be able to see the gesture. "That's exactly what I find odd about the news too. I assume that's because his publicist is trying to keep that aspect quiet. The company's value would plummet if Louis ever lost the cult of personality thing he has going for him."

"Well, the interesting thing is, according to my sources, the reason why alcohol isn't mentioned as a possible cause is because he had none of it in his bloodstream at the time. In fact, he had nothing in his system that would have impaired his judgment or his reflexes at all."

Juliane's eyebrow shot up. "Someone has to be altering the records then because he clearly was having a good time yesterday."

"I have been assured that the records are accurate. My source was there as the blood work was analyzed. She saw the results firsthand."

"How did you manage that? Doesn't that sort of information violate some confidentiality?"

Juliane didn't need to hear Durham's answer. She could picture him shrugging with a smug smile.

Durham sighed into his phone. "Juliane, I know all too well how it feels to be tossed aside, and I do apologize if you thought I had done the same to you."

His words forced Juliane to remember the day she was first introduced to Damien's team. Those terrible minutes when he had made her feel like a discarded plaything. Now, while he obviously had a relationship with this woman in the hospital, he was casually throwing around information that could cost the woman her career as if they were talking about the weather.

"We were on our way to being friends once. Now that everything is out in the open, I'd like to . . . um . . . do you think we could try to be friends again?"

Another friend. Aren't I just Ms. Popular all of a sudden? "Sure, but not right now. I've told you all there is to say about last night." Another headline crossed her newsfeed. "I need to go." She terminated the connection.

The headline said Louis's condition had stabilized. While he had suffered some severe trauma, he was expected to recover. The stock market was already responding with record purchasing on any company associated with one of Louis's business ventures.

The market action reminded Juliane that the weekend was over and it was time to return to the office. She had already wasted too much time lounging around the condo and had yet to receive an updated report regarding the factory's internal investigation. Once that was in, she would make her way to the hospital to visit Betty. Louis's news was terrible, but Juliane couldn't honestly say she was going to miss Elena. If that made her a terrible person, so be it.

As she reached her destination, Juliane's vision began blinking with another incoming communication request. She rolled her eyes. The call had to be from a reporter. Durham must not have been the only one to make the connection between Louis and the woman seen at the game.

"This is Juliane Faris." She braced herself for the onslaught of questions.

She was expecting a brash tabloid journalist to be on the other side of the line. Instead, the voice was weak and broken up as if every word was a struggle. It took Juliane several seconds to realize that the voice belonged to Betty.

"Betty? Is that you? I was just about to call you. We must have a terrible connection. I can barely make out what you're saying. Can you repeat that?" Juliane heard a large crash in the background, followed by a tear-fueled scream.

"Betty! Are you there? Are you all right? Betty? Betty!"

A male voice answered—one that Juliane was not familiar with. "Are you a friend of Dr. Dronigh's?"

"I was. Yes, I mean I am. I don't know. It's complicated. But yes, I know her. Is she okay?"

The person on the other end sighed. "Would it be possible for you to come this way?"

"Have you called her husband?"

"She refuses to see him. She's refused to allow us to call anyone."

"Is everything okay?"

The man on the other end cleared his throat. "I think it might be best if we spoke face to face. Can you come over? Please."

"I'm on my way."

TWENTY-EIGHT

Juliane hadn't bothered to ask the caller for additional information that might help her locate him when she reached the hospital. She had just assumed that she would be able to trace the call and locate the source.

However, when she entered the hospital's main entrance, her Internet connection was severed. Signs posted along the walls periodically suggested that wireless signals had been intentionally disrupted due to concerns about interference with medical equipment. As a result, Juliane had to rely on a series of signposts and building maps that took her down several hallways, across walkways, and in and out of no less than three elevators.

As she arrived at the suite of rooms, she couldn't be sure what floor she was on or even if she was still in the main hospital complex or some satellite building. She hadn't felt so lost in years. "How can people work like this?" she muttered under her breath.

The medical staff must have access to some limited network, thought Juliane. Her skin tingled as if she could sense wireless activity just outside of reach. After living with constant connection for so long, the lack of data made her itch.

Juliane had heard of the rise of technology retreat centers. They were spas designed to help clients relax by embracing similarly disruptive materials. She cringed at the thought. She would never be able to relax feeling this incomplete.

A tall, older man met her as she entered through the suite door. His eyes were nearly hidden under thick furry eyebrows. His skin around his neckline was loose as if he had recently lost significant weight, but his belly still extended. He reminded Juliane of one of the troll dolls she had seen in Chad's collection of old toys. All he lacked was a smile. Juliane pushed the comparison out her mind. She was here for Betty.

"Thanks for coming over so quickly. I am Dr. Thomas," said the man as he reached to shake her hand. "I am sorry you had to come down this way, but I just didn't feel like we could discuss this over the phone."

Juliane hesitated to meet the gesture. "Where's Betty?"

"We have her resting in a private room."

"What happened? What is wrong with her?"

"Frankly, that's why I asked you to come here. Would you happen to know if your friend has been under psychiatric care or on medication that could alter her mental state?"

"I don't know. We used to work together years ago, but haven't kept in touch as well as we should recently."

Dr. Thomas ran his hand through his hair as his shoulders sank. "You were listed on her information as her emergency contact." He sighed. "I was afraid that it might be a long shot, but I hoped that you might be able to provide us with a little more information than what the records show."

"I still don't understand why you aren't contacting her husband. I know that you said she doesn't want to allow it, but surely, he has to be able to provide better insight than I can."

"We've tried but have yet to reach him, and we are running out of time to react."

"What exactly are you trying to react to?"

"Well, at first we thought her behavior was merely a result of the strain caused by coping with her son's condition, but over the last twenty-four hours, she began to display symptoms of extreme paranoia. We attempted to sedate her, but it would seem our efforts may have made the condition worse."

He pressed his lips together. "Please understand I am only telling you this because of the severity of the situation and because she'd previously added you, specifically, to her disclosure forms."

"Which I still don't understand."

"That's between you and her. In any event, she suffered cardiac arrest, and her levels indicate some internal hemorrhaging, except we cannot seem to determine the source. There is a chance that the sedative triggered the attack if she was already being treated with other medication." He glanced at the contents of a manilla folder and frowned. "We may have successfully stabilized her heart, but unless we identify the source of the bleeding, we cannot be sure that other treatment options might not cause additional issues, and we don't have much more time to waste."

The doctor kept talking, but Juliane couldn't process the words. She sent a ping to Alan, only to receive a message delivery error. She cursed the hospital's signal suppression under her breath. He should be here, not her. "I am truly sorry. I wish I could help, I do, but I really don't know why she put me down as a contact."

He sighed. "I'd like you to try talking to her. She trusted you. Maybe hearing from a friend will rally her enough to respond to some basic questions."

The doctor ushered Juliane into a room the size of a closet. Her one-time colleague lay on the bed, connected to a multitude of machines and tubing, her skin washed out under the harsh ceiling lights. She looked much smaller than the woman who had entered Juliane's office just a few days prior, fragile and weak. As Juliane approached the bed, a machine whirred and a plastic cuff located around Betty's arm inflated.

Another machine sounded an alarm, and a nurse pushed Juliane to the side so that she could replace a depleted IV drip bag. After adding a quick notation to the chart located at the foot of the bed, the nurse disappeared as quickly as she had arrived.

Juliane tentatively reached out to touch Betty's skin. She felt like a plastic doll that had been left out under the sun for too long, soft and waxy. "Betty, it's me, Juliane. Can you wake up?"

Juliane and Dr. Thomas glanced up at the monitors to see if her words had resulted in any activity, only to see that there was no reaction. "Betty, you need to wake up. The doctors can't help you if they don't know what is wrong."

The machine attached to the arm cuff whirred again, punctuating her words.

Juliane walked over to Betty's chart, more out of a lack of better ideas rather than any expectation that it could offer any clues to the cause of Betty's condition. The numbers and readouts shown on the chart could have been written in a foreign language for as much help as they offered.

Another nurse entered the room and whispered into Dr. Thomas's ear. Dr. Thomas's lips tightened. "Keep trying," he encouraged Juliane as he spun and followed the second nurse back out into the hall.

Once again Juliane cursed the hospital's lack of network connectivity. If she only had access to her full capabilities, she would be able to access a whole slew of data. She could compare Betty's condition instantly with any number of case studies. She could run a simulation program and help rule out treatment options. She could do any number of things, but she was helpless. To do anything, she would either have to find a way to hack into the hospital's network or somehow get Betty's chart and all of her vital sign readings outside.

Juliane looked at the monitors again, weighing her choices. Either option would drain vital minutes. Minutes that Betty didn't have to spare.

"Betty, wake up!" Juliane tossed the chart back into its holder in frustration. She began to pace. "Why in the world wouldn't you call Alan?"

Juliane slapped the bed's railing, sending the chart clattering to the floor. "And you thought calling me instead was a good idea? What could be going on in your head? I may have made the occasional bad decision, but that one has to be worse."

She looked at the monitors again. Betty's readings showed no response to Juliane's diatribe. One of the other machines beeped, and the first nurse appeared to make an adjustment before returning the chart to its place at the foot of the bed. She vanished once again. The sound couldn't have been loud enough to have been heard at the nurses' station. Juliane realized she was looking for communication ports along the walls as if her eyes wanted to look at anything other than Betty lying still on the bed. All she saw were a handful of silver electrical outlets dotting the otherwise white walls.

Somehow the equipment must be communicating with the staff. Juliane became even more convinced that there was a form of private network managing the data inside the hospital walls. "Where one private network exists, so could others."

"This is for your own good," announced Juliane as she reached out to Betty's prone form. As her open palm connected to Betty's exposed skin, Juliane exerted her will. With Louis, she had established the connection in a heartbeat, but this time, it was like her mind was pressing up against a brick wall. She issued commands, breaking up the data packets. She visualized her commands as tendrils of ivy upon a wall and pulled. Betty's defenses were no match for her. The wall crumbled. She could feel Betty's mind open before her as she established the private connection. She could feel all of Betty's hurt and could sense Betty's life draining away as if it were her own.

Choking back a sob, Juliane closed her eyes and imagined their old lab, focusing on happier times. A few more seconds passed. Juliane wondered whether or not the effort had been enough. She glanced around the room. She hadn't seen the interior of the lab in years and expected some of her memory to be blurred, but everything showed as clearly as if she were physically standing in the room.

Movement along the length of one wall caught her eye, and Juliane watched as shadows converged into a solid dark mass. The shape seemed to pull itself from the wall's surface; some tendrils reached out farther than others, causing the mass to lighten as it stretched into a fine mist resembling the Betty that Juliane used to know.

"How did I get here?"

"You aren't really here, Betty. It is just the datasphere. I just had to come up with a location that we both knew."

"Where is my son?"

"I'm not sure, but I believe he is still in the hospital."

"I can't stay here. I need to go back to him." Betty began to run toward the lab door. The thought must have occurred to her that she didn't need to physically leave the room as she stopped moving in mid-stride. She frowned as she spun back on Juliane. "Why can't I wake up?"

"I wish I knew. It's been what I've been telling you to do for some time now."

Betty's forehead knit in confusion. "What do you mean?"

"Apparently, your doctors misjudged your dosage when they sedated you."

"Why have I been sedated?"

"Your doctor told me that you were suffering from an episode of paranoia. Unfortunately, something in your body decided to fight the medication. I am not going to sugarcoat this.

Your condition is now quite serious. Have you been taking anything recently that could have triggered a reaction?"

"I'm not taking anything. I never have been. They think I'm crazy, but it's not paranoia when it is the truth." Betty's form began to pulse.

"We didn't just undergo some cosmetic procedure," she continued. "We completely altered our DNA. The changes made by the Gene Assist serum. They'll pass to the next generation, and might well kill us unless we find an alternative power source."

"Alternative power source? What are you talking about? The technology doesn't need one."

Betty's lips pursed as she scolded. "Of course, it needs a power source, and right now, it is pulling from our natural energy reserves. The greater the processing need, the greater the drain. It's the same concept as your body burning calories during any other exercise. I started thinking about those times you passed out when you were still getting used to everything, and it was the only explanation that makes sense!"

"But I still don't see how that would destroy the human race."

Betty sighed. "All the mysteries of the world are open to you, yet you don't have a clue sometimes. It's kids, Juliane. We all start out as kids."

"I know that. I was one once too."

"Were you? Then you should remember that kids aren't as strong as adults. They can be insanely energetic at times, but only in bursts, and my son is proof that they are being born with the same amount of processing speed as I have. My son, your kid—assuming you ever get around to having one—or any child of an upgraded person is going to have the same issue. They will simply burn themselves out, a whole generation gone unless we can find a way to teach them control at an early age."

"Or redirect the energy pull," suggested Juliane. Betty's paranoia had a certain degree of logic to it.

"I've tried that, but so far, the fix is only temporary and won't last much longer." Betty's appearance had grown fainter as they were talking, reminding Juliane that she did not have time to waste on idle theories.

"Betty, I'd be happy to discuss all of this with you, but first, you need to wake up so that the doctors can help you."

Betty laughed, but there was no humor in the sound. When their eyes met again, Juliane saw pity reflected. "One day, with any luck, you'll understand." Betty faded further. "The doctors aren't going to be able to save me because I won't let them. My son is still alive only because he is pulling energy from me, but I am afraid he isn't going to last long after I'm gone. I am going to need you to pick up on my work, not just for my son, but for the thousands of other children who are going to be born with this same condition."

Suddenly, Juliane's vision of the landscape shifted. She was no longer in control. The lab morphed into a hospital complex, infinitely long, with children wasting away in their beds surrounded by helpless parents. Thriving cities emptied after a few short generations. Floating a short distance away, Betty was nearly transparent, having lost the majority of her form's definition.

"And Alan isn't able to help with any of this?"

The beds, children, and empty cities faded to black. Betty's semi-transparent form was all that remained, her head the only feature that still maintained some slight definition. Betty's voice hissed, "You can't trust Alan! Save my son. Chad knows where to find my research. Contact him. Do it quickly, while there's still time!"

Betty's face faded further into the darkness. Juliane watched her lips move, but no sound escaped. It was almost as if she had said, "I'm sorry."

Juliane's mind felt as if it was hit with a sledgehammer as she was pulled violently from Betty's bedside. It began to throb, quickly outpacing the pulsing sound of the machines as the doctor and nurse rushed the bed out toward an operating room. Betty hadn't been out of view long when Juliane felt her private network connection sever as sharply as if she had been physically cut in two. Juliane knew then that Betty would never wake again.

Juliane felt another pain crest, but this one was more distant, and her shoulder made contact with the tile floor. Her body screamed as the pain spread and intensified. Just like when she had broken the connection to Louis, it felt as if she had a gaping wound in her brain, except, this time, it felt even rawer around the edges. Juliane's vision began to blacken. *No!* she thought. *Not again! Never again!* She did not know if she was fighting against the impending unconsciousness or the lack of the network. She no longer cared.

TWENTY-NINE

Juliane blinked to clear her blurred vision as she pulled herself back upright. A handful of personnel in scrubs rushed past, barely noting her presence. As she made her way down the hall, Juliane was hit by waves of vertigo. She was in a hospital, but she couldn't quite remember the reason she was here. Her shoulder throbbed as she crashed into the hallway railing. She wondered if it might be better to take a day to recover before returning to work.

Juliane took more confident steps as her sight cleared. She would have Stuart begin rounding up the task force. The room spun again.

A patient, a young boy, was wheeled past her, strapped in a bed. A dull drone emitted from machines as they passed. Her vision blurred again as another wave of nausea hit. She hadn't felt this lethargic since she first severed the connection with Louis. A man in a white coat, looking much like a troll doll, rushed by. "Stay with me, buddy," he pleaded with the child.

"Are you all right, Ms.?" another male voice asked.

Juliane couldn't answer. It was as if the act of moving her lips required too much energy. The droning sound of the machine ceased, only to be replaced with a ping that reverberated in her ears. If she didn't get out of here soon, Juliane was certain she would go mad.

"I need you here stat," shouted the troll doll from down the hall. "We've got a reading." The person hovering near Juliane turned and sprinted toward the patient.

The sense of disorientation ebbed Juliane as the trio passed beyond a large pair of swinging doors. Why did the boy make her think of Betty? *Wasn't her son two years old?* It had been ages since she last saw them, or was it? Juliane turned and took a hesitant step forward, keeping the thought of her own office out of her mind. A thought danced in the back of her mind just out of reach. There was something she was supposed to do. Something she needed to remember. But it was like the information was on another side of a wall. Getting around that wall would require a significant effort, and all she wanted to do was go home and sleep until next week.

As drained as she felt, suddenly Juliane had the strangest compulsion to seek out Chad. It had to have been even longer since she had last seen him. She fought through exhaustion. *Did the hallway lights flicker?* With each step further away from the double doors, her vision cleared. By the time she made it to the exit, the ground was once again stable beneath her feet.

THIRTY

Juliane realized that she hadn't bothered to confirm Chad was still with the ACI before making the drive from the hospital. She accessed the online directory and released a breath as she spotted Chad's name in its listing. A specific office was not listed, but at least he should still be on the campus. Somewhere. Their old building would serve as a good starting point for her search.

As she made her way to the Gould building, she was struck by how every brick, every flower, along the ACI campus looked just as it had the day she left, as if the campus itself was impervious to the passage of time. A crow pecked at something on the ground as she reached the building's entrance, flying away only when she was close enough, she could have picked it up had she wanted to.

Entering the building, she felt hollow. She had spent so many years here, but it felt as if her memories of the place could fit into the span of a handful of days. Lost in her thoughts, she was startled when she heard someone approach from behind her.

"Dr. Faris? Is that you?" Chad stood inside the hall. His disheveled hair surrounded his head like a fiery halo, making him appear even more like the stereotypical mad scientist than she remembered. His arms were filled with stacks of folders covered in streaks of coffee stains. A pair of coffee cups balanced precariously on top.

"Chad! Just the person I was looking for!" Juliane smiled as Chad shifted his burden, jostling one of the cups and sending beads of coffee flying. *At least some things never changed*, she thought. She should have visited ages ago. Her smile faded. Why hadn't she looked him up over the last few years? She had always meant to, but it was as if every time she scheduled a moment to reach out, something would come up that required her immediate attention and the urge would evaporate.

"What happened to you? You just vanished. People here thought you might have died."

"Really? What were they saying?"

"Well, some people thought you must have had another episode while at home and got eaten by random dogs; other people thought you must have perished in one of your crazy experiments."

"That's one of the reasons I don't like to listen to gossip." Juliane laughed. "Ridiculous," she snorted. "What about you? What did you think happened?"

Chad paused before answering, and when he did, it was without humor or recrimination. "I just assumed that when opportunity knocked, whatever it was, you didn't hesitate to answer."

Juliane blinked. She must have been staring. She felt a heat rise in her cheeks and fought to control it. *Stop it, Juliane,* she thought. It was only Chad. There was no reason to react like this. After all the time they had spent together, of course, he knew her. It was a good thing Betty wasn't with them. She no doubt would tease her relentlessly.

Juliane felt her throat tighten as if there were bags of sand in her lungs, holding her down, preventing her from drawing a full breath. A piece of the mental wall chipped away as an image of Betty on a hospital bed flooded her mind. Her ears rang with the distinctive sound of a monitor's flat-line alarm. Pieces of the last few days and Betty's final words came rushing back.

Chad caught Juliane as she staggered, causing the coffee cup to spill onto the floor.

"Are you okay?" he asked.

Juliane's head pounded as she struggled to stand up again, but as quickly as the headache's onset began, it faded away to something like the pins-and-needles tingle of a limb allowed to fall asleep.

Chad's arm shifted under hers. Juliane pushed herself away. The vision of Betty in the bed remained behind her mind's eye, but it was muted. Like a dream. Colors were grayer. Details blurred. It was almost as if she hadn't even been in the room with her at all.

"Sorry about that. I must have slipped," she answered.

Chad scanned her face. "Are you sure?"

"Betty told me that you might have some of her research material." Juliane changed the subject.

Chad's face tightened. "She isn't going to be asking for it herself, is she?"

Juliane shook her head, unable to voice the words.

Chad's shoulders crumpled, sending a few papers to the floor where they landed dangerously close to the coffee spill. As they both bent down to pick them up, Chad whispered, "Come to my apartment later tonight."

When they were both standing once again, Chad spoke at regular volume, "Nadia is going to be so upset that she didn't get to see you."

"You two are still together?" Juliane tried to smile, but her lips refused to turn up. "I'm happy to hear that. Have you made it official yet?"

Chad shook his head. "Nothing formal yet, but that's her choice. She knows I will be ready to take that step whenever she is."

Juliane suppressed the urge to sigh. She wasn't surprised at all that Chad was content to wait for the lady to do the proposing. As much as she used to think Nadia treated her assistant like a doormat, she now could see he had always needed someone strong and opinionated. Chad smiled, and for a moment, Juliane wondered what it might have been like if their relationship had ever taken a romantic turn.

Chad glanced down at his wrist. "You wear a watch now?" she asked, stunned. Not only was it a watch, but it was an antiquated analog version.

"Well, you were always the one reminding me about how late I always was. Nadia, apparently, thought the same. She gave me her grandfather's watch a few Christmases ago. I find there is something nice about knowing that its sole function is to tell time and only requires a few spinning gears."

"But it's just so . . . so . . . unnecessary."

"Perhaps, but now and then, I've found it to be nice to do things the old-fashioned way." Chad glanced down at his wrist again and blanched. "Unfortunately, bad habits are hard to break. I really have to run these papers over to the team I am working with now. They have me running simulations on extreme climate change. Did you know that the Sahara went from green to a desert in a flash?"

"How thrilling for you. Do you think anyone will mind if I stick around the building a little longer?"

Chad hesitated in mid-stride. "I don't know if that's the best idea. If the wrong person saw you, who knows how they might react."

As Juliane made her way back to her car, she tried to call Stuart to see if the factory had sent in any further report. However, each time she attempted to instigate the call, she would be hit with another wave of vertigo. She decided that she would find a place to rest while she waited for the business day to end and

Chad to return home. *There has to still be a few cafes nearby.* She could not remember the last time she ate.

Rose light from the setting sun blanketed the parking lot as Juliane arrived at Chad's address. The apartment was located in a complex about twenty minutes away from the campus. It was a nice enough space, a definite step up from traditional student housing, with well-manicured common areas and clean lines.

Juliane spotted movement from one of the upper balconies. A short minute later, Nadia emerged, gesturing her inside while holding a finger to her lips.

"Why the whole cloak-and-dagger routine?" asked Juliane as the door closed behind her.

"Chad should be here in the next few minutes. I'll let him explain."

Nadia fidgeted under Juliane's glare. "He shouldn't be too much longer. Would you like me to make up some tea while we wait?"

Chad let himself into the apartment just as the kettle began its whistle. Nadia poured the steaming liquid into a pair of cups. To Chad, she said, "It's a beautiful night. I think I will go out for a bit while you two have a chance to get reacquainted." Without waiting for a response, she leaned over to kiss Chad briefly before grabbing her purse off the counter and departing.

"What's with all the secrecy?" Juliane asked.

"Betty did tell you what she was working on, right?"

"She explained her theory to me."

Chad paused before taking a quick sip of his tea. "And you think she was paranoid?"

Juliane left her cup on the end table and sat down on the couch across from Chad. "I am not as convinced that the situation is that dire. Alan would never design something he couldn't control." There was something else she needed to remember. Something else Betty wanted her to do. *What was it?*

Chad placed his teacup back on the countertop with care. "Betty seemed to think that was exactly what he did."

Pressure began to build behind Juliane's temples. *Not another headache,* she thought. It was harder to think straight when all she wanted to do was lie down. She needed something tangible to focus on. *The teacup.* "Maybe she allowed their marital problems to influence her opinion."

Chad shook his head. "That was my initial thought as well when she first discussed her theory with me, but think about it this way. What if what might appear to the rest of the world as a careless mistake wasn't so careless?"

"You mean, what if he purposely designed the virus to mutate so that he could intentionally put the entire population at risk?"

"Exactly."

THIRTY-ONE

Chad had handed Juliane a small metallic keychain fob. "Betty asked me to give you this."

It didn't look like much. It was just a small tube of plastic connected to an empty keyring with some unknown company's name printed on it. She turned the fob over and noticed a break in the material.

She pulled at the plastic. A portion of the device broke away, exposing a contact plate. It was an old throwaway flash drive—the type no one used anymore. Juliane closed her fist around the exposed metal surface. Immediately, a command prompt appeared behind her mind's eye, followed by a series of ones and zeroes. She issued a quick command, and the data packets were transformed into large high-definition photos of Betty's son in various poses.

Chad looked at her expectantly. Juliane shrugged and opened the next file.

File after file had been more of the same. Juliane began to uncurl her fist; Betty must have given Chad the wrong storage drive by mistake. Another wave of vertigo hit and Juliane ground her teeth in frustration as she sank further into Chad's couch.

When the room finally stopped spinning, Juliane noticed a framed picture placed on a nearby end table. Alan was behind a podium presenting something unclear while Chad and Betty looked on from the sidelines.

The shot must have been taken shortly after Juliane had left the team to join Damien's group. Chad looked embarrassed to be in the spotlight while Betty looked positively aglow; her eyes were locked on Alan with rapt attention.

Juliane's headache made it feel as if her brain were being torn in two. She felt a pain that was almost electric run down her spine, breaking her connection with the device. Juliane ground her teeth. *There has to be something on this drive worth all this trouble,* she thought. She clenched her fist again, and the files immediately reloaded. Once again, Juliane saw image after image of a young boy. His pale gray-blue eyes shone in the sunlight, carefree and happy. His eyes mirrored Betty's in shape, although his were a different color, but Betty's son was two. This boy was clearly a few years older.

There was something about the eyes. They just seemed wrong. On a whim, Juliane sent a command to change his iris color so that they would truly match Betty's. A few pixels in the image shifted. She adjusted the hue by a few points. Suddenly, the photo in her mind dissolved and was replaced by documents detailing out research notes and equations. Juliane sucked in her breath as the balance of files were decrypted. Another piece of the mental wall chipped away.

She glanced at Chad, and her brow wrinkled as she attempted to make sense of the scrolling data.

"Well?"

"I'm not sure, but I think I am looking at radiant energy transformation equations. But if that's what it is, why go to all the trouble of encrypting the formula?" The pictures dissolved, and Juliane felt lightheaded as the pressure of her headache eased. She blinked several times as Chad's face came back into focus.

"She stopped by here a few nights ago in a panic. I tried to get her to tell me what the matter was, but all she would say was that I was to give that to you and only you. You know how Betty used to always want us to go out to celebrate this, that, or another thing?"

Juliane nodded, the corner of her lip turning up at the mention of the memory.

"She was like that. Except not like that at all." Chad shook his hands. "Ugh. How to explain it . . . It was as if she had all the same intensity, but all the life had been drained away."

Juliane thought back to Betty's fierce reaction at the office when she had told her that she wouldn't be able to help. Betty had seemed like an animal backed into a corner.

"She looked awful, though," continued Chad. "I asked her if she wanted me to call Alan to come and get her, but all she would say was that she had already been away too long and had to get back." Chad picked his cup up and took another sip. "She looked terrified." He stared into his mug as if reading tea leaves. "I hate to say anything, but you look a little like that too."

Juliane traced her finger around the rim of her teacup, the file drive still clutched firmly in her other hand. "I've been under a bit of stress recently, but I was there, Chad. I was at the hospital when she died." Juliane sighed. "Alan wasn't. She had a bad reaction to the drugs the doctors gave her. It was a tragedy, not a conspiracy."

Chad jumped up. "I'm sorry, but I think you are wrong."

"Why?" Juliane allowed herself a half-smile. "Because you think Alan is an egotistical maniac?"

"Well, you have to agree he does have more than the average ego." Chad began to pace around the room.

"True, but that doesn't automatically mean that he is planning genocide." Chad spun to face her.

The door burst open, and Nadia came running in. Whatever Chad was going to say was lost in her entrance. "I know I promised you that I would let you have your meeting in private, but you have to see what is on the news," she pleaded.

Chad pressed a small button located on the wall, and a piece of artwork hanging nearby transitioned into a video display. Juliane toggled on her newsfeeds in her mind to run as a supplement to the images on the screen.

"Any particular channel?" Chad asked Nadia.

"He's on all of them."

The screen showed the exterior of the same hospital where Juliane had been not long ago. Louis sat in a wheelchair near a makeshift podium, supported on one side by a team of doctors dressed in the traditional white lab coats. Each stood straight, unafraid of the camera. Another man dressed in a sharply tailored business suit stood by Louis's other side. Juliane assumed this man must have replaced Durham in the role of go-to lackey.

The cameras zoomed in onto the man's face in anticipation of an official statement. The man said a few words, explaining that Louis was in recovery and would not be taking any questions.

The cameras panned over to Louis as he struggled to rise from his seat. He looked terrible in both senses of the word. He was bandaged and braced, with gray skin and several bruises, but his eyes shone with fierce determination.

His knuckles turned white as they clutched the podium, and his lips twisted in pain. Had the caption not identified the man as Louis, Juliane might not have recognized him. It appeared as if the man Juliane knew as Louis might have perished in the accident after all.

"As many of you have undoubtedly heard by now, I was involved in an accident that so tragically took the life of my beautiful wife, Elena. We as a society have become too trusting in our acceptance of technology. I was too trusting. We have ignored the fact that our devices are only as smart as the person who writes the code. We have allowed programs which we do not fully understand to run in the background alongside critical systems."

Juliane's brow wrinkled. Where was he going with this?

"Fifty years ago, society was afraid that the machines would rise one day to enslave humanity. That day came about years ago. There was no war, we went willingly, and I, I have been their biggest recruiter. No longer. From today on, I am redirecting my company and all of its available resources into reclaiming our independence. Elena, in life, was my sun."

Juliane's lip curled before she caught herself.

"She made every day brighter with her presence. In death, may she serve as a beacon of hope for others."

"He's lost his mind," mumbled Nadia. "Poor man."

Louis let go of the podium. One of the doctors moved as if to re-position the wheelchair closer. Louis waved him away, and after an initial tentative step, he left the conference. Several reporters shouted questions, but the man in the tailored suit waved them away before following Louis. Not having much else to focus on, the camera stayed fixed on the empty wheelchair Louis left behind.

The newsfeeds returned to stunned anchormen and women who offered their own opinions on what had and hadn't been said. One group speculated that Louis was only suggesting that there needed to be more emphasis on consumer education; another group believed that Louis had just declared war on the very products that had built his family's fortune.

Business feeds focused on the valuation of large public technology companies. If the overseas market activity was an indicator, the following day was going to be a busy one on the trading floor.

Juliane's vision flashed with incoming communication requests, the majority coming from Stuart. Fortunately, the alert did not trigger another wave of vertigo or pain.

Her assistant appeared in the corner of her vision. "Juliane, you need to come into the office."

"What is it? Is it the factory? Have we gotten their final report?"

"You aren't going to be happy."

"Let me guess, they determined that the worker was a troubled individual. They weren't able to find any evidence of poor working conditions or ways to improve the facility, all of his dorm mates have been transferred to a better place, and we won't be hearing from any disgruntled family members. Meanwhile, nothing has changed."

"You would be right except—"

"Except for what?" Juliane rubbed her hand over her forehead. The small burst of energy from the caffeine in the tea had already drained away. She glanced at Chad and Nadia who were still riveted to the video screen, their hands now clutched together.

"I think this will be better discussed face to face," answered Stuart.

Juliane stifled a groan. Aloud to Chad and Nadia, she said, "As entertaining as watching Louis commit career suicide is, I have some work to do." She left the apartment without waiting for them to respond.

Stuart's avatar remained in the corner of her vision. "I'm on my way to the office now."

She unclenched the fist which still carried the hard drive. She was somewhat surprised to have found she hadn't crushed it. She would take a more thorough look at the files after she finished the debriefing. *What am I missing?*

When she arrived at her office, Stuart stood at full attention. "I hope that this means you are ready to give me a full report."

He nodded. "You may want to take a seat though."

She made no move to sit. Her assistant shifted his weight from one foot to the next. "Perhaps you have forgotten where we left off. You were going to tell me how this incident was somehow different from the last three."

Stuart coughed once before speaking. "There won't be any further incidents from the factory, and we won't have to worry about disgruntled former employees or their families leaking information to the press, because there is no one left to report anything."

Juliane's forehead wrinkled. "And why did I have to come back to the office for this news?"

"They can't, because they are all dead. Someone executed everyone there and then torched the whole complex. Not just the factory, but the worker's village too."

Juliane gasped. "What? How is that even possible?"

Stuart shifted nervously from side to side. "The rumor is that whoever committed the act did it based on your orders."

Juliane realized her mouth was hanging open and quickly shut it. She took a step forward. Stuart jumped back.

Juliane cocked her head as she took in Stuart's panicked expression. "And do you believe them?" Juliane took another step forward. *It just wasn't possible.* Her assistant's matching step backward told her more than any verbal response he could have offered.

"I see." Her shoulder's slumped. Juliane felt that tightening pressure behind her eyes again. An icy rage filled her heart. *They can't all be dead. He had to be wrong. A story that sick had to be a lie. Why couldn't he see that?* She glared at Stuart. He thought she was a monster. She would show him a monster. "Under the circumstances, you must understand that your services are no longer required. I can't trust my sensitive information with someone who doesn't trust me, but I thank you for your professionalism."

Stuart stood motionless for a few awkward moments. "Was there anything else?" Juliane asked. *I'll get to the bottom of this myself.* She knew she hadn't ordered anyone's death, but if even a fraction of the story were true, someone would have contacted her much sooner. *Wouldn't they?*

She had failed Betty. If only she had gone to the hospital the day before, she might have been there before the doctors gave her those sedatives. *Why had they given her sedatives?* Now she may have failed hundreds of others.

"I believe it would be best if you took your leave now, otherwise I might have to notify the security team." She crossed the room toward the desk and pulled out her chair as her office began to spin. Out of the corner of her vision, she noted her former assistant back out of the room, but then he was out of her thoughts altogether before the door finished closing.

Left alone once again, her nails dug into her palm as she clasped her fist around the hard drive. The pain distracted her from the tears that threatened to consume her. Some dams could never be rebuilt. Opening her palm only long enough to expose the drive's connector, she accessed Betty's research files. She would not focus on anything except the drive in her hand.

THIRTY-TWO

Juliane awoke on her office's couch. The light from the rising sun filtered across the room. She had become so engrossed by trying to solve Betty's puzzle that she hadn't realized how exhausted she was until it was well beyond the point of safe travel. As she had delved deeper into Betty's theorem, she realized that the energy equation was only simple on the surface.

There were a few missing elements, but Betty's file appeared to be a bridge system that could wireless transfer power at a previously unheard-of rate. However, as far as she could tell, it had nothing to do with the upgrade or her son.

Betty's work had begun with a grand postulation; a deeply buried thermal energy matrix storage system could be paired with an orbital solar power plant. It was the sort of thing that the world could benefit from. *So why keep it a secret? Was she afraid Alan would steal her idea and take the credit?*

Juliane rubbed her temples. She had stayed up way too late reading over Betty's math. The few hours of sleep she had gained on the couch weren't nearly enough. She needed coffee to fully recharge her batteries.

She stretched her neck and rolled her shoulders to work out their stiffness before walking over to her office's "kitchen cabinet"—a coffee maker and food-based 3D printer built into part of the wall. She inserted a coffee pod into one orifice and a puree cartridge in the other. As brown liquid poured into her cup, a tan paste was extruded onto a heating tray. Within moments, the smell of a fresh-baked scone and Arabica blend filled the room.

The smell in both cases was more impressive than the taste. Neither appliance would win culinary awards, but they allowed her to fill her nutritional requirements and came in handy for days such as these. *Like eating at a hospital.* Betty was given sedatives because her son was in the hospital and she wasn't sleeping. *I wonder if he has been told yet about his mother.*

Together, the files represented a method of generating additional power. Power was already cheap, but Betty's proposal would make it nearly limitless. A single deployment of the system could potentially produce enough power to fuel half the planet. If Betty was right, it was the type of system that should be implemented immediately—not hidden away. There had to be something else on the drive she was missing.

Juliane frowned as an indicator light on the machine informed her that the device had initiated recharging mode. An idea struck her. *What if instead of powering small appliances, a building's power cells could help supplement people too?* She tapped a finger on the machine and shook her head. *The embedded power cells might be able to handle one-off jobs, but if everyone was upgraded that would create too much strain on the grid. Unless . . .* Unless Betty's generator came online.

The texture of her food felt like cardboard. Betty asked her to help her son. Her four-year-old son.

She considered calling Alan. *His wife just died. He isn't going to take calls.* She issued another communication command. "Durham, it's Juliane."

"Yes?"

"Listen, do you know if Alan's son is still in the hospital?"

"I don't know. Don't you want to ask Alan?"

"His wife . . . Betty passed away, and if their kid is still sick too, I . . . er . . . think it best not to intrude on his privacy. Unless I have to."

"Ah. I didn't know. Yeah, I'll need to offer my condolences to him, but why ask me? Or Damien? You're both closer to him than I am."

"I was hoping you might ask your friend."

Silence. "What friend?"

"The one that works at the hospital."

"I'm not sure that's a good—"

"On behalf of another friend," Juliane offered. "Please."

Durham sighed. "I'll ask, but you might wish I hadn't."

"I understand"—Juliane chewed her lip—"and Durham? Thank you."

After quick use of her office's shower, she pulled a spare set of clothing from another hidden cabinet and dressed quickly. She arranged for her clothing from the previous night to be sent out for dry-cleaning and returned to her condo.

She picked up Betty's drive and accessed the data once again. Now that her head no longer felt split in two and she could tell which way was up, Juliane identified the basic building blocks in Betty's proposal.

She closed her eyes, opening up her virtual senses to the building's infrastructure, searching for inductive modules. She attuned herself to a few of their signals. The light on her coffee maker turned off as she adjusted her body to the inductive power flow's signal. It did not take long before she felt a rush much like a triple espresso.

Her vision showed an incoming call from Durham. His voice told her the news was good. "Well, you'll be happy to hear that the boy was released yesterday evening. I was told he made a miraculous recovery. My friend is simply beside herself."

"That's a relief! Thank you so much for checking on that."

"No problem. You can pay me back with a rematch sometime."

"Mmhm." Juliane's mind raced as she ran through the implications of what she'd just done.

Durham paused. "It's nice to be able to talk to you again, Juliane."

"You too," said Juliane. She disconnected the call. An alarm sounded from the food printer as it went into battery mode. Juliane laughed to herself; the printer could go offline permanently for all she cared. Based on the way she felt now, she wouldn't need it again anytime soon.

Betty's equation would work. Juliane was sure of it. However, Betty hadn't been right about everything—not if her son was out of the hospital. Her son's condition couldn't have anything to do with Project Gene Assist.

Juliane's smile fell. *It was just in your head, Betty.* Juliane sighed. Betty might have succumbed to paranoia, but Juliane could still make sure her legacy was continued.

Juliane sat down to access the various newsfeeds before the workday officially began. Now to fix her own. She let the newsfeeds run in the background while she attempted to connect to someone at the factory.

She checked her contacts' online statuses. Everyone was marked away. She sent messages and frowned as they all came back with delivery failure notifications.

The building's lower floors housed the last remaining phone bank, installed as a courtesy for visitors who might need backup communication. Juliane wasn't even sure the devices were still operable. She'd never had reason to use them before.

Juliane rushed out of her office and into a waiting elevator. She punched a lower floor number with almost enough force to break through the keypad's plastic overlay.

A young man in a business suit scurried through the lobby as Juliane crossed the room. The man nervously adjusted his collar before running out of her line of sight. Juliane took a few calming breaths while she attempted to access the personnel directory for landline numbers or mobile numbers. Each time she dialed a number, a recorded voice answered that all lines were currently out of service.

Spinning on her heels so fast they threatened to crack the tile floor, she ran back toward the elevator. *Perhaps*, she thought, *I will have more success visiting the factory's site in the virtual world.* She didn't have to have an established meeting connection to go there.

She could just appear and then see who else might be using the location as a meeting site, just like the Internet chat rooms of old. *Alan did it all the time. Why can't I?* Her contacts might not be answering her pings, but there had to be someone goofing off in that environment who knew something.

Before she could reach the elevator, a bright light flashed outside the main doors. Turning her head, Juliane saw that several people were stationed just beyond the entrance. Another light flashed. At least a few of the people had cameras. "Reporters." Juliane's lips curled.

The various headlines that had been quietly scrolling in the corner of her vision became more insistent. She brought them up to her primary field of view. The stock market wasn't yet open, but analysts were already preparing for a tailspin of massive sell-offs in anything related to the world of technology. Reminders of similar events that happened nearly seventy years ago were only adding to the pre-open hysteria.

Then another headline, much further down in the world news report, caught her eye. Two American journalists had disappeared abroad. The pair had submitted their last report from a town close to the scene of a large factory explosion. Before their disappearance, the news source had asked the pair to investigate rumors of inhumane work conditions at the plant and now believed the pair were likely victims along with potentially hundreds if not thousands of other workers.

Juliane's face paled. She knew the part of the world referenced in the article all too well. The factory she used served as the chief employer for the entire region. It was extremely unlikely that the story could be about any other factory than the one she used.

A cold feeling settled deep in her stomach. She realized that Stuart may not have exaggerated as much as she had previously wanted to believe.

There wasn't much else to the story. The local government was acting tight-lipped and was not releasing much more as to the exact size of the explosion or its cause. Rumors as to the explosion's source ranged from the improper use of equipment to a raid by a rival company.

Juliane glanced at the lobby entrance. She could hear the sound of a growing crowd.

Her newsfeed flashed back to market commentators discussing the tech segment. Juliane felt her saliva consolidate into a wad when one commenter brought up her company only to suggest that Juliane might have intentionally caused the fire to collect on insurance claims based on the company's sinking value.

Juliane waited for someone to correct the commentator. The timeline of the explosion couldn't possibly support his theory. *Or did it?* The memory of Stuart's expression as he made his report came crashing to the top of her consciousness. Stuart seemed to think so, and he seemed to think it was somehow her fault.

But why would anyone think a catastrophic loss of life was what she wanted? She needed that factory to produce the pendants and earpieces which enabled people without genetic upgrades to access the virtual world she had created.

Everything she had done over the last five years had been to grant access to that world. There would be no grand insurance payout. She had no ownership stake in the factory. All her money had been tied up in producing product, and that inventory was now up in smoke, and she certainly had no motive to hurt anyone there.

Juliane spared the reporters another glance. *First, they made me out to be a whore, now they are making me a monster.* She toggled a setting on her communication program to automatically hide all but the most critical incoming call notifications.

She had to get away from the cameras. Punching elevator buttons, she quickly returned to her office. Stuart's report was laid open across her mind's eye before she had even closed the door.

One of the attachments in the file was an audio clip. Juliane's translation tool automatically adjusted the speech. On it, a woman could be barely heard, her voice trembling as she whispered. In the background, Juliane heard screams and a repeating metallic popping sound.

"Oh please God! Help me! There are bodies everywhere. Help me! Please!" The popping sound resumed, cutting off some of the whispers. " . . . to find me. You've got to do something. I can hear"—more pops and screams—"getting closer! Do something! Do something! Oh God! No!" There was a muffled sound like something being dragged away, and the audio ended.

Juliane's body shook as she took in the recording. If the popping sound was the explosion, then there had not been just one but instead, a fairly lengthy series of chain reactions. *It had to have been an accident.* Every fail-safe in the entire facility would have needed to be manipulated to achieve such an effect.

Juliane pounded her fist on the desk. Without being able to connect to a witness, she would have no means of determining exactly what happened, but she could no longer deny that something truly horrible had occurred.

Juliane flipped through more documents. The section related to the original investigation had shown much of what she had known from the beginning. The victim was described as a loner who had increasingly been the source of troubles on the line and who was facing disciplinary actions.

His superiors had performed all intervention activities per approved practices. They had even scheduled an all-hands assembly to discuss the matter and present support options, which was why there were so many people present in a single location when the explosion occurred.

A local team of first responders had made a handful of reports before they too seemed to disappear off the grid. Satellites provided WiFi around the world, but unless a person in the area was equipped with a pendant or ear clip, they had no access to it. It could be the reason why there were no further reports from the first responders, but it was becoming hard for Juliane to convince herself that there were any survivors.

A note showed that Stuart had tried reaching out to some of the locals. Only, his notes showed that people living in villages somewhat farther out had become superstitious and refused to assist in any further investigation. Juliane clenched her teeth. She didn't know if she should feel relieved. There was nothing in the report that suggested she or her company played any role in the disaster, but that didn't make the explosion any less tragic.

Juliane considered replaying the audio recording to determine if she might be able to pull out additional details but knew deep down it was unlikely that she would ever need to hear it again to remember the sounds of panic. *There is nothing else you can do, Juliane,* she told herself as she rocked back and forth, her arms wrapped around her chest. *Make the world better for those they left behind. Focus on the mysteries you can solve.*

Juliane may not be able to do anything to help those poor victims, but she still could make a difference. Reminded of Betty's equation, Juliane felt a stirring hope. She looked at the clippings adorning her office walls, and her shoulders slumped. Without production, she had no assets. She had no way to implement any of Betty's legacy on her own. Juliane considered her options. Her position within Damien's group granted her access to several potential investors, but her years of self-induced isolation limited her personal Rolodex.

She could beg Louis for funds. He already had a vested interest in the project, but that idea was repugnant, and he would be unlikely to accept her proposal based on his new position on technology anyway.

She could go to Damien, but to secure the level of funding she would need would require her to submit her proposal in front of the entire board, which meant that it would be impossible to honor Betty's wish to keep it a secret from Alan.

Juliane chewed her lip as she made her choice.

THIRTY-THREE

Juliane spent the next few days refining her needs and perfecting her proposal. The reporters had dispersed when she hadn't made an immediate appearance. Juliane, remembering her tabloid fame, did not trust the quiet. She assumed that while the whole press corps was no longer outside her door, at least one or two reporters or paparazzi were still camped out in more clandestine locations, either around her office or by her condo.

She sent a query to a real estate agent. Selling her condo wouldn't be enough to fund her next steps, but it would at least help her maintain a little more independence. She'd been homeless before. It didn't scare her, and Alan was right; she didn't live there anyway.

Juliane considered calling Durham to see if he might know a way to access some additional money but couldn't bring herself to ask for more help. She would have to follow through with her original plan.

As prepared as she could be, she made her way across town toward Damien's building. The building looked much as it had the first day she had seen it. The sandstone exterior was just as clean and bright as the day it had first been constructed. *Damien must spend a fortune in upkeep*, Juliane thought. The material was beautiful but prone to blacken as it absorbed everyday urban gases.

When she reached Damien's floor, his executive assistant met her at the door. Sarah had grown in confidence over the years. Gone was the people-pleaser. She had always been an extremely capable administrator, but there was now an edge about her. She seemed harder, less forgiving. She and Juliane hadn't gotten along any better since the day of their first meeting.

"Juliane. You finally decided to come out of hiding?"

"I need to talk to Damien about some recent developments."

"I'm sure you do, but you should know that he is well aware of the recent . . . unpleasantness."

Juliane fought the urge to bite her lip or otherwise signal to Sarah that her words meant anything to her. The other woman would only use them against her. Sarah's wounded pride from their first encounter was something that time would never heal.

"Then I am sure he would be willing to fit me into his schedule."

Sarah broke eye contact first, looking up and to the right, and yet at nothing in particular. Juliane watched as Sarah's body took on a slight glow. If Juliane hadn't been looking for it, she might not have noticed it.

"You're accessing the network," Juliane stated.

Sarah blinked, and the glow disappeared. Sarah allowed for one side of her mouth to twist in a half-smile. "How could you tell?"

"You glowed. I saw your skin interacting with the network."

Sarah's smiled melted into a frown. "I was told that the light fluctuations wouldn't be noticeable."

"And they probably aren't to the average eye, but I've had a few years of experience. I assume that you were checking Damien's calendar just then?"

Sarah's frown deepened. "You may go in. It seems he has been expecting you after all."

Juliane inclined her head in acknowledgment before turning and entering Damien's suite.

Damien was already walking toward the door as she crossed the threshold. "Ah, Juliane, you are looking lovely today. The fresh air from the other night seems to have done you some good."

"Thank you again for the tickets. It was . . . um . . . a new experience."

"One that I hope that you'll want to repeat again soon."

"We'll just have to see what time allows."

"Always so non-committal when it involves anything other than your work. How is everything going by the way? I heard that there may have been an explosion involving one of our manufacturing sites."

Juliane felt her eyes tighten at his choice in words. She had been operating Fair Use Jewelry independently for so long that she had forgotten that he also had an interest in the news story too. "That's what I've been able to ascertain as well, although communication seems to have been completely cut off."

"So why are you here telling me this?"

Juliane's forehead wrinkled. "I came here to discuss next steps. I've recently come into possession of some research that could—"

Damien's laughter interrupted Juliane's pitch.

"I meant why, Juliane, are you in my office when you could be at the site confirming the extent of the damage firsthand? Are you not at all curious as to what happened?"

"Of course, I am!" She couldn't eat. She couldn't sleep. Juliane could hear the screams of the woman on the audio file in her memory as if on constant playback. After the first two nights ruined by nightmares, Juliane had taken to pulling energy constantly from available inductive sources. "But that's not what I am here about."

"Oh?"

"I have recently inherited a big discovery. Potentially life-changing. I've already proved that a portion of the theory works, and now I just need a little help in deploying it on a much larger scale."

"Damien." Sarah did not even attempt to offer an apology for interrupting their meeting. "I just received word that there is a credible threat against several of our retail distribution sites."

"Threat?" he repeated. "What kind of threat?"

"Messages were intercepted between members of a radical anti-technology group, which detailed plans to blow up several major distribution hubs, ours included."

"Was anyone able to determine when this attack is expected to occur?"

"Unfortunately, no."

"And do they know how the bombs are expected to enter the buildings?"

Sarah shook her head. Damien continued as if he never anticipated that she might offer another answer. "Then we really have no choice but to increase our level of diligence internally, but we need to externally appear as if everything is business as normal. We don't want to incite a panic."

Sarah bowed her head and began backing out of the room. "Yes, sir. I'll notify the appropriate parties."

Damien turned back to Juliane. "It would seem that you might not be the only one with problems that need addressing. Perhaps it is for the best that you stay in the country after all. Now, why don't you tell me more about this theory you've come across?"

Juliane felt her shoulders relax. "Well, on the surface, it is quite simple," she began.

THIRTY-FOUR

For the hundredth time, Juliane squashed the urge to fling her arms towards the sky in celebration. Everything was working out better than she had originally anticipated. She couldn't remember why she had ever hesitated to confide in Damien.

She gazed up at the monument she and Damien had worked to erect and was momentarily blinded by its brilliant white surface. She grinned. The statue with its intricate whirls and detailed carvings was just a simple shell. The true marvel was the power transformation system inspired by Betty's equation.

Hidden underneath the stone was a series of converters, relays, and transformers. Once the complete system was online, it would also act as a receiver in addition to distributing power along the grid. Another monument located on the other side of the globe would perform a similar function. Juliane caressed the marble. This was a legacy to be proud of. *This is for you, Betty.*

To maximize the system's potential, the placement sites were critical. Unfortunately, as Juliane had realized in the months following her original discussion with Damien, alternative energy projects weren't always as well received in practice as they were on paper. No one wanted them in their backyard.

Damien had immediately thought of a way to get around the problem. He had suggested that they disguise the necessary antenna pairs as beautifully sculptured works of art. The land where they would be placed would be manicured like a park.

It added extra expense to the project, but as long as the monument didn't look like a power plant, the neighbors likely wouldn't attempt to delay the project. Once the plan was set, his speed to execution was dizzying.

Damien had commissioned a master artist to design both monuments in honor of his favorite scientists. The marble construction towering above her was dedicated to Marie Curie and showed the woman reaching toward the stars, a globe representing an atom perched on her extended fingertip.

The second statue had been dedicated to Charles Darwin. It too had a matching globe on top of a walking stick. The hand not resting on the walking stick was stretched out toward the sky, while a series of marble animals lay draped down the statue's steps.

Both statues had been beautiful on paper but were breathtaking in reality, especially if one ignored the real animal droppings that marked their surfaces within minutes of their unveiling.

Betty would have been bringing the champagne out around now, thought Juliane. Her grin slipped, thinking of her friend and former colleague. *You always did want to celebrate too soon.* Breaking ground on the park had been the easy part.

To complete the project, Juliane still had to deploy solar sheets into orbit and bury the thermal energy matrix storage system deep underground. Damien had been willing to sign off on the park's construction, but she was going to have to approach the board to request the rest of what was needed.

Juliane was confident the board presentation was a minor rubber stamp in the process, otherwise, Damien would not have already invested so much. However, she hadn't yet figured out how to continue to keep Alan from learning who originally came up with the system's equation. While she had figured out its potential, the idea's basis was far from her area of expertise.

Juliane's lips twisted. Thus far, honoring Betty's last wish to keep her work from Alan was proving to be less difficult than she first imagined it might be. As much as she wanted to verify that he was managing her loss and that Stevie was okay, she hadn't seen or heard from Alan since the day of the football game. *The poor man must be devastated. We'll talk when he's ready.*

Her vision flashed with an incoming call notification; it was Damien. She accepted the call without hesitation.

"Hi, Juliane, I just wanted to check in to see how the construction is going."

"You are an absolute magician. I don't know how you were able to pull it all together so fast! I thought we would still be knee-deep in the permit process."

"I take that to mean that you are pleased with the process."

"More than pleased. I almost wish that my proposal had required more than two towers."

"Well, I am glad to hear that. Any trouble with the locals?"

"A handful of people were opposed, but, for the most part, the majority of the locals are excited about what this park will do to their land values."

"Excellent."

"One of these days, Damien, I want you to share how you are able to accomplish so much so fast. Alan is good too, but you, sir, are a master."

"Perhaps now you will be more willing to visit my office on a regular basis. I have a few secrets I'd love to share with you."

Juliane's jaw began to ache from smiling so much. After so little use over the years, the expression felt unnatural.

"The board will meet in two weeks," Damien continued. "I'd like to add phase two to the agenda. Would you be ready by then?"

Juliane looked up toward the globe. The stone surface was so highly polished that Juliane thought she could just make out her reflection in its surface.

"I can manage that."

"Good. It will be worth your time. There are a number of other projects that have been developing that I believe you will be interested in learning more about."

"I look forward to it." Juliane disconnected the call and leaped from the stone stairs.

An early model Porsche 918 Spyder pulled up at the park's entrance just as Juliane reached the street. While the muscle car was aged, it had been well-maintained. The glossy exterior shone like black enamel. While the majority of vehicles on the roads were silent, this one still possessed the quiet roar of a tsunami. Even with the top down, it took a few moments for Juliane to break her attention away from the car to recognize its driver.

"Sarah? Is that you?"

Sarah smiled, although the expression never reached her eyes. "Who else would it be?"

"I just would have guessed you drove something more . . . er . . . practical."

Sarah tilted her head. "You aren't the only one who appreciates the benefits of being associated with the rich and powerful." She frowned. "But, in this case, you'd be correct. This is Camille's car. I'm to take you to her."

"Camille?" Her hand had risen as if it wanted to scratch her head on its own accord. She pulled it back to her side through conscious effort. "What does Camille need me for?"

Juliane had little reason to interact with the group's medical technologist over the years professionally and even less interest in forming any personal connection. Especially after noticing that she and Sarah seemed to be friends.

"Camille doesn't need you for anything . . . You need her."

Juliane's forehead wrinkled.

Sarah rubbed her temple. "Do you remember asking me about being upgraded?"

Juliane nodded.

"Well, accessing the Internet is just a fraction of our potential. Camille's been able to do so much more. Damien thought you would appreciate a little demonstration."

Sarah sent the car racing within seconds of Juliane strapping herself into the seat. The wind of their passage transformed Juliane's hair into a whip. She reached up to secure it into an informal ponytail as they drove. If she had a car like this, she would have to cut her hair short like Sarah's.

"Why weren't you at Betty's funeral? Weren't you two friends?"

"I'm honoring her memory in my own way." The truth was, Juliane hadn't learned there had been a memorial until after the fact. It would seem she hadn't been invited. *So much for being Betty's primary contact.*

It was just as well. Thinking of Betty lying lifeless in a box blackened her vision and caused her legs to lock into place. She remembered the feeling of their connection as it severed and shuddered. *Cursed private network*, Juliane thought once again. She would never, ever, establish one of those again.

"Such a tragic business. To lose one's spouse, well, that is a terrible thing, but at least he still has his son . . ." Sarah trailed off. Juliane wasn't sure if she was hearing Sarah correctly over the roar of the engine, but her tone seemed as if she were discussing a spring shower upsetting picnic plans.

Sarah continued. "I was told that I will likely never have children of my own, so I have always had to live vicariously through others." Sarah glanced in Juliane's direction. "You did know Alan had a son before this?"

"Of course."

Sarah mouthed "of course." More subdued, she said, "Well, *I* might never have known if Damien hadn't said something. I asked Alan once if I could see a picture, and do you know what he told me? He didn't carry a single photograph. He said Betty was the family photographer. He's regretting that now. He told me he can't find any of her files now. Can you imagine how awful that must be?"

"Oh, so you've talked to him?" Juliane asked

"Only for a moment," said Sarah.

Juliane kept her gaze locked on the road in front of them. "Alan was never much for clutter, hard copies or electronic. Betty was always the less organized one. I am sure she has a few scattered about."

"I heard you were with her when she died. Is that true?"

"I visited her at the hospital."

"Did she ever share photos with you? I only ask because I am worried about how Alan is holding up in this situation."

"She was unresponsive when I got there." If Juliane told Sarah about the private network, she had little doubt that Sarah would try to establish one just to prove she could. *No one deserves that*, thought Juliane. *Not even Sarah.*

They pulled into the parking lot. "You're late." Camille met them at the door of her facility and escorted them back to her office.

"I thought you would appreciate it if I didn't damage your car," Sarah retorted with a warm-hearted laugh.

"What have you told her?"

"Very little. You know me. I just do the filing."

Camille's eyes twinkled at what had to be an inside joke and turned toward Juliane. "Are you at all aware of the works of Jonathan Hutchinson or a condition known as progeria syndrome?"

"I can't say that either has come up in my field of study."

Camille closed her eyes and took a breath. "It is an extreme genetic condition which manifests as premature aging in afflicted individuals. Those with the condition typically age at a rate eight to ten times faster than normal, all because of a mutation in a simple protein."

"That sounds terrible. I assume you have been working on a cure?"

Camille tilted her head, stretching the muscles in her neck before answering. "A cure would only help a small portion of the population. No, Juliane, we are thinking bigger. Once we were able to isolate the cause of the mutation, it took little imagination to see the benefit in applying the same technique to normal human cells."

"Are you telling me that you are working on creating a technique that could potentially cause people to appear to age only one year when, in fact, ten years have passed?"

Camille turned her nose up, allowing the hallway light to shine fully upon her face. "We aren't working on a technique. We've perfected it."

Only then did Juliane see that neither Camille nor Sarah possessed the fine lines around their eyes that would have normally given away their ages. "You've undergone the procedure."

"Yes. Everyone on the board has. By the way, I imagine your visit here today will cause at least one person to lose their wager. Most of us thought that after spending so much time with avatars, you might never notice un-aging people in real life long enough to question why we always looked so young."

"We're effectively immortal now," interjected Sarah.

"No, Sarah," corrected Camille. "We are still very much mortal. The process only slows down aging and even appears to reverse its effects to a point, but the process doesn't stop aging altogether."

"I'm surprised this technique of yours hasn't already been blasted on the news," Juliane said.

Camille smiled and shook her head. "The fountain of youth doesn't exactly need help with advertising."

"I suppose you're right. But don't you want to share this accomplishment with the world?"

"The idea of being a public figure has never appealed to me."

"But you could have the world eating out of your hand," Juliane sputtered. *How can he be so nonchalant?*

"Why do you think I can't have that while remaining private?"

"But if you don't release what you have done, how would anyone realize your service is any different from the dozens of other cosmetic procedures?"

"The difference would be that my clients could potentially reach their seven-hundredth birthday. However, I would imagine that the word would have gotten out long before then."

"But you could have it all tomorrow. Don't you want that?"

"Juliane, I've already undergone the procedure. Time is no longer my enemy. I can afford to be patient. Until then, rest assured that those who have the means and the motivation will find me. Now that you understand the full implication of what we have achieved here, would you be interested in giving the procedure a try for yourself?"

If what Camille said was true, she would have several lifetimes to continue her work. Juliane caught her reflection on a mirror hung in Camille's office. By accepting, she would not only remain mentally in her prime but physically as well.

"Absolutely."

Sarah and Camille exchanged a glance, and Sarah exited the room, returning later with a small rod.

"For this procedure to work, a candidate must have first gone through the original upgrade. So not just anyone will be eligible for treatment, which is another reason I've held back from releasing this news to the press. At least, they're not eligible today. We're working on a way to apply both sequences at the same time."

Camille pressed a button and the rod hummed to life. "Next, this rod will upload a command sequence to the code already running in your DNA. Once that is done, the specific protein in your DNA will be isolated and modified by your own natural chemistry."

"So, in theory, I might have been able to modify the protein without its assistance?"

Camille shrugged. "And enough monkeys typing at random could replicate Shakespeare. You might have stumbled upon it one day if you tried hard enough. This just speeds the process along. Think of it as a cheat code in a game."

"I was never much one for video games." Juliane felt a pinching along the length of her body as if she had been bitten by hundreds of mosquitoes. She hissed.

"That uncomfortable feeling is your cells responding to the treatment as your skin begins to firm and tighten. Don't worry; it's only a temporary effect. You won't even notice the sensation an hour from now."

Juliane glanced back at the mirror. She did not realize how many lines had begun to etch her face around the corners of her eyes until they blurred away. She still held herself with the confidence of someone experienced with the world but had the smooth skin of a twenty-year-old.

"I'll admit, I am impressed."

"I'm so glad my work meets your approval," Camille said, putting the rod down on a nearby table. She looked at Sarah. "I believe I have done what I said I would. Now may I return to my real work?"

Sarah nodded. Camille turned and exited the room without saying good-bye.

As the sound of her footsteps faded, Juliane asked Sarah, "I take it that bringing me here wasn't her idea."

"Damien made it clear that he wanted all board members to have the opportunity to improve themselves."

Juliane thought of the football game. "I understand. It's hard to say no to him."

Sarah's lips tightened. "You have no idea." She appeared to chew on her response. "Not all of us are treated like the prodigal daughter. Some of us have to earn our place."

Juliane gazed into the mirror, patting her hair smooth. It would take a while to get used to her new reflection. "I earned my place, just the same as you. I may have just done so a little differently than the others."

Sarah slammed her fists down upon the table with such force that Juliane had to return her attention to the enraged woman.

"What—"

"You cannot begin to comprehend what I have done, what I have sacrificed, to have a place by Damien's side."

Juliane's forehead wrinkled. "I'm sorry, I—"

Sarah picked up the rod from where Camille had left it and examined it for obvious damage before pocketing the device away. "Why don't I take you home?"

Juliane, stunned by the venom in Sarah's voice, took a step back. "Okay."

Juliane and Sarah did not speak again until they were both secured in Camille's vehicle and the medical complex was a mere speck in the rearview mirror. "Look, about today . . ."

"I know I shouldn't be mad, but I am. You like to think you're smart, but there are so many things you don't seem to comprehend at all. For example, you have no clue how easy you've had it being Damien's favorite, how much freedom he has allowed you over the years. Even now, when he is bringing you back into the fold after your epic failure, he is doing so with gifts."

Juliane sat in silence for a few moments. "What epic failure are you referring to?" The sound of the woman suffering in the factory audio played in her mind. *It was an accident. A terrible, terrible accident.*

Sarah rolled her eyes. "This is what I mean about you being treated differently from the rest of us. I bet you never once asked yourself why the press let that disaster at your factory go so quickly. Two of the victims were reporters," said Sarah. "*American* reporters. The disaster at *your* facility should be the *only* thing people are talking about."

Juliane steeled her jaw. Was what Sarah implying true? Damien had the means, but she'd never asked him to do anything on her behalf. Was she now involved in a cover-up? Her reputation had taken enough hits. Her career, and more importantly her credibility would never recover if rumors were to get out. "It might not be the news story you think it is. Everyone knows that there is always a risk of corners being cut when dealing with low-cost manufacturing regions."

"So that's it? You admit that corners were cut."

"I am not admitting anything to you or anyone else. I am only saying that I recognize that there was a risk. Funds for a formal investigation went up in flames with the factory, and the local government isn't talking. If they don't want to pursue justice for the victims, then I have to respect their sovereignty."

Sarah snorted. "That's rather convenient for you."

Juliane shrugged.

"So instead of doing the right thing and funding an inquiry, you are playing gardener and building statues."

Sarah doesn't know the real purpose for the statues, realized Juliane. That meant that Damien didn't trust his own assistant with the information. Juliane replayed her conversations with Sarah in her head. *What if Sarah hadn't been making simple conversation when she asked about Alan's missing photos? Was paranoia a side effect of Camille's procedure?*

But what if she wasn't being paranoid? What would Sarah or Alan stand to gain from the files now, that they weren't eventually going to have access to in a few months when the project was completed?

It just didn't make sense. The statues would provide billions with clean, renewable energy. *Why hide that from the board?* Juliane felt her temples begin to throb. *Was this how Betty felt during her final days?*

THIRTY-FIVE

The car pulled to an abrupt stop, startling Juliane out of her thoughts. Traffic was at a standstill in all directions. Sarah's knuckles were white where they gripped the steering wheel.

Chunks of concrete and piles of glass lay scattered across the street. A number of people stood on the sidewalk. A handful, however, had their faces concealed behind red and white masks that looked like lizard heads.

One of the masked individuals stood out ahead of the others. The figure lifted his or her fist into the air and let a scrap of cloth fall. This must have been some cue for the others as they seemed to melt into the cityscape.

Within seconds, all that remained was the red and white cloth as it came to rest upon the broken glass remains of a burnt-out storefront's windows. Those on the sidewalk who hadn't worn a mask took this as their signal to run as well.

The gaping holes where a pair of destroyed shops' front windows once stood called to her. Juliane was out of the car before she even realized what she was doing.

From the car, Sarah said something, but Juliane couldn't make out her words. Screams of panic, the stampede of feet, and squealing tires filled the air. Juliane shook her head in confusion. Sarah shifted the car into gear and sped off.

A large chunk of a shop's sign lay among the rubble. Based on the few words that remained legible, as well as the pieces of inventory scattered about that were not destroyed, the store had provided basic, run-of-the-mill electronics.

She ran a mental search query. The neighboring shop had been a high-end pet boutique. *The masked figures had definitely targeted one of the two shops, if not both, but why?*

Juliane accessed the newsfeeds. Traffic cameras clocked the event within seconds of Sarah and Juliane's arrival. Had they arrived a moment sooner, they too might have been hit by flying debris.

The masked figures appeared on her newsfeed. At least one person nearby had been live-streaming at the time and had captured footage of them leaving. However, they hadn't recorded the explosion itself. Headlines scrolled across announcing it was a developing story.

The masked figures looked even more serpentine on the amateur video as they had when Juliane spotted them outside the car. As a group, they even moved with the undulating motions of a reptile. The red cloth floating on the breeze appeared on the feed like a tongue tasting the air.

The lizard people melted into the alleyways as quickly on the feed as it had appeared live. The reporters weren't able to provide any concrete evidence as to who the group was or what their purpose might be. They ended the report by asking for anyone with more information to give the news desk a call.

An eerie silence fell over the street and Juliane became aware of how very much alone she was. *Sarah ditched me.* The people responsible for the attack could be anywhere. She needed to get out of sight and quickly.

Without thinking, she darted through the closest shop's doorway. *What am I doing?* wondered Juliane. *There was just a major explosion, there are crazy people out there, and what do I do? I jump into a building that has just been destabilized.* Juliane spun. She needed to get out of the building before more of it came down.

Blue-white lights flashed near the entranceway. Juliane could see exposed wires arc overhead. She heard a pop as a sprinkler head was engaged. *A little late*, she thought. A black liquid began to pool near the entranceway.

Juliane glanced toward the shop's back. Perhaps there was an alternate exit.

Racks of twisted metal blocked her path. The air was thick with smoke and melted silicon. "I can't see a thing in here," Juliane said to herself.

Juliane looked down at her hands. She imagined making them glow as Louis had done during the football game. At first, there was light only at the center of her palm where the skin was thinnest, but it gradually spread out to her fingertips. *Much better than a party trick.*

She curled her digits, encasing and consolidating the light until it was transformed into a directionless orb. *It would have to be enough*, thought Juliane. *At least I might not break my ankle getting out of here.*

Two doors stood at the shop's back. The remains of an exit sign hung from a broken ceiling tile near the larger of the two. Juliane began to reach for the larger door's handle, then paused. There was something odd about the smaller door. *Probably just a storage closet*, she told herself and took another step toward the larger door.

A pink-blue light arched from the door's handle to Juliane's outstretched hand. A shock of pain broke her concentration, causing what light she was able to generate to go out.

Juliane reached toward the wall with her other hand. She was blind in the darkness. She inched her way toward the smaller door. Maybe there was something in the closet she could use to ground the exit door so that she could open it safely.

It took a few tries to jostle open the second door, but finally, it gave way. Juliane concentrated. Once again, she was able to create a soft glowing light from her palm.

This was no storage closet. The space had been spared from much of the damage that ruined the rest of the store. Empty animal crates lay open, scattered across the room. The floor was heavily scarred as large equipment had been moved without regard for surface damage.

The backroom must be a shared space with the pet shop, thought Juliane. *If the wiring next door is a little safer, I might just be able to get out of here.*

"Where is everyone?" whispered Juliane. She wasn't exactly looking forward to seeing a dead body but based on the level of damage surrounding her, Juliane was a little surprised she hadn't yet seen any evidence of human casualty.

As she gingerly made her way across the room, Juliane thought she could hear voices coming from the other side of the wall. Juliane let out a relieved breath. *Thank goodness. The first responders are here.* She swiped her hand along the wall, hopeful that its light would soon illuminate the second doorway she knew had to be there.

The voices grew louder. Juliane could just make out their words. *Where was that door?* she wondered. *Oh, forget about the door. I'll just make a new one.* Juliane raised a fist. She would break through the wall herself or at least get her would-be rescuer's attention.

"The news is making the attack out to be the work of an animal rights group," laughed a male voice.

"Animal rights? Why would they think that?" asked another.

"It seems the owner of the pet shop was engaged in some illegal side business. Trading exotic animals or something like that."

The voices grew louder. Juliane pounded on the wall.

"We're looking for a lady, right?" asked the second voice.

Juliane shouted, "Hello? Hello? I'm back here!" She hit the wall again.

"What does she look like again?" continued the second voice.

"Tall, brunette, mid-thirties," answered the first. "You'll recognize her when you see her."

Juliane's blood ran cold. They weren't looking for just some lady. *They're looking for me.* Were they members of the group responsible for the explosion? Had they seen her duck into the building?

She jumped back from the wall, scanning the room for a place to hide. As she did, the light from her hand reflected her image off a sheet of metal near the pile of crates. She lifted a hand to her face.

Camille had stated that a person might learn how to take command of their cellular structure without the need for her program. If that was true, what else might a person be able to do?

"I'll get an ax out of the truck," she heard the second voice say.

Juliane bit back a scream. *This has to work,* she thought as she knelt closer to the metal sheet making her reflection almost as clear as if she was looking in a mirror. Her dark eyes stared back unblinking. She fired off mental commands as if she were changing the parameters of a computer program. Did the rim of her irises lighten?

"Stay put, ma'am. Help is on the way," shouted the first voice. More softly he said, "Call the boss."

Yes. Her irises lightened. Juliane let out a sigh of relief. Within moments, the eyes in the reflection were a silver hazel. The overall effect looked alien on her face, and she blinked, breaking her concentration. When she looked back, her eyes had resumed their natural color.

The wall shook from the impact of the ax on the wall.

"Focus, Juliane." She starred at her reflection again. Three large freckles appeared over the top of a natural blush. The ax struck again, and her visage was once again flawless alabaster.

"There has got to be another way," she muttered, standing upright once more. "If only I had something like an invisibility cloak." The thought reminded Juliane of her old office at the ACI campus with the setup of cameras that fooled the eye into thinking that the lower levels weren't there. The ax struck again, this time breaking through. She was nearly out of time.

She reached out with her mind as if she was interfacing with her emulator program. Suddenly, it was as if she could see and feel the man's neurons firing as if she was setting up a private network but with far less intimacy. She visualized herself twisting and pulling at their endings.

"It's not her. Just some kid," yelled the man at the wall to his partner as the ax broke through the rest of the way. "Blonde girl, probably seventeen . . . nineteen tops."

The man was dressed in a thick dark jacket of heavy material. *A firefighter* realized Juliane. She shivered. Her first thought that they were first responders must have been correct, but that didn't mean that was all they were.

"She must have gotten away."

The words served to confirm her fears. *They're not here to rescue me.* Her heartbeat raced. The wail of sirens could be heard in the distance. *There is no way I am going to be able to keep this disguise up with that many people,* thought Juliane.

"Keep your eyes out. She can't have gotten far."

To Juliane, the firefighter said, "Don't worry, Miss. We'll have you out of here in no time."

The hole in the wall widened.

"Now how did you get stuck back there?"

Juliane shook her head, afraid to speak.

"Wrong place, wrong time?"

Juliane nodded eagerly.

"Did you see anything—notice anything strange before the explosion?"

Juliane vigorously shook her head.

"Anyone else back there with you?"

Juliane shook her head again, this time more slowly.

"Maybe this is your lucky day after all." To his partner, he yelled, "All clear."

Turning back to Juliane, he continued, "Miss, if I were you, I'd be a bit more careful where I go alone. There may be some dangerous people in the area. Do you have someplace else you can go?"

Juliane nodded.

As he pulled the last bit of wall separating them away, the firefighter glanced in the direction of his partner. The other man was turned away, still talking on his phone. "Then you'd better get out of here, kid."

Juliane ran out of the pet shop and down the street as fast as her feet would carry her as the sound of additional fire trucks and police cars could be heard arriving on the scene.

THIRTY-SIX

Juliane stared at her reflection in the bathroom mirror as she fought back another wave of panic. A breaking news alert flashed across her vision. It was a report of yet another bombing attributed to the lizard-masked individuals, but in another city, states away.

What was happening out there? She closed her eyes, filling her lungs with slow breaths as she reminded herself that it had been several days since she had found herself in the shop's backroom. No one had come to her door making threats. Maybe the lizard people didn't know who she was after all. She had no reason to keep looking over her shoulder, but they could be anyone.

The Apex advisory board waited for her upstairs. As far as Damien was concerned, business was expected to operate as usual. He'd called for a meeting with the board immediately following the explosion down the street and explained it was their responsibility to show strength in times of uncertainty. They needed to set an example for the masses.

She opened her eyes to examine her outfit for the tenth time. It was pure white, tailored and pressed to perfection. It screamed power. Now all she had to do was master her features so that her expression matched. Today was not the day to appear to be anything but completely in control. Damien had made it clear that she had his backing, but she still needed to convince the rest of the group. Her stomach turned over.

Juliane frowned as she fought the urge to vomit; Sarah and likely Camille would be looking for a reason to reject her proposal out of personal dislike. For the first time, she regretted not attending more of these meetings in person. Then maybe she would have a better sense of who her true allies might be.

She arrived at Damien's tower and proceeded to the sixth floor, where she was the first to enter the hexagonal conference room. Her gaze took in the artwork on the walls. The piece was really quite lovely, whether it was viewed up close or afar. One of these days, she needed to ask Damien who the artist was.

Juliane heard voices in the hallway. Her pulse quickened as she imagined the voices belonged to masked men. She clenched her fists. Her nails bit into her palms as she fought the urge to flee from the room.

Her legs threatened to lock as she pulled out the chair opposite from Damien's usual spot. Once seated, she crossed her ankles, locking her feet behind the chair's rollers as she waited for the rest of the board to file in. The door opened, allowing Durham and Sarah to enter. So distracted by their conversation, neither acknowledged her presence.

"Eithan is exasperated," Sarah pronounced.

"Well, I would think that's an understandable response, all considering," replied Durham.

"It's making him reckless."

Durham shrugged. He stopped in his tracks when he noticed Juliane in the room.

"Miss, I believe you are in the wrong room."

Juliane felt her body begin to relax. As she leaned back into the chair, Durham stuttered. His mouth flapped open and close, yet no sound escaped.

Sarah's eyes narrowed to slits. She stared at Juliane until Juliane thought the glare could bore a hole through her skull. "Juliane?"

Juliane forced a smile. "In the flesh."

"Well that was a neat trick," said Sarah.

Juliane willed her features to remain serene. *What trick? What had they seen? Oh no,* she thought, *the near panic attack.* She must have involuntarily modified her features. How could she explain what she had done without letting Sarah know how easily she had been affected by what was going on miles away? Sarah would make sure someone so jumpy couldn't be trusted with making sound decisions related to Apex resources.

"I thought it would be nice to share what I've learned," Juliane replied. *Nicely done,* she thought.

"Juliane? Here and sharing? The world truly has gone mad." Camille entered the room, standing close to Sarah.

"After you were kind enough to share your youth program with me, I thought it would be rude not to return the favor."

Durham's face also showed an ageless quality, except no one would mistake a person possessing a chin that strong to be anything other than a full-grown adult. He had shaved his head recently, and only pale white stubble broke up the gleam of his scalp. The effect did nothing to help hide a small, round red-gray bruise from the center of his forehead.

She forced her gaze to return to Sarah and Camille. Juliane could not decide if it was only the room's lighting, but it appeared that they too had a similar mark.

"Juliane." Alan had arrived. Juliane had been expecting to see a broken man, or if nothing else, a grieving one. She did not expect the carefree individual who strode into the room. Out of curiosity, Juliane glanced at his forehead but found no shadow mark.

"I truly am sorry for your loss."

"Are you?" Alan purred. "Well, that's small comfort." His stride remained unbroken until he stood directly across from Juliane, his hand caressing the leather of the seatback. "I am glad to see that you were able to join us today. I know I am not alone when I say that the board has missed your presence."

The room was silent. Alan tapped the chair where he stood three times before taking a step back and sitting down one position over. Sarah glanced at Alan with her eyebrows raised as she took the chair immediately to his right. Durham said nothing as he sat at the table a few chairs down from everyone.

Damien had continued recruiting additional team members throughout the years. Their group was now thirteen, in addition to Damien, and the others began filing in, filling seats where there was room. Eventually, the only ones missing were Eithan and Damien himself.

Sarah rose from her seat and placed a finger on a small pad mounted on the wall. A portion of the artwork moved to become a video monitor. It was definitely different to see the room from this side of the screen. Juliane took a deep breath. She could get through this.

"Good afternoon to you all. I am so glad that you were all able to make it today. Eithan and I are not able to join you in person for reasons which will be made evident soon enough." He paused, and several of the others exchanged questioning looks. *It seems that I am not the only one who has secrets for Damien to keep*, she thought.

"As all of you know, many of our firm's efforts have centered on technology to improve the human experience. Juliane is here today to pitch a new energy collection, storage, and disbursement strategy."

Juliane saw several eyebrows rise. She wasn't surprised. The way Damien described it made the project seem a world away from her area of expertise. Only a few years ago, they would have been right.

She could feel the throb of energy coming from the walls as if the room were alive. It felt like the building itself was encouraging her to continue. As Alan leaned forward in her seat, she told herself she had no reason to be afraid—not of the board, or a bunch of psychos running around outside in masks.

Damien's words brought her attention back to the meeting at hand. "Following her presentation, I will be turning the discussion over to Eithan, who has been hard at work cracking the next big advancement in nanorobotics and bioengineering. Juliane, you have the floor."

Juliane rose and began her presentation. Alan watched her every move like a raptor but remained silent throughout the entire proceeding as if he had been given an advance copy of the script. The vote passed without a single voice of dissent. She hadn't needed to worry at all.

Before she regained her seat, memos were sent instructing various outlets to move forward with the balance of land and material acquisition. They had authorized the construction of orbital solar sheets, which would harness the energy and then convert the power into a signal that could be received by the statues' antennas.

Juliane slumped in her chair. Now that it was over, the entire experience felt rather anticlimactic. Even so, she couldn't stop feeling like she should be far away from the room and everyone in it.

The video screen focused on Eithan. The geneticist appeared frazzled and altogether out of sorts, yet triumphant. "As many of you know, my workspace over the last few weeks has been rather . . . fluid." Several of the others in the room chuckled. Juliane frowned in confusion. *Must be an inside joke*, she thought.

Eithan continued after the laughter died down. "However, my primary research location has remained secure, and I am pleased to state that I am ready to begin phase two. I would like to thank those who have already volunteered to act as test subjects; I am honored by your trust."

Eithan paused again to collect his thoughts. Juliane glanced around the room. Sarah seemed to be struggling to keep a smug smile from her face. Durham rubbed the mark on his forehead.

Juliane scanned the rest of the room. At least two of the others shared a pale bruise in the center of their forehead, though she would not have seen it had she not been looking for it. *Was Eithan's work related to the mark?* thought Juliane to herself.

Her attention was drawn back to the video monitor as the camera zoomed out. Damien could be seen in the background leaning against a white and chrome cylinder that had to be at least seven feet long.

Eithan joined Damien. He caressed the metallic surface before turning back to address the board. "We were told by our elders from the time we were children that there are only two certainties in life, death, and taxes. I am here to say that we were lied to. While there is still no easy way to get around taxes, death should consider itself officially on notice."

Juliane realized she had been holding her breath. As she released it, she heard at least one person in the room snort in derision.

"The road ahead will not be painless. Some of us already have firsthand experience." Juliane heard more chuckles. "But there will always be some pain in any worthwhile change."

Juliane looked around for the source of the laughter in time to see Sarah nod her head at Eithan's words.

"Fifty years ago, technology such as cryogenics was relegated to the science fiction bin, and those of us who pursued it were ridiculed out of the scientific community. That is until we discovered nanorobotics."

Juliane took another look at the cylinder on the screen and raised an eyebrow. To her knowledge, those that were researching pseudo-sciences such as cryogenics were still laughed out of any worthwhile positions. Just what was Eithan suggesting?

"Thanks to Camille's research, we have unlocked the ability to rebuild cellular structures. However, that technique is limited by its very nature. She has admitted that all she can do is slow down the natural aging process."

Juliane glanced at Camille, who looked as if she had just tasted something sour. Juliane found herself feeling sorry for the woman. If what Eithan implied was true, Camille's work would wind up being only a footnote in the annals of history rather than the headline it deserved to be.

"I would like to introduce you all to my hard-working assistants."

The video feed switched over to a super magnified image. The nanobots looked similar to cartoon renditions of bombs. Tendrils extended out from their base and could be seen interacting with cellular platelets.

"Nanobots have been around for several decades. Studies in the early twenty-tens found that nanobots could be used to repair muscle damage and made the repaired muscle more resistant to future damage. Researchers took it a step further and began using nanobots to aid in cardiac surgery, effectively dropping the mortality rate for heart disease by a quarter."

Eithan paused again. Juliane suspected that he must be scanning his audience to ensure that everyone followed his presentation. While the science was not her specialty, Juliane was aware of the technology. Likely the rest of the room was too. Shortly before Louis's press conference, the ACI had announced they were going to be using similar bots instead of a virus for the Gene Assist upgrade procedure.

"Now, thanks to Camille's work, we have identified the root of aging within the human body, but her technique is indiscriminate. Cancerous cells will receive the same rejuvenating treatment as healthy cells. My projections show that brain tumors, particularly in men, would become especially difficult to treat if left alone."

If Camille looked any more displeased by the direction of the conversation, laser bolts would begin shooting out of her eyes. Eithan blanched. He must have also noted the expression on Camille's face.

"I am sure you were fully aware of the risk." Camille's lack of interest in promoting her work made a great deal more sense now. She wouldn't want to be known for increasing cancer's strength.

"Why is the risk more pronounced in men than women?" asked John, one of the newer board members.

Eithan smiled, and his shoulders relaxed. "That's due to the shortened Y chromosome in male DNA." Eithan's skin returned to its more natural coloring. "An injection combined with a deployment of nanobots delivered directly into the prefrontal cortex will become critical. This injection will improve a subject's internal ability to differentiate between healthy and unhealthy cells. The nanobots would then be deployed to damaged areas and commanded to either repair good tissue or destroy cancerous cells."

"So, you've cured cancer?" asked Lillian, another board member. Juliane noted that no one was laughing now.

"No, not cure. We may never fully understand the reasons why one cell turns, versus another. What I am saying is that we now have a treatment that does not require chemotherapy, does not place a person's immune system at risk, and is completely effective."

Eithan grinned from ear to ear. Damien stepped up to pat him on the shoulder.

"But what happens when your nanobots run out of power?" asked Lillian. "As you said, the cancer risk will still be there.

What happens when your treatment stops working? Will we all be expected to be jabbed in the forehead every couple of years with a large needle? It looks like some of you are okay with that, but I—for one—am not a fan of needles."

Damien spoke up, "The tube you see behind me should alleviate your concern." Damien gestured for Eithan to continue.

"Yes, of course. Before I learned of Camille's technique, I had been working with the nanobots as a means of inducing a hibernation-like state designed to prevent muscle dystrophy for deep space missions. The tube you see behind me is one of a dozen prototypes. It is designed not only to perform routine body scans, but it also administers replacements as needed. Sarah, Durham, both of you received your injections this way. Would you like to describe the experience?"

Durham spoke up, "I honestly can't. It was nothing like I've ever experienced before. You could feel the pain, but at the same time, there was almost a dreamlike quality to it. Sarah?"

Sarah's eyebrow arched. "I think that it will become an extremely individual experience, just like any other form of treatment. What could be agony for you, could feel like nothing more than a bee sting to me." She continued, "So are you proposing that we advertise this as something like a spa or rejuvenation center?"

Damien laid a finger aside his lips. "That is an interesting proposition, Sarah."

Sarah looked like a child who had just been given the last cookie in front of her siblings.

Camille tilted her head. "I suppose, that would allow us to move forward much more quickly." Sarah's smile deepened. "What do you think Durham? What are the legal risks?"

For a brief moment Durham's eyes tightened, but then he said, "We'd have to be very careful how we market it, but in theory, it could work. But—"

Another board member, Lillian joined in. "If we pull from Juliane's power supply and control this specific nanobot's production, there would be little cost of operation. If we included Camille's treatment as part of the rejuvenating package, we really would control the fountain of youth." She clapped her hands.

"You might not want to start counting those dollars quite so soon," stated Alan. "What if people found out a way to keep the nanobots charged without visiting your so-called fountain? There goes the monopoly."

"It's not like you can just plug yourself into the wall," countered Eithan. "There has to be an active power source."

Alan inched his chair around so that his back was toward the screen. "Oh, I believe Juliane has a workaround for that. Don't you, Juliane? We've shared all our tricks with you. I believe it is now time for you to return the favor."

Juliane pushed back from the desk. Alan knew about Betty's equation. A cold shiver ran up her spine. If that was the case. Why then had Betty gone to such lengths to keep her notes hidden from him? "I am not sure I understand what you are asking."

"Oh, I believe you do." Alan stood and crossed the room over to her. "But you've always been the coy one, haven't you?"

Juliane stood. "I have nothing else to share."

"Oh, Juliane, you wound me. After everything we've meant to each other, everything I've given you freely, you say something like that."

Juliane glanced about the room again. "Perhaps we should take this conversation elsewhere?" she suggested.

"No, Juliane. I am done playing our games. All of our games. Let's be honest with one another. You've always been mine, and I think it is time you paid me my due."

Juliane took a step back. "Yours? Due?" Alan halved the distance. "What are you even talking about?"

"You know very well what I'm talking about."

"No. Frankly, I don't." She raised a hand in defense.

"And now what are you trying to do? Set me on fire like you did that poor Elena woman?"

Juliane gasped before gritting her teeth and hissing out the words. "That was an accident, and you know it."

Alan laughed. "Do I? You once told me quite emphatically that I didn't know your precious boy-toy. You thought then that you knew him better than I did. I hope you've since realized who was right. You keep trying to start over, but you always forget that I know the real you. I've always known you."

Juliane's back touched the wall. Until that moment, she hadn't realized that she had taken additional steps backward. She raised her other hand in an attempt to slow Alan's forward progress. Without a thought, she began to pull on the building's power grid. An electric blue web danced between her fingertips and her thumb.

Alan's eyes flashed like fire. Juliane scanned the room for potential allies. Dull eyes stared back as if they were obvious to the exchange. Except for Sarah. Sarah smiled like a shark. No, there were allies in the room, just not hers.

Alan paused in his approach, although his grin became even more menacing. His brow wrinkled. He raised his hand, mirroring her gesture. The room lights faded as a matching web materialized against his outstretched palm. "And here I was, beginning to worry you weren't going to share after all. Now let me share what I can do."

A series of banging noises followed by the sound of shattered glass from outside the building broke the tension. An office worker ran into the conference room, her arm punctured with a series of small cuts. "Crows! Dozens of them just crashed into the building."

THIRTY-SEVEN

The other board members looked as if they were waking from a dream as they exited the room to view the extent of the damage. Then, only Juliane and Alan remained. The blue glow from the monitor's interrupted signal sharpened the angles of his face.

The light flashed like lightning as the monitor attempted to regain its signal. Juliane glanced behind her as Alan took another step closer. Against the wall, his shadow appeared to have grown wings.

"Crows!" Juliane exclaimed as the memory of her first experience following the Gene Assist upgrade struck her. She covered her mouth. "They aren't just crashing into the building on their own out there. Are they? They're a distraction. They're you. You're controlling them."

Alan shrugged. "Do you realize how crazy you sound?"

"Absolutely," said Juliane. "But it doesn't make it any less true."

Alan threw back his head in laughter. "No, I guess it doesn't. Fine, I'll admit it. Yes, they're mine. Think of them as another side project. Helped me stay up to date better than any news source. I've been using them to keep an eye on you for years, ever since the first upgrade."

"You've been spying on me? Why? We're on the same team." Juliane's forehead knit in confusion as her eyes glanced toward the exit.

"You have to know that I care about you. In the past, you've suffered from poor judgment. I wanted to make sure that you didn't relapse."

"But Betty . . . Stevie . . . You have a family!" Juliane wanted to dismiss Alan's confession as being nothing more than his grief talking. She wanted to, but couldn't.

Alan's grin grew wider. "In any experiment, you never jump straight into trials with subjects who matter. You first start with animal trials to prove your theory and then build up from there. I know that you've been away from academia for a while, but surely you remember that much about the scientific process."

Bile rose in the back of Juliane's throat as Alan took a step closer. "Oh my . . . Betty was right. You did want the virus to mutate. But that means—" She gasped. "You . . . you wanted them dead. Your own family."

"We were never a family," Alan sneered. "We were barely even the same species. Betty was only a means to an end and Stephen proof of concept. However, I will admit, I was pleasantly surprised the boy pulled through. Then again, he does have half of my genes. Maybe there's a use for him after all."

His eyes shone as the monitor flashed again. "I've told you we evolved. Soon, we will be like Gods to people like them, but my son will still need a mother. A mother who I can consider my equal."

The building shook, dropping Juliane and Alan to the floor. "Oof," said Alan. His grin slipped.

Sarah appeared in the doorway. "There was another explosion, this time just down the street." She walked over and helped Alan rise. "All the roads around here are blocked."

"Dammit," muttered Alan. "Their timing—"

"Changes nothing," said Sarah.

Durham ran into the room. His face looked twisted in pain as if he were running with a broken bone. "Juliane, you have to come with me. We have to get out of here. Now!"

Sarah blocked his way. He attempted to push her to the side to get to Juliane, but she remained locked in place. He might as well have attempted to topple the statue in the park. Juliane recalled what Alan had said about some of the Sharks having undergone muscle enhancement surgery. Alan had mentioned he was considering having the surgery as well. It dawned on Juliane that Alan might not have been the only one.

Sarah and Alan exchanged a glance. She placed her hand on Durham's back. A glow surrounded her arm while the lights dimmed again. Durham crumpled to the floor at her feet. "Durham, when you wake up, we will need to have to have a serious discussion about where your loyalties lie," said Alan.

Juliane crawled toward the conference room door. Sarah walked over to Juliane, stepping on her hand while blocking the exit. Juliane couldn't have dislodged Sarah's foot if she tried. To Alan, Sarah said, "I've always said she was beneath you. What more proof do you need?"

Sarah placed her finger to her ear as if receiving a call. The corners of her lips curled up. "He's here." She nudged Juliane with her toe. "Stay down if you know what is good for you."

An icon in the video monitor showed that a connection had been made. The screen then flickered back to an image from the front desk lobby's security camera.

A solitary figure stood in the center of the room. He was tall and muscular, his face covered with a crimson lizard mask. The doors to the building were barred, and the security guards lay slumped in their seats.

The figure tapped his neck three times. The video monitor's speakers protested as the connection was made. "Come out, come out wherever you are . . ." The figure pulled the mask off his face.

"Louis," whispered Juliane.

"How he was ever considered to have leadership potential is beyond me," scoffed Alan. Not looking away from the monitor Alan commanded, "Figure out a way to connect me to downstairs." Sarah nodded. Removing her foot from Juliane's hand she walked over to the wall console and pulled out a small microphone from a hidden cabinet.

"Louis. I had a feeling we hadn't seen the last of you. I've just been informed that there has been some nearby unpleasantness. You wouldn't happen to know anything about that, would you?"

"Just as I am sure you wouldn't know anything about the death of my wife, Alan."

"I'm afraid I don't, but as a recent widower myself, I sympathize with the pain you must be going through."

Juliane knew she should run while Alan was distracted, but at the same time, she wanted to slap the condescending look off his face. The hand that had been damaged under Sarah's foot throbbed. Juliane pulled herself upright, tightening her muscles in advance. An electric blue light flickered in her vision.

"Tsk, tsk, Juliane. You don't want to give me a reason," gloated Sarah. The electricity danced across the length of her arm as static played across the video monitor.

"Trouble in the ranks?" asked Louis.

"Nothing I can't handle," replied Alan.

"Louis, call for help. Alan has gone insane," Juliane shouted.

"I'm afraid that's not an option, my dear," chuckled Alan. "Haven't you realized? Louis is one of the terrorists. Possession of that mask alone would put him away for a very, very long time."

"I've joined the liberators. It is people like you who are the real threat."

Alan's eyes rolled. "Please don't pretend that you are any better than the rest of us. Your company funded most of everything you are now so intent on destroying."

"Which is why I am taking responsibility for cleaning up my mess now."

"Just like you are taking responsibility by blaming me for your wife's death," Alan sneered. "You are just like your father. It's never your family's fault."

"You did something to me that night. I felt you in my head."

"You were roaring drunk. You carelessly got behind the wheel and over-corrected into oncoming traffic."

Juliane felt a chill move up her spine at Louis's accusation. Alan wasn't denying he did something to Louis. She felt pressure build behind her eyes. Her peripheral vision began to darken. *No*, she thought, *I can't pass out now*. She suddenly had the urge to focus on anything other than the scene unfolding before her. She stared at the artwork on the walls as if she could anchor her awareness.

Her thoughts floated to the first time she had seen the artwork and Damien's serenity fountain. What had he said that day? Something about taking a step back. She really did need to ask Damien about the artist one day. The pressure eased as Juliane's breath calmed. Her eyes traced one of the patterns on the wall. It looked so different from this vantage point. Sleep would be nice. Juliane frowned. Why am *I on the floor?* she wondered.

Sarah snorted at something Alan said. Juliane blinked, and the memory of the last several minutes came back. *I am on the floor because everyone around me has lost their minds.* Her stomach tightened. How could she have forgotten any second of the last few minutes?

She felt the pressure increase once again. It was sharp and cutting. Juliane tasted blood. She's bitten her tongue. She closed her eyes and focused on the pain, willing it back. It felt as if hooks were latching onto her psyche, each attached to alien tendrils of thought that crept and probed her mind like ivy exploiting the cracks of a wall.

Betty must have felt something similar at the hospital when she forced the private connection. Something . . . no, *someone* was trying to manipulate her, just like he had with the crows outside. Juliane's eyes narrowed at Alan. His skin looked paler than it had a moment before.

She wouldn't make it easy for him. Juliane closed her eyes. She issued commands to her processors, isolating each unwelcome data strand. She issued another command, and the data strands were corrupted like ivy taking fire. All except one. The last strand felt different than the others. It pulsated with sorrow and confusion, yet there was wonder in it too.

As she focused on the strand, it widened, filling in the cracks and strengthening her psyche's wall. Suddenly, Juliane understood the reason Stevie survived. The pressure behind her eyes shattered as tears cascaded down her cheeks.

Juliane looked at Alan and saw that he had turned from the screen and now watched her. He deepened his smile as if he could read her thoughts and found them amusing.

Not taking his eyes off her, he responded to Louis. "I believe you've made the mistake of believing we are lacking defenses here."

Nothing happened at first. Then, Juliane saw Louis drop to the floor on his knees.

"What did you do to him?" she demanded.

"I've just exposed him to a blast of high-frequency noise, used effectively in crowd control for years. Don't worry. It will daze him for a bit, but I haven't done anything permanent. Yet."

Sarah chuckled as she and Alan shared a smile. As soon as they returned their attention to Louis and the monitor, Juliane mentally isolated Alan's and Sarah's bioelectric auras. She twisted the signals so that light would appear to pass around her as if she wasn't present in the room like she had done in the wrecked shop.

She had to move quickly but silently to get past them. She sprinted toward the door on tiptoes and down the hall. Juliane caught a sigh of relief from giving away her position as she spotted an open elevator door. She raced inside and commanded the vessel down toward the lobby floor.

THIRTY-EIGHT

Louis was still kneeling on the marble floor when the elevator doors opened. He held his head in his hands as his body shuddered.

Juliane knew at once than Alan had brought Louis to his knees with more than a blast of noise. She could feel his anguish as clearly as if she had never cut the connection between them. Waves of hurt and want crashed against her with each step overpowering her senses.

Juliane slowed her approach, worried that she might startle him like a wild animal. "Louis?" she whispered.

Louis bolted upright. He shouted something unintelligible, causing Juliane to halt in mid-stride. "Elena?" he asked, taking a step toward her.

Juliane looked behind her but saw no one.

"My golden goddess, I've missed you so much." He reached out, eyes shining.

Juliane took a step backward. "I have to get you out of here."

"No, don't go!" Louis rushed toward her, closing the remaining distance. His next words were indecipherable as he crushed her body against his in a fierce embrace and began to nuzzle her neck. Juliane briefly wondered if his mind had shattered, but as his arms tightened around her, she found she didn't care.

Her body relaxed, accepting his caresses. Louis immediately responded, his hands becoming much more demanding. He forced her face upward, meeting her lips with his own with a possessive fury. He pushed aside a lock of blonde hair for better access.

Blonde? She twisted in his arms. Louis pulled her closer. The heat from his lips on hers could have caused the sun to blister.

Alan's voice over the speaker was a slap to reality. "And here I thought that you were mourning."

Right. Get it together, thought Juliane. They had to get away.

"I was almost feeling sorry for you, but I see now that I shouldn't have wasted the energy. You seem all too eager to move on."

Juliane felt her cheeks burn as Louis snapped back to full attention.

"I wish I could say I was surprised," Alan continued, "but I'm disappointed all the same. While you still have good taste"—Alan paused—"I must regretfully inform you that Juliane is no longer on the market."

Louis looked into her eyes and pulled away as if scalded. He didn't need to say anything for her to know her hair was once again black as night.

"You bitch. What did you make me do?" he said. "Oh, Elena, I am so sorry," he cried.

"Nothing. I did nothing." Her eyes widened. "I didn't . . . that wasn't . . . I was only trying to get us out of here. I didn't mean for that to happen." Juliane willed Louis to understand.

"You always hated her. Everyone knew it." His nostrils flared. "You wanted her dead, and now you think you can just take her place. You disgust me."

"It's not like that. I mean I never meant . . . I would never—"

"Enough. It's not like I would believe a single word out of your mouth," Louis interrupted.

Juliane's skin, flushed by the combination of adrenaline and desire, pimpled as if his words caused a physical drop in the temperature of the room. Her eyes widened in confusion.

"I know all about what you've done. After killing hundreds, do you honestly think I would believe you incapable of killing one more just because you know how to bat your eyelashes?" His lips, still roughened from their encounter, curled back and showed his teeth. "I've seen you turn on the charm when it helps you get what you want."

"No! It's not that!" Juliane glanced toward the barred door and back toward the elevator. Louis locked his hand around her wrist.

"I heard the rumors before, but I never wanted to believe them. I was so blind then, but I see everything perfectly now."

"Let me go! You're hurting me!" Juliane twisted in his grip.

"At least you aren't trying to deny it anymore."

"Deny what?" she exclaimed.

"I am talking about the night you and Dr. Dronigh murdered my wife. I'm talking about that factory and all those people you had executed. Or have you killed so often the events all blend together?"

She finally escaped his grasp and darted backward, massaging the blood back into her hand.

"I had nothing to do with either of those things."

"Ah, that may not be an entirely accurate statement, my dear," interrupted Alan over the speaker. "I'll make a deal with both of you," Alan's voice echoed in the lobby. "Join me on the basement level, and I'll do my best to clear this whole business up in person. I'd come up there, but I don't exactly trust the company either of you've been keeping lately.

Juliane looked longingly at the exits. A storm crossed Louis's features.

"Afterward, I'll even turn myself in to the authorities for whatever transgressions I may be responsible for," Alan continued, "but you'll need to bring Juliane along to pass the elevator's biometric security."

Juliane looked into Louis's eyes as her vision blurred behind a well of tears.

"Louis, don't listen to him. We can still walk away. We just go out those doors and pretend none of this ever happened."

Louis glanced toward the entrance. It could have been made of stone for all the light that was able to pass through its doors. Faint sirens could be heard in the distance.

Juliane's wrist throbbed as Louis relaxed his grip. If she could only get him away from the immediate danger, she would explain the severed network and how it must have affected him. It might take him a while to forgive her for the accidental impersonation, but at least they would be safe. "I have so much to tell you. You want to make the world a better place? We can do it"—she reached toward him—"together."

"You have a deal, Alan." Louis's iron grip shackled her wrist again, and he dragged Juliane back toward the elevator shaft.

THIRTY-NINE

The elevator closed behind them. Louis released her wrist with such force that Juliane's back slammed into the wall. At her grunt, Louis shot her a look of such disdain, further words died on her tongue.

Juliane had never had reason to visit the lowest levels of the Apex building before. The space was filled with a raised platform and a series of thick cables and insulated piping.

Damien and Eithan stood on the platform in front of the white and chrome tube. The video feed upstairs had only captured the single tube, but in this larger space, Juliane saw that there were several identical components scattered around the dais.

Conference chairs had been positioned on the ground level and were filled with the various board members, who must have made their way down during her unsuccessful escape attempt. Durham was among them. He was seated upright, his eyes glazed and unseeing, and flanked by Alan and Sarah. Juliane overheard Sarah tell Camille, "It was lucky we found him when we did. Something must have hit him during the initial panic."

Juliane rushed over to the stage's edge in front of Damien. She tried to keep panic from flavoring her voice as she gestured for him to come closer. "Alan's gone mad," she whispered. Her eyes darted to Sarah and then to Louis. "The whole world has. You have to get everyone out of here before something happens."

Damien leaned down and whispered back, "Louis might have disrupted the video, but Eithan and I were able to hear everything upstairs. The situation will be under control in no time. Just don't make any more sudden moves, and let this next part play itself out. We'll be okay."

Alan gestured to the other board members. "Why don't you share with the group? You've got yourself a captive audience."

"We had a deal, Alan," Louis said with the monotone voice of a man defeated.

"That we did, and I am more than happy to complete my part, but why don't we first allow Eithan to finish the presentation you so rudely interrupted?"

Juliane glanced back toward the elevator door. Sarah sneered at her; blue-white light danced along her arm as she brought a single finger up to her lips.

Eithan turned toward Damien, who shrugged and nodded toward the seated board.

"Er . . . Ah, well, yes, um, where was I?"

"You were in the process of telling us all about how you've found a way for us all to live forever," Sarah said as she examined the nails on one hand.

"Right. Well, yes, I mean in theory. I still have some work to do, but it is promising."

"And you need more volunteers for the next round of testing," suggested Sarah.

"Precisely." Eithan seemed much more at ease. Juliane glanced about. Everyone did. *How could they possibly think this was business as usual?* It was like watching drones.

"Assuming you are released for additional human testing," supplied Camille.

"Of course," Eithan responded.

"Isn't that going to be somewhat of a more difficult problem for you now?" Sarah asked.

Snippets of forgotten conversation flashed in Juliane's memory like puzzle pieces. Juliane suddenly recalled the scratches on the floor in the room behind the wrecked electronics and pet boutique. "That was your lab. The one that was bombed," stated Juliane.

"You and Damien keep saying how smart that woman is, yet she is always the last to figure anything out," laughed Sarah to a scowling Alan.

The smile slipped from Eithan's face. "Yes, yes it was. It was one of a few sites. Luckily, I caught wind of a rumor that activists were targeting my work. I was able to get most of the critical projects out of harm's way, but even so, I have had to deal with significant setbacks." Eithan glared at Louis. "All thanks to you I presume."

Louis shrugged. "You were trying to play God. There were bound to be consequences." Eithan's eyes bulged, and he scurried toward the steps, only to be held back by Damien.

"You aren't above the law, Evans," said Eithan.

"Nor are you." Louis scanned the room, resting his gaze on Alan. "Nor is anyone in this room. I've had enough. Tell me why I came down here."

"Whatever you say." Alan laughed. "Where to begin, where to begin?" Alan said in a singsong voice. "You may want to have a seat." Alan gestured toward an available chair. Sarah rolled it over, forcing her down into the cushion.

"I guess we should start back on the day of our first upgrade. You probably remember it as the day you and Juliane first . . . blacked out.

"I remember that day somewhat differently. Shortly after the procedure, Juliane here started mumbling about connecting with a bird, and the next thing we knew she was running out of the office talking about flying."

Juliane's cheeks heated. She couldn't help remembering that initial disorientation combined with an exhilarating sense of freedom.

"Luckily, I was able to catch her and bring her back to the lab just before she was about to attack a random passerby."

Alan began to pace around the room, before stopping to address Juliane directly. "I'll admit it. I began to worry. I grabbed you in a last-ditch effort to capture your attention, and you were back, only you didn't seem to have any awareness of what you had just done. I realized later that when I reached for you, I did so with more than just my hands. I could sense your mind working. I could feel what you felt. I tried to pull back but was afraid I would only do more damage. Until that moment, I had no idea how fragile you were back then. You were desperate to connect with anything or anyone. But I also understood that I had seen only a fraction of your potential. You just needed a gentle hand to guide you."

Juliane didn't know what to make of Alan's words. He had to be lying. She would never have lost control like that. She certainly wouldn't have forgotten about it. It just wasn't possible. *Or was it?*

"I worried that you might break if you knew what I had done. All that potential might be wasted, so I figured out how to wipe the memory away." He swiped his hand in the air.

"Actually, it was surprisingly easy to do. Your subconscious must have wanted the memories gone as much as I did." He shook his head. "I knew then what I had previously only suspected. We were destined to be together." Alan grinned, reaching out his hand.

"I could have claimed you then," he said, dropping his arm back to his side. "Perhaps I should have, but other experiments needed my attention."

"And the fact that I was with Louis at the time wasn't at all an issue," said Juliane.

"Of course, it wasn't." Alan gestured toward Louis. "He never saw you as anything more than a casual distraction. Everyone could see that." He sniffed.

"Louis loved me," Juliane responded.

"You keep saying that, but did you ever hear those words from Louis? Even once? Did you ever ask his friends what he said to them about you?" Alan swung his arm toward Durham. "Because I did." Durham seemed to be frozen in place, oblivious to the exchange. A bead of drool began to descend from the corner of his mouth.

Juliane glanced at Louis. *Alan's a liar,* she wanted to scream. *It hadn't been like that.*

Louis remained silent. Sarah threw back her head and cackled. Juliane wished she could blast them all away. A machine hummed over in the corner of the room, and she felt a surge of energy.

"You've still not been able to get a hold of that temper of yours, have you Juliane. Sarah? Would you mind?"

Sarah walked over to the machine, which had to be a generator of some sort, and punched a button. The humming ceased, and Juliane felt her energy drain from her body as if her body were a sieve.

Juliane felt sickened to her stomach. The person prancing about the room was some twisted caricature of her former colleague. It had to be the madness Camille warned them about. She attempted to meet Damien's gaze; whatever Damien was planning, she wished he would get on with it.

"Where were we?" Alan glanced at Sarah, who rolled her eyes. "Ah, yes. The factory." Alan strolled over to Juliane.

Juliane felt her blood crystallize. Her brain ached trying to follow the conversation. All she wanted was to leave this room and continue the work that had been so promising an hour ago. She looked longingly toward the elevator door.

The humor left Alan's voice. "For this next part, Juliane, I am sorry. Truly I am. I preferred you never knew."

He left her side, returning to the center of the room. "As many of you know, Juliane here chose to set up her center of operations in a region of the world that had less than ideal working conditions." He paused, and several of the other board members bobbed their heads like marionettes.

"Recently, she was notified of the tragic ending of a simple line worker. A day after this tragic event, she came to me looking for a confidant. A shoulder to cry on." Alan paused.

Juliane imagined that she possessed a quiver of poisoned darts. *That wasn't how it happened. Wasn't what I did. How could anyone believe any of this?* The panic she felt earlier paled against her desire to find a way to remove that smug expression from his face.

"There had been other messes, but this one felt different."

Juliane fantasized about tying Alan to a post and burying him in the ground up to his neck only after dribbling honey all over his body.

"It didn't take much convincing on her part before we were booked on the next flight out." Juliane glanced toward the door. Death by ants was not nearly enough for a liar like him. Perhaps she would need to slice him up with a million paper cuts and then dose him with a spray of lemon juice.

"I arrived at dawn and met with the inspection committee. I originally had signed on for the trip, only in the role of a concerned friend, but within the first few minutes, it became clear that Juliane was not going to be satisfied with a few signatures on a report. She had made it clear that heads should roll."

Juliane decided that being eaten alive by ants was too easy. No, Alan needed to truly wish for death before she was done with him. Perhaps it would be better to tie him to a post and remove each lung individually like the Vikings had done centuries before.

"As I was in discussions with the welcoming committee, I caught sight of a man scribbling on a notepad. I knew what would happen if the story got out, but I must not have been the only one to notice. Another team showed up. I assumed they were third-party inspectors. They told me to wait outside while they took care of the matter per Juliane's wishes."

Even though Alan was twisting events, his words cut close to her darkest fear. Could the threats she made in the virtual world actually be the cause behind the massacre at the factory? The audio from the recording came tumbling back in her mind.

"Oh, please God! Help me! There are bodies everywhere. Help me! Please!" She listened again to the popping sound in between the whispers. " . . . to find me. You've got to do something. I can hear"—more pops and screams—"getting closer! Do something! Do something! Oh God! No!"

When she had listened to it the first time, she had thought the sounds of the screams would be permanently lodged in her brain. Could it be possible that she was in some way responsible for pulling the trigger?

No, Alan had to still be lying about everything. The Viking death would be too quick. The Persians had it right. She would lock him in a box and cover him with a combination of milk and honey. Flies would then visit, depositing their eggs. The larvae would then begin to devour him days later.

"An hour later, they brought me down to the factory floor. Her entire staff was there, and the people with me opened fire on them. It only took a few seconds to decimate the first rows. What could I do?" Alan shrugged.

"It was one of those moments where you have to decide whether you want to do the wrong thing and live or the right thing and die. I'll have to live with my decision for the remainder of life, but up until today, thanks to my kindness, Juliane wasn't going to have to."

"Enough," shouted Juliane. "Tell me you're lying. You've got to be lying. I wasn't there. I never left the office. You're making it all up. The fire at the factory was an accident. It had to be just a terrible accident."

"An accident. Just like when the generator exploded and just happened to burn Louis's wife and only Louis's wife." Alan shrugged. "I am not surprised that you don't want to accept these events, but it doesn't make them any less true. Look up your travel records. You'll see a ticket."

Juliane glanced around the room for support and once again found none. Those in chairs nervously fidgeted as if afraid to make eye contact. Hating herself for listening, she pulled up her calendar. There, mixed in with other meeting notes and attachments was a printed flight confirmation with her name on it. "That doesn't prove I was there with you."

Juliane turned toward Louis. He recoiled. She pulled her hand back instantly. "You can't possibly believe him." Juliane reduced her voice to a whisper. "You know me. You know I'm not capable of something like that. Anything like that."

Louis met her gaze. "When we first met, nothing was going to stand in your way. Why should I think that you would be any different now?"

"But he's describing a brutal massacre of hundreds," she shouted.

"Hundreds that you probably considered beneath your notice, or worse, a threat to the idea of your legacy." Louis's eyes tightened. "I've seen firsthand how you respond to those who threaten you."

Juliane stared into his eyes, urging him to take back his words. Instead, Louis turned toward Alan, showing her his back.

Alan laughed. "So, Juliane, still convinced you two were meant to be together?"

"It doesn't matter what she thinks," Louis said. "None of this does." A small beeping sound emitted from Louis's pocket. He smiled as he unfastened the buttons of his shirt. A large belt fitted with wires was exposed as he pulled back one side of the garment. Louis pulled another device from his pocket and held it out for everyone to see.

"It seems your time is up, Alan," Louis said with a smile. "That sound tells me that my associates have now placed devices similar to the one I am wearing near key structural positions throughout the building. I will only have to press this button to bring this entire building down."

Louis nodded toward the other members of the board who were looking around as if wondering how they had gotten into the room. "I wasn't originally going to target all of you, at least not at the same time, but when Alan invited me down here, it was just too tempting of an offer. However, I am not the monster some of your associates are. I'm willing to make a deal. If Alan tells me what happened the night of Elena's death to my satisfaction, I'll give the rest of you a sporting chance at survival."

"Tell him what he wants to know!" screeched Camille. She ran up to Alan, pulling him by his sleeve.

As if Camille can force Alan to do anything he doesn't already want to do, Juliane thought. Camille would have had more luck convincing a shark that tofu was the better option for dinner.

Others in the room began pressing their backs against their chairs as if a few inches of distance could help save them. Juliane's stomach twisted. Damien, however, remained on the dais, looking as confident as he had from the time she entered the room. "Anytime you want to take charge, Damien," she muttered.

Juliane glanced at Alan. Alan appeared to be leaning toward Louis and the device. The smile plastered on his face was one of satisfaction, not madness. Alan wasn't acting surprised. He met her gaze, and his smile deepened. No, if anything, Alan had anticipated this development. For all she knew, he had orchestrated all the events leading up to this moment. But why? Why would he want to put them all in a position to be blown to bits?

Sarah equally looked nonplussed, although paler than usual. She must have had some inclination of what could potentially occur today.

"Now, Alan, I've been more than patient with you. Tell me what I want to know . . . now."

"First, send Juliane over. She's proven to have more than a few tricks up her sleeves, and I would hate for her to miss the rest of the show."

"You two really were made for each other." The disgust rolling off Louis's tongue was palpable. "You want her so badly even after all you say she's done? Fine. She's yours." Louis shoved Juliane painfully toward Alan's outstretched arms.

Alan whispered into her ear as he claimed her abused wrist, "You have always been mine."

FORTY

"Now that is settled, where were we? Oh yes, you want to know about the night of your unfortunate accident." He nodded to Sarah, who proceeded to adjust the controls on the video monitor. "You've already been told what happened, but as they say, a picture is worth a thousand words."

Still pulling painfully on Juliane's wrist, he dragged them both over to an open chair and forced her down into its seat.

"You should know that Damien is very invested in the Sharks organization and takes the security and safety of his players extremely seriously. And, like any responsible owner, he had positioned several security cameras throughout the facility. Some of these cameras are fairly obvious, and that public footage he freely shared with the police. However, other cameras are more innocuous."

Alan paused as the image on the screen transitioned to a playback. The time and date stamp were visible to all. Louis and Elena could be seen sashaying down the corridor, their arms interlocked. Louis stumbled and Elena pulled him back upright. Louis could be seen throwing his head back in laughter as the two stumbled out of the camera's field of vision.

"Just what are you trying to prove with these? I freely admit that I was at the game and that I had enjoyed myself, but I know how to pace myself otherwise everyone would have heard a different story when the toxicology report was published."

The video flashed, and the time stamp showed the image to be only a few minutes from the first scene. This time, Louis and Elena were one of the several couples loitering in the concession lobby. It had to be halftime and the moment of their confrontation. Juliane had no sooner placed the scene when the crowds parted and she could see Alan and herself.

There was no sound, but their body language spoke volumes. A security guard entered the shot several feet away. Juliane hadn't realized that their conversation had been noticed, but it must have raised at least one person's concern.

Juliane watched as Louis fell on her with Alan pushing him back toward Elena. It was just a moment, but in that moment, Alan's body flickered and the video feed was temporarily disrupted by static. Louis and Elena were already on their way when the static cleared.

There was something different about Louis though. His steps, as they moved back toward the concession line, were straight and sure. Elena, on the other hand, appeared even more intoxicated. It was Louis's turn to provide additional support.

"Are you going to tell me that you didn't do something to me just then?" demanded Louis.

"Absolutely not," scoffed Alan.

"I fired you and you wanted revenge. But it didn't go as planned, did it? I survived your little trick."

Alan roared with laughter. "Oh, Louis, you have such an inflated sense of self-importance."

Louis growled, "I don't see the humor."

"No?" Alan rubbed his hand over his mouth. "Of course, you don't." The smile was replaced with bored indifference.

"Then let me explain this in a way you would understand. For me to worry about outdoing a rival, I would first have to recognize that an equal is in some way threatening my position. I have never been threatened by you. If I was, would I have ever agreed to upgrade you on that first day?"

"You expected the process would kill me."

"I accepted that outcome and I did reassess my opinion of you that day. Even so, I still didn't view you as an equal or a true rival. You are as much of a rival to me as a sparrow hawk is to an eagle. Sure, they might both be at times interested in the same meat, but only the eagle has the strength and stamina to bring the larger game home."

Louis's skin erupted into a sea of red. "So, you were targeting my wife. What did Juliane do? Beg you to finish what she started in the lab? I can guess what she promised you in return." Louis leered at Juliane.

Juliane reminded herself how terrible the loss of the private connection could be. Louis was only lashing out because he didn't know how to control its loss. She wasn't his enemy, and if he would just calm down enough to see that, they could still walk out of this room. No one had to get hurt.

"Between you and me, you aren't getting the better end of the bargain," continued Louis. "I've had better."

Durham made a choking sound. A valve located behind Sarah blew, hurtling a piece of plastic into the room. Sarah called out as she was struck in the side.

A hiss of steam escaped while backup controls on the equipment powered into their fail-safe mode. Juliane wished she could similarly lash out. Juliane felt her skin tingle and realized that she had called forth another electric web across her palms.

"I don't think that is a good idea, my dear," noted Alan. "The man is outfitted in an explosive belt. As much as I've always loved that brain of yours, I have no wish to see it on the outside."

Juliane flicked her fingers and the web was dispelled.

"That's better." Returning his attention to Louis, Alan continued.

"You still have it wrong. Neither Juliane nor I ever plotted against your precious wife. Elena had already ensured herself a lifetime of suffering when she married you. Why should I harbor her any further ill will?"

"Then what exactly did you do? Answer me honestly, and I will leave this room, taking my vest and the detonator with me."

"I know you would like to believe otherwise, but I'm really not a terrible person. You had too much to drink that day. All I did was introduce a program that would redirect the existing alcohol in your bloodstream so that you didn't make a complete fool of yourself. It is that simple."

"You didn't want me to be drunk?" Louis sounded incredulous. Juliane had to agree with his assessment.

"Seeing you in the news, happy, sad, or otherwise distracts Juliane, and I want her focused. The way you were acting was going to get you noticed by the gossip channels, which could then undo weeks of progress. That could be all the reason I needed, or maybe I did it just to prove I could. You should know now that I enjoy experimenting. In either case, there was nothing nefarious behind my motivation.

"But you interpreted my gift as a challenge. Rather than slowing down, you eventually outpaced my program. You passed out while driving, and we all know where you were when you woke up. Only by then, my program had caught up and the alcohol was out of your bloodstream. There. Mystery solved."

"You, Louis, you are the sole cause of your wife's death. Shake your fist at technology all you want, but technology could have actually saved her. She's gone because of your irresponsibility, and no amount of exploding labs or war against technology will bring her back."

The red sheen of Louis's face had faded and only the color of gray ash remained. He looked down toward his belt and scanned the room. With meticulous care, he casually covered the belt with his shirt and returned the detonator to his pocket.

Louis's shoulders dropped, and he suddenly looked as if he had aged twenty years as he turned toward the board members. "I made a deal. Truth for a sporting chance. If I am not in the room with you when the explosives detonate, then you will still have a chance to make your way back to the surface."

Louis turned and made his way back toward the elevator shaft. Juliane struggled to run after him, but her wrist was still held in a manacle-like grip.

"Louis! Please! You don't have to do this," Juliane called out.

Louis turned as he reached the doors. His eyes met hers, and in that brief moment, she saw all that might have been drown under an infinite sea of regret and sadness.

FORTY-ONE

"So now what?" asked Sarah.

"We wait," replied Alan.

"What? Down here? Did you not hear Louis say that several bombs are going to go off any minute?"

"There's no safer spot to be. Why do you think I worked so hard to get us all down here?"

"I understand why you and I are here, but why did you invite *him* down here too? I thought the plan was to drive Louis to those anti-tech serpentine nut jobs and make a few billion as the ACI tanks. Personally, I—for one—would prefer not to be blown to bits before I can spend my fortune."

"Juliane needed to hear the truth. And you heard Louis; we won't be blown to bits down here. We have a sporting chance."

"Being buried alive isn't high on my to-do list either. Why put us at risk?" Sarah asked.

"Were you not paying attention?"

"To what, you professing your undying love for Juliane? Oh yes, that was made perfectly clear."

Alan snorted. "To the presentations today."

"What about them?"

"We are in a room filled with several personal cryogenic chambers suitable for space missions. There are enough for all of us. All we have to do now is take a nap. It's that simple."

"We don't know that Eithan's little toys work."

"They work," stated Eithan.

"You see. Nothing to worry about. Now, how about you pick out which one would suit you first? I don't imagine our friends upstairs will allow us too much more time to argue."

Sarah glanced toward the elevator doors with longing in her eyes.

"An elevator is probably not where you want to be when the explosion begins."

Her forehead creased while she considered his words. She rubbed the darkened spot in its center before shrugging and ascending the dais. She traced her fingers along the length of the canister before stepping in. Others began following her cue. Alan stepped into a cylinder as the lights flickered. A sound like thunder could be heard above. Alan blew her a kiss as his lid closed and the LED showed the device activating. Soon, only Damien—who had assisted placing a still vegetative Durham into a tube—and Juliane were left.

The ground began to shake as additional devices were detonated above. Bits of ceiling tile began to drop like autumn leaves. Damien placed his hand on the side panel of one of the last cylinders. "There isn't much time, Juliane."

"You said you had everything under control," she said.

"And it is," said Damien, extending his hand.

Juliane took one last look at the elevator door before accepting his hand and climbing into the tube. Damien's hands flew across the control panel. Within seconds, her toes and fingertips were numb. Damien glanced down at her and smiled, like a father easing his child into bed. "It's just a short nap. Everything will be exactly as it should when you wake up."

"But what about you?" she asked.

"You don't need to worry about me. I've taken care of everything."

Juliane could no longer feel her legs beyond her knees. Her arms were reduced to icy weights pulling her body down, but at the same time, she felt as if she were floating. Everything seemed to slow down around her. More debris came tumbling down, but to Juliane, it moved like a bubble in the breeze.

She found herself thinking of Alan's explanation for the events at the factory. The pieces simply did not fit. She accepted that her memory might have been manipulated, but she hadn't been there. She knew it to her bones.

She couldn't care what the others thought of her, but couldn't bear that Damien might view her as being less than she knew she was. "Damien, you don't believe that I ordered all those people dead, do you?"

Damien smiled and stroked her cheek with a finger like a father would a daughter as the dais swayed. "I know you didn't."

Juliane sighed. She felt an icy chill up her spine as more of her body was put to sleep. A thought entered into her mind like a pebble in a shoe. "But how?" she asked.

"How?"

"How do you know?"

Damien smiled. "I know because I was the one who gave that order."

Juliane felt tendrils of fog enter her thoughts. Something Damien had just said was wrong. Very wrong. She felt she should be shocked right now. She felt she should be pulling away from his touch, but she could no longer move her head.

"Why?" she whispered.

"The factory had served its purpose. Loose ends had to be eliminated."

She mumbled a sound, her mouth no longer functioning.

"Shh. Remember it's always easiest if you don't fight these things. I am truly sorry that you had to go through all that, but Louis showed up too early. I told Alan I needed him to cause a delay."

He sighed. "It made it so much easier to convince you all to enter the tubes willingly. However, I am surprised you accepted Alan's story so readily. I had thought that you, compared to all the others, would be least likely to doubt yourself. But it is for the best. As it was once said, 'It's okay for people to respect you, but when they fear you, you know you have the power.' And you, my dear, wear power so beautifully."

The tiny grain of Juliane still awake wanted to scream and run away, but neither option was available. Damien returned his attention to the side panel. The sound of gas escaping could be heard as a glass screen began to inch over her face. Even covered, she could still make out Damien's words thundering in between crashes of destruction.

"Sometimes the only way to save something is to break it down to its foundation and rebuild; give it a fresh start. I believe that's a concept you are familiar with. It has become clear to me for some time that humanity was on a collision course with self-destruction."

Damien's tapped the edge of the tank. "Alan's a purest. He believes that the future of the world should be decided purely by the survival of the fittest. His belief might be a tad extreme, but that doesn't mean he is entirely wrong. We accelerated the process while there was still hope for our future. I chose each of you for a very special reason. You each represent the best minds in your respective fields. When you wake up, you will be like Gods to the children left behind."

His hand brushed errant hair away from her forehead. "And there will be children left behind, thanks to you. We will be able to make real the vision of the future we all share. And I will be there to guide you all along the way."

The lights in the room flashed as fixtures fell from the ceiling. The dais shook as if the earth was readying itself to swallow them whole. Damien could no longer be seen. Juliane was now completely sealed within the cryogenic unit. The lights flashed one more time before only a few emergency lights remained.

Juliane hung onto consciousness by a fingernail. Everyone around her had gone mad. Louis, Alan, and now Damien. Betty hadn't been paranoid. Rather, she had been the only sane person in Juliane's life. Damien was wrong. He hadn't recruited all the best minds. He hadn't recruited Betty.

She heard another sound whirling within her tube and saw a mechanical arm extend out over her forehead. The motion of a mechanical finger descending brought her consciousness back to the forefront. Juliane suddenly remembered Eithan's nanobots. They were supposed to be beneficial, but could she trust anything produced by Damien's group? Alan had done enough damage from hacking her mind. Could she risk her body being hacked as well? She willed her body to move. This time, her will wasn't enough. Her body betrayed her, remaining stationary in the cylinder's cradle.

The pain as the needle penetrated her skin was like nothing she had ever imagined. Her eyes burned, but tears would not form and no sounds escaped her throat.

She had to find the strength to reject the nanobots just as she had once instructed Betty to do during the test in the emulator. By now, thousands of the tiny machines must be navigating her bloodstream. Her thoughts grew cloudy and more difficult to form. She was powerless to fight their onslaught.

Then, there was nothing. No pain, no worries, and no heartache. Each of her senses departed, and Juliane's consciousness was left floating like a disembodied presence expanding into the vacuum of space.

"I'm so sorry," Betty's voice whispered. A photograph of a smiling child briefly came into focus. Powerless. An equation. Out of time.

"Coffee?" asked Chad. Energy. Fountain of Youth. Hope.

Light. A web of light shone through the darkness. Her mind instinctively floated closer. Feelings of warmth, innocence, and stubborn determination—the emotions of a child—wrapped around her consciousness like a net, preventing her mind from drifting further into the nothing. *Thank you, Betty. I'll try to be worthy.* She clung to the net's webbing and pulled from its strength just enough to solidify her thoughts. She was not powerless, but she could ensure the nanobots were.

Juliane summoned the will for one last command, pulling energy from the machines. It wouldn't be enough to halt the cryogenic process, but she hoped her mind would be her own when she woke. Because if it was, this time, she wouldn't start over; she'd finish what she started.

End of Book One: The Fair & Foul
The experiment continues in
Project Gene Assist Book 2: The Watch & Wand

THE WATCH & WAND — SNEAK PREVIEW

Stephen removed his headset and held the power button until the whirl of the computer's fan confirmed complete system shutdown. Why he bothered escaped him. The machine would have powered itself down in another two minutes, but it was just one of those things he had gotten into the habit of doing. Once off, he closed the screen and hid the device beneath a loose board in the barn floor.

He rustled the crease in his hair from the headset before stepping out of the barn. The windmill a few yards away caught his gaze. Its propellers remained stationary even though a gust of a fall wind caused Stephen to shiver. He zipped up his cotton jacket.

"Generator's out again, Ed," Stephen announced, entering the farmhouse on the other side of a dirt and gravel path connecting the two buildings. A slew of screws, nuts, and metal plates littered the kitchen table. "But it looks like you already knew that."

His adoptive father, Ed Thomas, appeared from the other room. A cream and brown cloth wrapped around his left hand highlighted the swath of dark freckles running up the rest of his arm.

"What happened?" Stephen asked.

"I think squirrels must have gotten into it. Again."

"No. I meant to your hand." Stephen said, pointing.

"Oh. That. Driver slipped." Ed gestured at the offending tool on the table. As he did so, Stephen noticed a red circular stain on the cloth. Stephen didn't need to see the wound underneath to know that it would be ugly. They always were. No doubt in the coming weeks he would have yet another pale line to add to the collection of scars along his hands, arms, and legs—assuming, of course, he'd manage to sew himself up without infection.

They'd been lucky so far, but Ed had always been more than a little clumsy and seemed to be growing even more accident-prone every year. A serious injury was no longer an *if*, but a *when*.

"How bad?"

"Needs a new solenoid."

"Once again, not what I meant," Stephen asked, nodding in the direction of the bandage.

"I should live. But I may need you to pick up a little more around here for the next few days."

Stephen glanced back toward the kitchen door and the barn across the way. Sneaking in thirty minutes between his chores already created a stiff challenge. If he had to pick up Ed's too, it was going to be difficult if not impossible to get the machine rebuilt in time for the next virtual meet-up with Wes.

"Yeah. Not how I intended to spend my golden years either." Ed grinned at his joke, but Stephen failed to see the humor in his comment. It wasn't right. Ed was far from what should have been considered old. He wouldn't have even been called middle-aged, but now… Stephen glanced again out the window to avoid looking at the white-laced hair where fiery red should be or at the spots of age that now dotted his skin in between the freckles.

"You see something?" Ed asked, on guard.

Stephen sighed, rubbing his face as he pulled his gaze from the barn. It didn't take much to spook the man. Edward's paranoia made Stephen's feelings about rats seem downright sensible. "Just checking to see how much sunlight we have left. If I leave now, I can get to Earthaven by nightfall."

"You aren't going to Earthaven." Ed arranged the tools and fasteners on the table using an indecipherable, system-bucking sort of logic.

"Someone has to." Stephen pointed at the components scattered on the table.

"And where would you go then? You know it's too dangerous to be out at night."

"It's only Earthaven." Stephen imagined walking over to the table and switching out one bolt for another just to see how long it would take the older man to notice.

"Yes, and there are reasons we're here and not there." Components clinked together as Ed moved the piles around.

"But…Earthaven…" Stephen turned his face before Ed could see him roll his eyes.

"Just because nothing has ever happened in the town doesn't mean nothing ever will." Ed gestured with his bandaged hand as he spoke, scattering the contents of one of the piles.

"And we're still talking about Earthaven," repeated Stephen as he bent down, picked up a screw from the ground, and placed it back on the table with the others. Ed picked it up and placed it in another pile.

"Not this again." Helen Thomas entered the farmhouse holding a bowl of vegetables. Dirt smeared her otherwise reddened cheeks. Strands of her hair, also whiter and grayer than the brown it should be, rebelled against the plaited braid.

"Let me help you with that" Ed reached for the vegetables, sending more metal parts to the floor.

"Oh no, you don't. I harvested them. I can wash them." As she batted his arm away, Edward winced. "Operating on yourself again, I see? I swear, Stephen, I turn my back on him for one second…"

Stephen grinned. "Sorry. Didn't realize it was my turn to watch him."

"So, what were you two arguing about?" Helen asked as she turned the dial on the faucet, allowing water from the rain barrel to flow for a few seconds into the sink basin. The contents of the barrel could fill the basin with more to spare, but the summer had been dry, and a little conservation now could make a huge difference in the days or weeks ahead unless the weather turned.

Then again, Stephen thought, *it could rain for a month and Helen would still act as if they were in a drought.* "My ability to walk five miles." Stephen reached down and handed her a small potato that had rolled away from the others.

"After dark," grumbled Ed as he rearranged the contents of the piles, making their composition even less consistent.

"I'm nineteen now. Weren't you both considered adults at this point?"

Helen's shoulders slumped. "Honey, we know you aren't a kid anymore, but the world is nothing like it was when we were your age. There were millions of more people for starters." She looked at Ed's piles of components. "Not to mention reliable power." She paused. Her lips twisted. "And if we got into trouble, we had phones."

"Yeah, and yet you somehow have managed to live all this time without those things. All I am asking is the chance to do the same. To actually live."

Helen scrubbed the potato with a stiff brush before transferring it to a cardboard box near the sink.

Ed broke the silence first. "This isn't the life either of us wanted for you, but—"

"No, he's right." Helen put the brush down. "Good or bad. It's time we give him the opportunity to make the occasional decision." Helen moved to the table and picked up the component that had thus far eluded Ed's notice. She placed it in his good hand. "Goodness knows you could have used a little more practice back then."

The two shared a grin over some secret joke before Helen turned back to the basket of vegetables. She turned the root over in her hand as she cleaned it, inspecting its skin and eyes before placing it to the side of the basin rather than in the box with the others. "Besides, as he said, it is only Earthaven. Jim will keep an eye on him."

"My point exactly." Stephen raced over to kiss Helen on the cheek, grabbing a washed sweet pepper harvested along with the potatoes.

"But what if…?" Ed gestured again. A piece of fabric from the bandage caught on one of the components, sending the piles tumbling once again to the floor.

Helen came over to Ed's side and helped him gather his supplies. "Who's left to remember, let alone care about—Helen started. She glanced in Stephen's direction and dropped the sentence. Returning to the sink, she continued as if the words had never been spoken. "Besides, you clearly aren't fit to go."

Stephen didn't want to risk Helen changing her mind by asking either of the two to go into more details about whatever it was. *More of Ed's paranoia, I bet.* Stephen bit into the pepper, tasting dirt as much as vegetable as he raced to the door. He wiped the pepper's skin on the side of his jacket as he threw open the door and jumped down the stairs. "I'll be back in the morning," he shouted without looking back.

"Keep your eyes open," Ed called out as Stephen ran into the woodlands hiding the farm from casual view. Stephen's ears barely caught Ed's last words. "And don't trust anyone."

You can purchase the rest of the Watch & Wand from your favorite online book retailer

ACKNOWLEDGMENTS

Just like raising a child, creating a book takes a village. Special thanks go to Lora Denton, Libby Green, and Kristen Pham for taking the time to read through my early drafts, and more importantly, continuing to talk to me afterwards. I have re-read those early drafts. You each deserve a medal. To Tony Miltich for dropping everything at a moment's notice to help locate missing words. To my mom, Ann Jordan, for dropping by with a hand written review after reading an early printing from cover to cover because short notes on the novel's pages simply wouldn't do. It is gestures like that which prove little things in life have the biggest impact. To the hundreds of bloggers on WordPress who have encouraged me by sharing their own stories and experiences, and to my family and friends for continuing to be the reason I write a single word.

I would also like to thank readers like you, willing to take a chance with small to medium press and / or independent publications. The only way we can compete is through reviews and word of mouth. If you have enjoyed this novel, I encourage you to contact me, leave a review, or tell a friend.

ABOUT THE AUTHOR

Allie Potts, born in Rochester Minnesota was moved to North Carolina at a very early age by parents eager to escape to a more forgiving climate. She has since continued to call North Carolina home, settling in Raleigh, halfway between the mountains and the sea, in 1998.

When not finding ways to squeeze in 72 hours into a 24 day or chasing after children determined to turn her hair gray before its time, Allie enjoys stories of all kinds. Her favorites, whether they are novels, film, or simply shared aloud with friends, are usually accompanied with a glass of wine or cup of coffee in hand.

A self-professed science geek and book nerd, Allie also writes at www.alliepottswrites.com.

Want to connect?

Email Allie at: allie@alliepottswrites.com
Subscribe to Allie's mailing list: http://eepurl.com/c0fcSj
Facebook: https://www.facebook.com/alliepottswrites
Twitter: @alliepottswrite
Pinterest: @alliepottswrite
Instagram: @alliepottswrites
Bookbub: https://www.bookbub.com/profile/allie-potts

OTHER TITLES BY ALLIE POTTS

Project Gene Assist

Ready or not, the next era of human evolution is here

The Fair & Foul
The Watch & Wand
Lies & Legacy

Rocky Row Novels

Living happily ever after is a full-time job

An Uncertain Faith
An Uncertain Confidence